THE OUTLINE OF HISTORY

Being a Plain History of Life and Mankind

BY
H. G. WELLS

WRITTEN WITH THE ADVICE AND EDITORIAL HELP OF

MR. ERNEST BARKER,
SIR H. H. JOHNSTON, SIR E. RAY
LANKESTER
AND PROFESSOR GILBERT MURRAY

AND ILLUSTRATED BY
J. F. HORRABIN

VOLUME I

New York
THE MACMILLAN COMPANY
1920
All rights reserved

𝔑𝔬𝔯𝔴𝔬𝔬𝔡 𝔓𝔯𝔢𝔰𝔰
J. S. Cushing Co.—Berwick & Smith Co.
Norwood, Mass., U.S.A.

INTRODUCTION

"A philosophy of the history of the human race, worthy of its name, must begin with the heavens and descend to the earth, must be charged with the conviction that all existence is one—a single conception sustained from beginning to end upon one identical law."—FRIEDRICH RATZEL.

THIS *Outline of History* is an attempt to tell, truly and clearly, in one continuous narrative, the whole story of life and mankind so far as it is known to-day. It is written plainly for the general reader, but its aim goes beyond its use as merely interesting reading matter. There is a feeling abroad that the teaching of history considered as a part of general education is in an unsatisfactory condition, and particularly that the ordinary treatment of this "subject" by the class and teacher and examiner is too partial and narrow. But the desire to extend the general range of historical ideas is confronted by the argument that the available time for instruction is already consumed by that partial and narrow treatment, and that therefore, however desirable this extension of range may be, it is in practice impossible. If an Englishman, for example, has found the history of England quite enough for his powers of assimilation, then it seems hopeless to expect his sons and daughters to master universal history, if that is to consist of the history of England, plus the history of France, plus the history of Germany, plus the history of Russia, and so on. To which the only possible answer is that universal history is at once something more and something less than the aggregate of the national histories to which we are accustomed, that it must be approached in a different spirit and dealt with in a different manner. This book seeks to justify that answer. It has been written primarily to show that *history as one whole* is amenable to a more broad and comprehensive handling than is the history of special nations and periods, a broader handling that will bring it within the normal limitations of time and energy set to the reading and education of an ordinary citizen. This outline deals with ages and races and nations, where the ordinary history deals with reigns and pedigrees and campaigns; but it will not be found to be more crowded with names and dates, nor more difficult to follow and understand. History is no exception amongst the sciences; as the gaps fill in, the outline simplifies; as the outlook broadens, the clustering multitude of details dissolves into general laws. And many topics of quite primary interest to mankind, the first appearance and the growth of scientific knowledge for example, and its effects upon human life, the elaboration of the ideas of money and credit, or the story of the origins and spread and influence of Christianity, which must be treated fragmentarily or by elaborate digressions in any partial history, arise and flow completely and naturally in one general record of the world in which we live.

The need for a common knowledge of the general facts of human history throughout the world has become very evident during the tragic happenings of the last few years. Swifter means of communication have brought all men closer to one another for good or for evil. War becomes a universal disaster, blind and monstrously destructive; it bombs the baby in its cradle and sinks the food-ships that cater for the non-combatant and the neutral. There can be no peace now, we realize, but a common peace in all the world; no prosperity but a general prosperity. But *there can be no common peace and prosperity without common historical ideas*. Without such ideas to hold them together in harmonious co-operation, with nothing but narrow, selfish, and conflicting nationalist traditions, races and peoples are bound to drift towards conflict and destruction. This truth, which was apparent to that great philosopher Kant a century or more ago—it is the gist of his tract upon universal peace—is now plain to the man in the street. Our internal policies and our economic and social ideas are profoundly vitiated at present by wrong and fantastic ideas of the origin and historical relationship of social classes. A sense of history as the common adventure of all mankind is as necessary for peace within as it is for peace between the nations.

Such are the views of history that this *Outline* seeks to realize. It is an attempt to tell how our present state of affairs, this distressed and multifarious human life about us, arose in the course of vast ages and out of the inanimate clash of matter, and to estimate the quality and amount and range of the hopes with which it now faces its destiny. It is one experimental contribution to a great and urgently necessary educational reformation, which must ultimately restore universal history, revised, corrected, and brought up to date, to its proper place and use as the backbone of a general education. We say "restore," because all the great cultures of the world hitherto, Judaism and Christianity in the Bible, Islam in the Koran, have used some sort of cosmogony and world history as a basis. It may indeed be argued that without such a basis any really binding culture of men is inconceivable. Without it we are a chaos.

Remarkably few sketches of universal history by one single author have been written. One book that has influenced the writer very strongly is Winwood Reade's *Martyrdom of Man*. This *dates*, as people say, nowadays, and it has a fine gloom of its own, but it is still an extraordinarily inspiring presentation of human history as one consistent process. Mr. F. S. Marvin's *Living Past* is also an admirable summary of human progress. There is a good *General History of the World* in one volume by Mr. Oscar Browning. America has recently produced two well-illustrated and up-to-date class books, Breasted's *Ancient Times* and Robinson's *Medieval and Modern Times*, which together give a very good idea of the story of mankind since the beginning of human societies. There are, moreover, quite a number of nominally Universal Histories in existence, but they are really not histories at all, they are encyclopædias of history; they lack the unity of presentation attainable only when the whole subject has been passed through one single mind. These universal histories are compilations, assemblies of separate national or regional histories by different hands, the parts being necessarily unequal in merit and authority and disproportionate one to another. Several such universal histories in thirty or forty volumes or so, adorned with allegorical title pages and illustrated by folding maps and plans of Noah's Ark, Solomon's Temple, and the Tower of Babel, were produced for the libraries of gentlemen in the eighteenth century. Helmolt's *World History*, in eight massive volumes, is a modern compilation of the same sort, very useful for reference and richly illustrated, but far better in its parts than as a whole. Another such collection is the *Historians' History of the World* in 25 volumes. *The Encyclopædia Britannica* contains, of course, a complete encyclopædia of history within itself, and is the most modern of all such collections.[1] F. Ratzel's *History of Mankind*, in spite of the promise of its title, is mainly a natural history of man, though it is rich with suggestions upon the nature and development of civilization. That publication and Miss Ellen Churchill Semple's *Influence of Geographical Environment*, based on Ratzel's work, are quoted in this *Outline*, and have had considerable influence upon its plan. F. Ratzel would indeed have been the ideal author for such a book as our present one. Unfortunately neither he nor any other ideal author was available.[2]

The writer will offer no apology for making this experiment. His disqualifications are manifest. But such work needs to be done by as many people as possible, he was free to make his contribution, and he was greatly attracted by the task. He has read sedulously and made the utmost use of all the help he could obtain. There is not a chapter that has not been examined by some more competent person than himself and very carefully revised. He has particularly to thank his friends Sir E. Ray Lankester, Sir H. H. Johnston, Professor Gilbert Murray, and Mr. Ernest Barker for much counsel and direction and editorial help. Mr. Philip Guedalla has toiled most efficiently and kindly through all the proofs. Mr. A. Allison, Professor T. W. Arnold, Mr. Arnold Bennett, the Rev. A. H. Trevor Benson, Mr. Aodh de Blacam, Mr. Laurence Binyon, the Rev. G. W. Broomfield, Sir William Bull, Mr. L. Cranmer Byng, Mr. A. J. D. Campbell, Mr. A. Y. Campbell, Mr. L. Y. Chen, Mr. A. R. Cowan, Mr. O. G. S. Crawford, Dr. W. S. Culbertson, Mr. R. Langton Cole, Mr. B. G. Collins, Mr. J. J. L. Duyvendak, Mr. O. W. Ellis, Mr. G. S. Ferrier, Mr. David Freeman, Mr. S. N. Fu, Mr. G. B. Gloyne, Sir Richard Gregory, Mr. F. H. Hayward, Mr. Sydney Herbert, Dr. Fr. Krupicka, Mr. H. Lang Jones, Mr. C. H. B. Laughton, Mr. B. I. Macalpin, Mr. G. H. Mair, Mr.

F. S. Marvin, Mr. J. S. Mayhew, Mr. B. Stafford Morse, Professor J. L. Myres, the Hon. W. Ormsby-Gore, Sir Sydney Olivier, Mr. R. I. Pocock, Mr. J. Pringle, Mr. W. H. R. Rivers, Sir Denison Ross, Dr. E. J. Russell, Dr. Charles Singer, Mr. A. St. George Sanford, Dr. C. O. Stallybrass, Mr. G. H. Walsh, Mr. G. P. Wells, Miss Rebecca West, and Mr. George Whale have all to be thanked for help, either by reading parts of the MS. or by pointing out errors in the published parts, making suggestions, answering questions, or giving advice. The amount of friendly and sympathetic assistance the writer has received, often from very busy people, has been a quite extraordinary experience. He has met with scarcely a single instance of irritation or impatience on the part of specialists whose domains he has invaded and traversed in what must have seemed to many of them an exasperatingly impudent and superficial way. Numerous other helpful correspondents have pointed out printer's errors and minor slips in the serial publication which preceded this book edition, and they have added many useful items of information, and to those writers also the warmest thanks are due. But of course none of these generous helpers are to be held responsible for the judgments, tone, arrangement, or writing of this *Outline*. In the relative importance of the parts, in the moral and political implications of the story, the final decision has necessarily fallen to the writer. The problem of illustrations was a very difficult one for him, for he had had no previous experience in the production of an illustrated book. In Mr. J. F. Horrabin he has had the good fortune to find not only an illustrator but a collaborator. Mr. Horrabin has spared no pains to make this work informative and exact. His maps and drawings are a part of the text, the most vital and decorative part. Some of them, the hypothetical maps, for example, of the western world at the end of the last glacial age, during the "pluvial age" and 12,000 years ago, and the migration map of the Barbarian invaders of the Roman Empire, represent the reading and inquiry of many laborious days.

The index to this edition is the work of Mr. Strickland Gibson of Oxford. Several correspondents have asked for a pronouncing index and accordingly this has been provided.

The writer owes a word of thanks to that living index of printed books, Mr. J. F. Cox of the London Library. He would also like to acknowledge here the help he has received from Mrs. Wells. Without her labour in typing and re-typing the drafts of the various chapters as they have been revised and amended, in checking references, finding suitable quotations, hunting up illustrations, and keeping in order the whole mass of material for this history, and without her constant help and watchful criticism, its completion would have been impossible.

SCHEME OF CONTENTS

BOOK I
THE MAKING OF OUR WORLD

CHAPTER VII. THE AGE OF MAMMALS

BOOK II
THE MAKING OF MEN

CHAPTER VIII. THE ANCESTRY OF MAN

CHAPTER IX. THE NEANDERTHAL MEN, AN EXTINCT RACE.
(THE EARLY PALÆOLITHIC AGE)

CHAPTER X. THE LATER POSTGLACIAL PALÆOLITHIC MEN, THE FIRST TRUE MEN.
(LATER PALÆOLITHIC AGE)

CHAPTER XI. NEOLITHIC MAN IN EUROPE

CHAPTER XII. EARLY THOUGHT

CHAPTER XIV. THE LANGUAGES OF MANKIND

BOOK III
THE DAWN OF HISTORY

CHAPTER XV. THE ARYAN-SPEAKING PEOPLES IN PREHISTORIC TIMES

CHAPTER XVI. THE FIRST CIVILIZATIONS

CHAPTER XVII. SEA PEOPLES AND TRADING PEOPLES

CHAPTER XVIII. WRITING

CHAPTER XIX. GODS AND STARS, PRIESTS AND KINGS

BOOK IV
JUDEA, GREECE, AND INDIA

CHAPTER XXI. THE HEBREW SCRIPTURES AND THE PROPHETS

CHAPTER XXIII. GREEK THOUGHT AND LITERATURE

CHAPTER XXIV. THE CAREER OF ALEXANDER THE GREAT

CHAPTER XXV. SCIENCE AND RELIGION AT ALEXANDRIA

CHAPTER XXVI. THE RISE AND SPREAD OF BUDDHISM

BOOK V
THE RISE AND COLLAPSE OF THE ROMAN EMPIRE

CHAPTER XXVII. THE TWO WESTERN REPUBLICS

CHAPTER XXVIII. FROM TIBERIUS GRACCHUS TO THE GOD EMPEROR IN ROME

CHAPTER XXIX. THE CÆSARS BETWEEN THE SEA AND THE GREAT

BOOK VI
CHRISTIANITY AND ISLAM

CHAPTER XXX. THE BEGINNINGS, THE RISE, AND THE DIVISIONS OF CHRISTIANITY

LIST OF MAPS AND ILLUSTRATIONS

{vl-1}

BOOK I

THE MAKING OF OUR WORLD

{vl-2}
{vl-3}

THE OUTLINE OF HISTORY

I

THE EARTH IN SPACE AND TIME

THE earth on which we live is a spinning globe. Vast though it seems to us, it is a mere speck of matter in the greater vastness of space.

Space is, for the most part, emptiness. At great intervals there are in this emptiness flaring centres of heat and light, the "fixed stars." They are all moving about in space, notwithstanding that they are called fixed stars, but for a long time men did not realize their motion. They are so vast and at such tremendous distances that their motion is not perceived. Only in the course of many thousands of years is it appreciable. These fixed stars are so far off that, for all their immensity, they seem to be, even when we look at them through the most powerful telescopes, mere points of light, brighter or less bright. A few, however, when we turn a telescope upon them, are seen to be whirls and clouds of shining vapour which we call nebulæ. They are so far off that a movement of millions of miles would be imperceptible.

One star, however, is so near to us that it is like a great ball of flame. This one is the sun. The sun is itself in its nature like a fixed star, but it differs from the other fixed stars in appearance because it is beyond comparison nearer than they are; and because it is nearer men have been able to learn something of its nature. Its mean distance from the earth is ninety-three million miles. It is a mass of flaming matter, having a diameter of 866,000 miles. Its bulk is a million and a quarter times the bulk of our earth.[vi-4]

These are difficult figures for the imagination. If a bullet fired from a Maxim gun at the sun kept its muzzle velocity unimpaired, it would take seven years to reach the sun. And yet we say the sun is near, measured by the scale of the stars. If the earth were a small ball, one inch in diameter, the sun would be a globe of nine feet diameter; it would fill a small bedroom. It is spinning round on its axis, but since it is an incandescent fluid, its polar regions do not travel with the same velocity as its equator, the surface of which rotates in about twenty-five days. The surface visible to us consists of clouds of incandescent metallic vapour. At what lies below we can only guess. So hot is the sun's atmosphere that iron, nickel, copper, and tin are present in it in a gaseous state. About it at great distances circle not only our earth, but certain kindred bodies called the planets. These shine in the sky because they reflect the light of the sun; they are near enough for us to note their movements quite easily. Night by night their positions change with regard to the fixed stars.

It is well to understand how empty space is. If, as we have said, the sun were a ball nine feet across, our earth would, in proportion, be the size of a one-inch ball, and at a distance of 323 yards from the sun. The moon would be a speck the size of a small pea, thirty inches from the earth. Nearer to the sun than the earth would be two other very similar specks, the planets Mercury and Venus, at a distance of 125 and 250 yards respectively. Beyond the earth would come the planets Mars, Jupiter, Saturn, Uranus, and Neptune, at distances of 500, 1806, 3000, 6000, and 9500 yards respectively. There would also be a certain number of very much smaller specks, flying about amongst these planets, more particularly a number called the asteroids circling between Mars and Jupiter, and occasionally a little puff of more or less luminous vapour and dust would drift into the system from the almost limitless emptiness beyond. Such a puff is what we call a comet. *All the rest of the space about us and around us and for unfathomable distances beyond is cold, lifeless, and void.* The nearest fixed star to us, *on this minute scale,* be it remembered,—the earth as a one-inch ball, and the moon a little pea—would be over 40,000 miles away.

The science that tells of these things and how men have come{vi-5} to know about them is Astronomy, and to books of astronomy the reader must go to learn more about the sun and stars. The science and description of the world on which we live are called respectively Geology and Geography.

The diameter of our world is a little under 8000 miles. Its surface is rough; the more projecting parts of the roughness are mountains, and in the hollows of its surface there is a film of water, the oceans and seas. This film of water is about five miles thick at its deepest part—that is to say, the deepest oceans have a depth of five miles. This is very little in comparison with the bulk of the world.

About this sphere is a thin covering of air, the atmosphere. As we ascend in a balloon or go up a mountain from the level of the sea-shore the air is continually less dense, until at last it becomes so thin that it cannot support life. At a height of twenty miles there is scarcely any air at all—not one hundredth part of the density of air at the surface of the sea. The highest point to which a bird can fly is about four miles up—the condor, it is said, can struggle up to that; but most small birds and insects which are carried up by aeroplanes or balloons drop off insensible at a much lower level, and the greatest height to which any mountaineer has ever climbed is under five miles. Men have flown in aeroplanes to a height of over four miles, and balloons with men in them have reached very nearly seven miles, but at the cost of considerable physical suffering. Small experimental balloons, containing not men, but recording instruments, have gone as high as twenty-two miles.

It is in the upper few hundred feet of the crust of the earth, in the sea, and in the lower levels of the air below four miles that life is found. We do not know of any life at all except in these films of air and water upon our planet. So far as we know, all the rest of space is as yet without life. Scientific men have discussed the possibility of life, or of some process of a similar kind, occurring upon such kindred bodies as the planets Venus and Mars. But they point merely to questionable possibilities.

Astronomers and geologists and those who study physics have been able to tell us something of the origin and history of the earth. They consider that, vast ages ago, the sun was a spinning, flaring[vi-6] mass of matter, not yet concentrated into a compact centre of heat and light, considerably larger than it is now, and spinning very much faster, and that as it whirled, a series of fragments detached themselves from it, which became the planets. Our earth is one of these planets. The flaring mass that was the material of the earth broke as it spun into two masses, a larger, the earth itself, and a smaller, which is now the dead, still moon. Astronomers give us convincing reasons for supposing that sun and earth and moon and all that system were then whirling about at a speed much greater than the speed at which they are moving to-day, and that at first our earth was a flaming thing upon which no life could live. The way in which they have reached these conclusions is by a very beautiful and interesting series of observations and reasoning, too long and elaborate for us to deal with here. But they oblige us to believe that the sun, incandescent though it is, is now much cooler than it was, and that it spins more slowly now than it did, and that it continues to cool and slow down. And they also show that the rate at which the earth spins is diminishing and continues to diminish—that is to say, that our day is growing longer and longer, and that the heat at the centre of the earth wastes slowly. There was a time when the day was not a half and not a third of what it is to-day; when a blazing hot sun, much greater than it is now, must have moved visibly—had there been an eye to mark it—from its rise to its setting across the skies. There will be a time when the day will be as long as a year is now, and the cooling sun, shorn of its beams, will hang motionless in the heavens.

It must have been in days of a much hotter sun, a far swifter day and night, high tides, great heat, tremendous storms and earthquakes, that life, of which we are a part, began upon the world. The moon also was nearer and brighter in those days and had a changing face.[3]

{vl-7}

II

THE RECORD OF THE ROCKS

§ 1. *The First Living Things.* § 2. *How Old Is the World?*

§ 1

W E do not know how life began upon the earth.[4]

Biologists, that is to say, students of life, have made guesses about these beginnings, but we will not discuss them here. Let us only note that they all agree that life began where the tides of those swift days spread and receded over the steaming beaches of mud and sand.

The atmosphere was much denser then, usually great cloud masses obscured the sun, frequent storms darkened the heavens. The land of those days, upheaved by violent volcanic forces, was a barren land, without vegetation, without soil. The almost incessant rain-storms swept down upon it, and rivers and torrents carried great loads of sediment out to sea, to become muds that hardened later into slates and shales, and sands that became sandstones. The geologists have studied the whole accumulation of these sediments as it remains to-day, from those of the earliest ages to the most recent. Of course the oldest deposits are the most distorted and changed and worn, and in them there is now no certain trace to be found of life at all. Probably the earliest[vi-8] forms of life were small and soft, leaving no evidence of their existence behind them. It was only when some of these living things developed skeletons and shells of lime and such-like hard material that they left fossil vestiges after they died, and so put themselves on record for examination.

The literature of geology is very largely an account of the fossils that are found in the rocks, and of the order in which layers after layers of rocks lie one on another. The very oldest rocks must have been formed before there was any sea at all, when the earth was too hot for a sea to exist, and when the water that is now sea was an atmosphere of steam mixed with the air. Its higher levels were dense with clouds, from which a hot rain fell towards the rocks below, to be converted again into steam long before it reached their incandescence. Below this steam atmosphere the molten world-stuff solidified as the first rocks. These first rocks must have solidified as a cake over glowing liquid material beneath, much as cooling lava does. They must have appeared first as crusts and clinkers. They must have been constantly remelted and recrystallized before any thickness of them became permanently solid. The name of Fundamental Gneiss is given to a great underlying system of crystalline rocks which probably formed age by age as this hot youth of the world drew to its close. The scenery of the world in the days when the Fundamental Gneiss was formed must have been more like the interior of a furnace than anything else to be found upon earth at the present time.

After long ages the steam in the atmosphere began also to condense and fall right down to earth, pouring at last over these warm primordial rocks in rivulets of hot water and gathering in depressions as pools and lakes and the first seas. Into those seas the streams that poured over the rocks brought with them dust and particles to form a sediment, and this sediment accumulated in layers, or as geologists call them, *strata*, and formed the first Sedimentary Rocks. Those earliest sedimentary rocks sank into depressions and were covered by others; they were bent, tilted up, and torn by great volcanic disturbances and by tidal strains that swept through the rocky crust of the earth. We find these first sedimentary rocks still coming to the surface of the{vl-9} land here and there, either not covered by later strata or exposed after vast ages of concealment by the wearing off of the rock that covered them later—there are great surfaces of them in Canada especially; they are cleft and bent, partially remelted, recrystallized, hardened and compressed, but recognizable for what they are. And they contain no single certain trace of life at all. They are frequently called *Azoic* (lifeless) Rocks. But since in some of these earliest sedimentary rocks a substance called graphite (black lead) occurs, and also red and black oxide of iron, and since it is asserted that these substances need the activity of living things for their production, which may or may not be the case, some geologists prefer to call these earliest sedimentary rocks *Archæozoic* (primordial life). They suppose that the first life was soft living matter that had no shells or skeletons or any such structure that could remain as a recognizable fossil after its death, and that its chemical influence caused the deposition of graphite and iron oxide. This is pure guessing, of course, and there is at least an equal probability that in the time of formation of the Azoic Rocks, life had not yet begun.

Long ago there were found in certain of these ancient first-formed rocks in Canada, curious striped masses, and thin layers of white and green mineral substance which Sir William Dawson considered were fossil vestiges, the walls or coverings of some very simple sort of living thing which has now vanished from the earth. He called these markings*Eozoon Canadense* (the Canadian dawn-animal). There has been much discussion and controversy over this Eozoon, but to-day it is agreed that Eozoon is nothing more than a crystalline marking. Mixed minerals will often intercrystallize in blobs or branching shapes that are very suggestive of simple plant or animal forms. Any one who has made a lead tree in his schooldays, or lit those queer indoor fireworks known as serpents' eggs, which unfold like a long snake, or who has seen the curious markings often found in quartz crystals, or noted the tree-like pattern on old stone-ware beer mugs, will realize how closely non-living matter can sometimes mock the shapes of living things.

Overlying or overlapping these Azoic or Archæozoic rocks come others, manifestly also very ancient and worn, which do[vi-10] contain traces of life. These first remains are of the simplest description; they are the vestiges of simple plants, called algæ, or marks like the tracks made by worms in the sea mud. There are also the skeletons of the microscopic creatures called Radiolaria. This second series of rocks is called the Proterozoic (beginning of life) series, and marks a long age in the world's history. Lying over and above the Proterozoic rocks is a third series, which is found to contain a considerable number and variety of traces of living things. First comes the evidence of a diversity of shellfish, crabs, and such-like crawling things, worms, seaweeds, and the like; then of a multitude of fishes and of the beginnings of land plants and land creatures. These rocks are called the Palæozoic (ancient life) rocks. They mark a vast era, during which life was slowly spreading, increasing, and developing in the seas of our world. Through long ages, through the earliest Palæozoic time, it was no more than a proliferation of such swimming and creeping things in the water. There were creatures called trilobites; they were crawling things like big sea woodlice that were probably related to the American king-crab of to-day. There were also sea-scorpions, the prefects of that early world. The individuals of certain species of these were nine feet long. These were the very highest sorts of life. There were abundant different sorts of an order of shellfish called brachiopods. There were plant animals, rooted and joined together like plants, and loose weeds that waved in the waters.

It was not a display of life to excite our imaginations. There was nothing that ran or flew or even swam swiftly or skilfully. Except for the size of some of the creatures, it was not very different from, and rather less various than, the kind of life a student would gather from any summer-time ditch nowadays for microscopic examination. Such was the life of the shallow seas through a hundred million years or more in the early Palæozoic period. The land during that time was apparently absolutely barren. We find no trace nor hint of land life. Everything that lived in those days lived under water for most or all of its life.

--

Life in the Early Palæozoic

Between the formation of these Lower Palæozoic rocks in which the sea scorpion and trilobite ruled, and our own time, there have intervened almost immeasurable ages, represented by layers[VI-12] and masses of sedimentary rocks. There are first the Upper Palæozoic Rocks, and above these the geologists distinguish two great divisions. Next above the Palæozoic come the Mesozoic (middle life) rocks, a second vast system of fossil-bearing rocks, representing perhaps a hundred millions of swift years, and containing a wonderful array of fossil remains, bones of giant reptiles and the like, which we will presently describe; and above these again are the Cainozoic (recent life) rocks, a third great volume in the history of life, an unfinished volume of which the sand and mud that was carried out to sea yesterday by the rivers of the world, to bury the bones and scales and bodies and tracks that will become at last fossils of the things of to-day, constitute the last written leaf.

(It is, we may note, the practice of many geologists to make a break between the rest of the Cainozoic system of rocks and those which contain traces of humanity, which latter are cut off as a separate system under the name of Quaternary. But that, as we shall see, is rather like taking the last page of a book, which is really the conclusion of the last chapter, and making a separate chapter of it and calling it the last chapter.)

These markings and fossils in the rocks and the rocks themselves are our first historical documents. The history of life that men have puzzled out and are still puzzling out from them is called the Record of the Rocks. By studying this record men are slowly piecing together a story of life's beginnings, and of the beginnings of our kind, of which our ancestors a century or so ago had no suspicion. But when we call these rocks and the fossils a record and a history, it must not be supposed that there is any sign of an orderly keeping of a record. It is merely that whatever happens leaves some trace, if only we are intelligent enough to detect the meaning of that trace. Nor are the rocks of the world in orderly layers one above the other, convenient for men to read. They are not like the books and pages of a library. They are torn, disrupted, interrupted, flung about, defaced, like a carelessly arranged office after it has experienced in succession a bombardment, a hostile military occupation, looting, an earthquake, riots, and a fire. And so it is that for countless generations this Record of the Rocks lay unsuspected beneath the{vi-13} feet of men. Fossils were known to the Ionian Greeks in the sixth century B.C.,[5] they were discussed at Alexandria by Eratosthenes and others in the third century B.C., a discussion which is summarized in Strabo's *Geography* (?20-10 B.C.). They were known to the Latin poet Ovid, but he did not understand their nature. He thought they were the first rude efforts of creative power. They were noted by Arabic writers in the tenth century. Leonardo da Vinci, who lived so recently as the opening of the sixteenth century (1452-1519), was one of the first Europeans to grasp the real significance of fossils,[6] and it has been only within the last century and a half that man has begun the serious and sustained deciphering of these long-neglected early pages of his world's history.

§ 2

--

Speculations about geological time vary enormously.[7] Estimates of the age of the oldest rocks by geologists and astronomers starting from different standpoints have varied between 1,600,000,000, and 25,000,000. The lowest estimate was made by Lord Kelvin in 1867. Professor Huxley guessed at 400,000,000 years. There is a summary of views and the grounds upon which the estimates have been made in Osborn's *Origin and Evolution of Life*; he inclines to the moderate total of 100,000,000. It must be clearly understood by the reader how sketchy and provisional all these time estimates are. They rest nearly always upon theoretical assumptions of the slenderest kind. That the period of time has been vast, that it is to be counted by scores and possibly by hundreds of millions of years, is the utmost that can be said with certainty in the matter. It is quite open to the reader to divide every number in the appended time diagram by ten or multiply it by two; no one can gainsay him. Of the relative amount of time as between one age and another we have, however, stronger evidence; if the reader cuts{vl-14} down the 800,000,000 we have given here to 400,000,000, then he must reduce the 40,000,000 of the Cainozoic to 20,000,000. And be it noted that whatever the total sum may be, most geologists are in agreement that *half or more than half of the whole of geological time had passed before life had developed to the Later Palæozoic level.* The reader reading quickly through these opening chapters may be apt to think of them as a mere swift prelude{vl-15} of preparation to the apparently much longer history that follows, but in reality that subsequent history is longer only because it is more detailed and more interesting to us. It looms larger in perspective. For ages that stagger the imagination this earth spun hot and lifeless, and again for ages of equal vastness it held no life above the level of the animalculæ in a drop of ditch-water.

Not only is Space from the point of view of life and humanity empty, but Time is empty also. Life is like a little glow, scarcely kindled yet, in these void immensities.{vl-16}

III

NATURAL SELECTION AND THE CHANGES OF
SPECIES

Now here it will be well to put plainly certain general facts about this new thing, *life*, that was creeping in the shallow waters and intertidal muds of the early Palæozoic period, and which is perhaps confined to our planet alone in all the immensity of space.

Life differs from all things whatever that are without life in certain general aspects. There are the most wonderful differences among living things to-day, but all living things past and present agree in possessing *a certain power of growth*, all living things *take nourishment*, all living things *move about* as they feed and grow, though the movement may be no more than the spread of roots through the soil, or of branches in the air. Moreover, living things reproduce; they give rise to other living things, either by growing and then dividing or by means of seeds or spores or eggs or other ways of producing young. *Reproduction* is a characteristic of life.

No living thing goes on living forever. There seems to be a *limit of growth* for every kind of living thing. Among very small and simple living things, such as that microscopic blob of living matter the *Amœba*, an individual may grow and then divide completely into two new individuals, which again may divide in their turn. Many other microscopic creatures live actively for a time, grow, and then become quiet and inactive, enclose themselves in an outer covering and break up wholly into a number of still smaller things, spores, which are released and scattered and again grow into the likeness of their parent. Among more complex creatures the reproduction is not usually such simple division, though division does occur even in the case of many creatures[vi-17] big enough to be visible to the unassisted eye. But the rule with almost all larger beings is that the individual grows up to a certain limit of size. Then, before it becomes unwieldy, its growth declines and stops. As it reaches its full size it *matures*, it begins to produce young, which are either born alive or hatched from eggs. But all of its body does not produce young. Only a special part does that. After the individual has lived and produced offspring for some time, it ages and dies. It does so by a sort of necessity. There is a practical limit to its life as well as to its growth. These things are as true of plants as they are of animals. And they are not true of things that do not live. Non-living things, such as crystals, grow, but they have no set limits of growth or size, they *do not move of their own accord* and there is *no stir within them*. Crystals once formed may last unchanged for millions of years. There is *no reproduction* for any non-living thing.

This growth and dying and reproduction of living things leads to some very wonderful consequences. The young which a living thing produces are either directly, or after some intermediate stages and changes (such as the changes of a caterpillar and butterfly), like the parent living thing. But they are never exactly like it or like each other. There is always a slight difference, which we speak of as *individuality*. A thousand butterflies this year may produce two or three thousand next year; these latter will look to us almost exactly like their predecessors, but each one will have just that slight difference. It is hard for us to see individuality in butterflies because we do not observe them very closely, but it is easy for us to see it in men. All the men and women in the world now are descended from the men and women of A.D. 1800, but not one of us now is exactly the same as one of that vanished generation. And what is true of men and butterflies is true of every sort of living thing, of plants as of animals. Every species changes all its individualities in each generation. That is as true of all the minute creatures that swarmed and reproduced and died in the Archæozoic and Proterozoic seas, as it is of men to-day.

Every species of living things is continually dying and being born again, as a multitude of fresh individuals.{vi-18}

Consider, then, what must happen to a new-born generation of living things of any species. Some of the individuals will be stronger or sturdier or better suited to succeed in life in some way than the rest, many individuals will be weaker or less suited. In particular single cases any sort of luck or accident may occur, but *on the whole* the better equipped individuals will live and grow up and reproduce themselves and the weaker will *as a rule* go under. The latter will be less able to get food, to fight their enemies and pull through. So that in each generation there is as it were a picking over of a species, a picking out of most of the weak or unsuitable and a preference for the strong and suitable. This process is called *Natural Selection* or the *Survival of the Fittest.*[8]

It follows, therefore, from the fact that living things grow and breed and die, that every species, so long as the conditions under which it lives remain the same, becomes more and more perfectly fitted to those conditions in every generation.

But now suppose those conditions change, then the sort of individual that used to succeed may now fail to succeed and a sort of individual that could not get on at all under the old conditions may now find its opportunity. These species will change, therefore, generation by generation; the old sort of individual that used to prosper and dominate will fail and die out and the new sort of individual will become the rule,—until the general character of the species changes.

Suppose, for example, there is some little furry whitey-brown animal living in a bitterly cold land which is usually under snow. Such individuals as have the thickest, whitest fur will be least hurt by the cold, less seen by their enemies, and less conspicuous as they seek their prey. The fur of this species will thicken and its whiteness increase with every generation, until there is no advantage in carrying any more fur.

–

Diagram of Life in the Later Palæozoic Age.
Life is creeping out of the water. An insect like a dragon fly is shown. There were amphibia like gigantic newts and salamanders, and even primitive reptiles in these swamps.

Imagine now a change of climate that brings warmth into the land, sweeps away the snows, makes white creatures glaringly visible during the greater part of the year and thick fur an encumbrance. Then every individual with a touch of brown in its colouring and a thinner fur will find itself at an advantage, and very white and heavy fur will be a handicap. There will be{vi-20} a weeding out of the white in favour of the brown in each generation. If this change of climate come about too quickly, it may of course exterminate the species altogether; but if it come about gradually, the species, although it may have a hard time, may yet be able to change itself and adapt itself generation by generation. This change and adaptation is called the *Modification of Species*.

Perhaps this change of climate does not occur all over the lands inhabited by the species; maybe it occurs only on one side of some great arm of the sea or some great mountain range or such-like divide, and not on the other. A warm ocean current like the Gulf Stream may be deflected, and flow so as to warm one side of the barrier, leaving the other still cold. Then on the cold side this species will still be going on to its utmost possible furriness and whiteness and on the other side it will be modifying towards brownness and a thinner coat. At the same time there will probably be other changes going on; a difference in the paws perhaps, because one half of the species will be frequently scratching through snow for its food, while the other will be scampering over brown earth. Probably also the difference of climate will mean differences in the sort of food available, and that may produce differences in the teeth and the digestive organs. And there may be changes in the sweat and oil glands of the skin due to the changes in the fur, and these will affect the excretory organs and all the internal chemistry of the body. And so through all the structure of the creature. A time will come when the two separated varieties of this formerly single species will become so unlike each other as to be recognizably different species. Such a splitting up of a species in the course of generations into two or more species is called the *Differentiation of Species*.

And it should be clear to the reader that given these elemental facts of life, given growth and death and reproduction with individual variation in a world that changes, life *must* change in this way, modification and differentiation *must* occur, old species *must* disappear, and new ones appear. We have chosen for our instance here a familiar sort of animal, but what is true of furry beasts in snow and ice is true of all life, and equally true of the soft jellies and simple beginnings that flowed and crawled for hundreds of millions of years between the tidal levels and in the shallow, warm waters of the Proterozoic seas.

The early life of the early world, when the blazing sun rose and set in only a quarter of the time it now takes, when the warm seas poured in great tides over the sandy and muddy shores of the rocky lands and the air was full of clouds and steam, must have been modified and varied and species must have developed at a great pace. Life was probably as swift and short as the days and years; the generations, which natural selection picked over, followed one another in rapid succession.

Natural selection is a slower process with man than with any other creature. It takes twenty years or more before an ordinary human being in western Europe grows up and reproduces. In the case of most animals the new generation is on trial in a year or less. With such simple and lowly beings, however, as first appeared in the primordial seas, growth and reproduction was probably a matter of a few brief hours or even of a few brief minutes. Modification and differentiation of species must accordingly have been extremely rapid, and life had already developed a very great variety of widely contrasted forms before it began to leave traces in the rocks. The Record of the Rocks does not begin, therefore, with any group of closely related forms from which all subsequent and existing creatures are descended. It begins in the midst of the game, with nearly every main division of the animal kingdom already represented.[9] Plants are already plants, and animals animals. The curtain rises on a drama in the sea that has already begun, and has been going on for some time. The brachiopods are discovered already in their shells, accepting and consuming much the same sort of food that oysters and mussels do now; the great water scorpions crawl among the seaweeds, the trilobites roll up into balls and unroll and scuttle away. In that ancient mud and among those early weeds there was probably as rich and abundant and active a life of infusoria and the like as one finds in a drop of ditch-water to-day. In the ocean waters, too, down to the utmost downward limit to{vl-22} which light could filter, then as now, there was an abundance of minute and translucent, and in many cases phosphorescent, beings.

But though the ocean and intertidal waters already swarmed with life, the land above the high-tide line was still, so far as we can guess, a stony wilderness without a trace of life.{vl-23}

IV

THE INVASION OF THE DRY LAND BY LIFE

§ 1. *Life and Water.* § 2. *The Earliest Animals.*

W HEREVER the shore line ran there was life, and that life went on in and by and with water as its home, its medium, and its fundamental necessity.

The first jelly-like beginnings of life must have perished whenever they got out of the water, as jelly-fish dry up and perish on our beaches to-day. Drying up was the fatal thing for life in those days, against which at first it had no protection. But in a world of rain-pools and shallow seas and tides, any variation that enabled a living thing to hold out and keep its moisture during hours of low tide of drought met with every encouragement in the circumstances of the time. There must have been a constant risk of stranding. And, on the other hand, life had to keep rather near the shore and beaches in the shallows because it had need of air (dissolved of course in the water) and light.

No creature can breathe, no creature can digest its food, without water. We talk of breathing air, but what all living things really do is to breathe oxygen dissolved in water. The air we ourselves breathe must first be dissolved in the moisture in our lungs; and all our food must be liquefied before it can be assimilated. Water-living creatures which are always under water, wave the freely exposed gills by which they breathe in that water, and extract the air dissolved in it. But a creature that is to be exposed for any time out of the water, must have its body and its breathing apparatus protected from drying up. Before the seaweeds could creep up out of the Early Palæozoic seas into[vı-24] the intertidal line of the beach, they had to develop a tougher outer skin to hold their moisture. Before the ancestor of the sea scorpion could survive being left by the tide it had to develop its casing and armour. The trilobites probably developed their tough covering and rolled up into balls, far less as a protection against each other and any other enemies they may have possessed, than as a precaution against drying. And when presently, as we ascend the Palæozoic rocks, the fish appear, first of all the backboned or vertebrated animals, it is evident that a number of them are already adapted by the protection of their gills with gill covers and by a sort of primitive lung swimming-bladder, to face the same risk of temporary stranding.

Now the weeds and plants that were adapting themselves to intertidal conditions were also bringing themselves into a region of brighter light, and light is very necessary and precious to all plants. Any development of structure that would stiffen them and hold them up to the light, so that instead of crumpling and flopping when the waters receded, they would stand up outspread, was a great advantage. And so we find them developing fibre and support, and the beginning of *woody fibre* in them. The early plants reproduced by soft spores, or half-animal "gametes," that were released in water, were distributed by water and could only germinate under water. The early plants were tied, and most lowly plants to-day are tied, by the conditions of their life cycle, to water. But here again there was a great advantage to be got by the development of some protection of the spores from drought that would enable reproduction to occur without submergence. So soon as a species could do that, it could live and reproduce and spread above the high-water mark, bathed in light and out of reach of the beating and distress of the waves. The main classificatory divisions of the larger plants mark stages in the release of plant life from the necessity of submergence by the development of woody support and of a method of reproduction that is more and more defiant of drying up. The lower plants are still the prisoner attendants of water. The lower mosses must live in damp, and even the development of the spore of the ferns demands at certain stages extreme wetness. The highest plants have carried freedom from{v1-25} water so far that they can live and reproduce if only there is some moisture in the soil below them. They have solved their problem of living out of water altogether.

The essentials of that problem were worked out through the vast æons of the Proterozoic Age and the early Palæozoic Age by nature's method of experiment and trial. Then slowly, but in great abundance, a variety of new plants began to swarm away from the sea and over the lower lands, still keeping to swamp and lagoon and watercourse as they spread.

And after the plants came the animal life.

There is no sort of land animal in the world, as there is no sort of land plant, whose structure is not primarily that of a water-inhabiting being which has been adapted through the modification and differentiation of species to life out of the water. This adaptation is attained in various ways. In the case of the land scorpion the gill-plates of the primitive sea scorpion are sunken into the body so as to make the lung-books secure from rapid evaporation. The gills of crustaceans, such as the crabs which run about in the air, are protected by the gill-cover extensions of the back shell or carapace. The ancestors of the insects developed a system of air pouches and air tubes, the tracheal tubes, which carry the air all over the body before it is dissolved. In the case of the vertebrated land animals, the gills of the ancestral fish were first supplemented and then replaced by a bag-like growth from the throat, the primitive lung swimming-bladder. To this day there survive certain mudfish which enable us to understand very clearly the method by which the vertebrated land animals worked their way out of the water. These creatures (*e.g.* the African lung fish) are found in tropical regions in which there is a rainy full season and a dry season, during which the rivers become mere ditches of baked mud. During the rainy season these fish swim about and breathe by gills like any other fish. As the waters of the river evaporate, these fish bury themselves in the mud, their gills go out of action, and the creature keeps itself alive until the waters return by swallowing air, which passes into its swimming-bladder. The Australian lung fish,[v1-26] when it is caught by the drying up of the river in stagnant pools, and the water has become deaerated and foul, rises to the surface and gulps air. A newt in a pond does exactly the same thing. These creatures still remain at the transition stage, the stage at which the ancestors of the higher vertebrated animals were released from their restriction to an under-water life.

The amphibia (frogs, newts, tritons, etc.) still show in their life history all the stages in the process of this liberation. They are still dependent on water for their reproduction; their eggs must be laid in sunlit water, and there they must develop. The young tadpole has branching external gills that wave in the water; then a gill cover grows back over them and forms a gill chamber. Then, as the creature's legs appear and its tail is absorbed, it begins to use its lungs, and its gills dwindle and vanish. The adult frog can live all the rest of its days in the air, but it can be drowned if it is kept steadfastly below water. When we come to the reptile, however, we find an egg which is protected from evaporation by a tough egg case, and this egg produces young which breathe by lungs from the very moment of hatching. The reptile is on all fours with the seeding plant in its freedom from the necessity to pass any stage of its life cycle in water.

The later Palæozoic Rocks of the northern hemisphere give us the materials for a series of pictures of this slow spreading of life over the land. Geographically, all round the northern half of the world it was an age of lagoons and shallow seas very favourable to this invasion. The new plants, now that they had acquired the power to live this new aerial life, developed with an extraordinary richness and variety.

There were as yet no true flowering plants,[10] no grasses nor trees that shed their leaves in winter;[11] the first "flora" consisted{v1-27} of great tree ferns, gigantic equisetums, cycad ferns, and kindred vegetation. Many of these plants took the form of huge-stemmed trees, of which great multitudes of trunks survive fossilized to this day. Some of these trees were over a hundred feet high, of orders and classes now vanished from the world. They stood with their stems in the water, in which no doubt there was a thick tangle of soft mosses and green slime and fungoid growths that left few plain vestiges behind them. The abundant remains{v1-28} of these first swamp forests constitute the main coal-measures of the world to-day.

Amidst this luxuriant primitive vegetation crawled and glided and flew the first insects. They were rigid-winged, four-winged creatures, often very big, some of them having wings measuring a foot in length. There were numerous dragon flies—one found in the Belgian coal-measures had a wing span of twenty-nine inches! There were also a great variety of flying cockroaches. Scorpions abounded, and a number of early spiders, which, however, had no spinnerets for web making.[12] Land snails appeared. So too did the first-known step of our own ancestry upon land, the amphibia. As we ascend the higher levels of the Later Palæozoic record, we find the process of air adaptation has gone as far as the appearance of true reptiles amidst the abundant and various amphibia.

The land life of the Upper Palæozoic Age was the life of a green swamp forest without flowers or birds or the noises of modern insects. There were no big land beasts at all; wallowing amphibia and primitive reptiles were the very highest creatures that life had so far produced. Whatever land lay away from the water or high above the water was still altogether barren and lifeless. But steadfastly, generation by generation, life was creeping away from the shallow sea-water of its beginning.{v1-29}

V

CHANGES IN THE WORLD'S CLIMATE

§ 1

THE Record of the Rocks is like a great book that has been carelessly misused. All its pages are torn, worn, and defaced, and many are altogether missing. The outline of the story that we sketch here has been pieced together slowly and painfully in an investigation that is still incomplete and still in progress. The Carboniferous Rocks, the "coal-measures," give us a vision of the first great expansion of life over the wet lowlands. Then come the torn pages known as the Permian Rocks (which count as the last of the Palæozoic), that preserve very little for us of the land vestiges of their age. Only after a long interval of time does the history spread out generously again.

It must be borne in mind that great changes of climate have always been in progress, that have sometimes stimulated and sometimes checked life. Every species of living thing is always adapting itself more and more closely to its conditions. And conditions are always changing. There is no finality in adaptation. There is a continuing urgency towards fresh change.

About these changes of climate some explanations are necessary here. They are not regular changes; they are slow fluctuations between heat and cold. The reader must not think that because the sun and earth were once incandescent, the climatic history of the world is a simple story of cooling down. The centre of the earth is certainly very hot to this day, but we feel nothing of that internal heat at the surface; the internal heat, except{vI-30} for volcanoes and hot springs, has not been perceptible at the surface since first the rocks grew solid. Even in the Azoic or Archæozoic Age there are traces in ice-worn rocks and the like of periods of intense cold. Such cold waves have always been going on everywhere, alternately with warmer conditions. And there have been periods of great wetness and periods of great dryness throughout the earth.

A complete account of the causes of these great climatic fluctuations has still to be worked out, but we may perhaps point out some of the chief of them.[13] Prominent among them is the fact that the earth does not spin in a perfect circle round the sun. Its path or orbit is like a hoop that is distorted; it is, roughly speaking, elliptical (ovo-elliptical), and the sun is nearer to one end of the ellipse than the other. It is at a point which is a focus of the ellipse. And the shape of this orbit never remains the same. It is slowly distorted by the attractions of the other planets, for ages it may be nearly circular, for ages it is more or less elliptical. As the ellipse becomes most nearly circular, then the focus becomes most nearly the centre. When the orbit becomes most elliptical, then the position of the sun becomes most remote from the middle or, to use the astronomer's phrase, most eccentric. When the orbit is most nearly circular, then it must be manifest that all the year round the earth must be getting much the same amount of heat from the sun; when the orbit is most distorted, then there will be a season in each year when the earth is nearest the sun (this phase is called *Perihelion*) and getting a great deal of heat comparatively, and a season when it will be at its farthest from the sun (*Aphelion*) and getting very little warmth. A planet at *aphelion* is travelling its slowest, and its fastest at *perihelion*; so that the hot part of its year will last for a much less time than the cold part of its year. (Sir Robert Ball calculated that the greatest difference possible between the seasons was thirty-three days.) During ages when the orbit is most nearly circular there will therefore be least extremes of [vi-31] climate, and when the orbit is at its greatest eccentricity, there will be an age of cold with great extremes of seasonal temperature. These *changes in the orbit of the earth* are due to the varying pull of all the planets, and Sir Robert Ball declared himself unable to calculate any regular cycle of orbital change, but Professor G. H. Darwin maintained that it is possible to make out a kind of cycle between greatest and least eccentricity of about 200,000 years.

But this change in the shape of the orbit is only one cause of the change of the world's climate.

There are many others that have to be considered with it. As most people know, the change in the seasons is due to the fact that the equator of the earth is inclined at an angle to the plane of its orbit. If the earth stood up straight in its orbit, so that its equator was in the plane of its orbit, there would be no change in the seasons at all. The sun would always be overhead at the equator, and the day and night would each be exactly twelve hours long throughout the year everywhere. It is this inclination which causes the difference in the seasons and the unequal length of the day in summer and winter. There is, according to Laplace, a possible variation of nearly three degrees (from 22° 6' to 24° 50') in this inclination of the equator to the orbit, and when this is at a maximum, the difference between summer and winter is at its greatest. Great importance has been attached to this variation in the inclination of the equator to the orbit by Dr. Croll in his book *Climate and Time*. At present the angle is 23° 27'. Manifestly when the angle is at its least, the world's climate, other things being equal, will be most equable.

And as a third important factor there is what is called the *precession of the equinoxes*. This is a slow wabble of the pole of the spinning earth that takes 25,000 odd years. Any one who watches a spinning top as it "sleeps," will see its axis making a slow circular movement, exactly after the fashion of this circling movement of the earth's axis. The north pole, therefore, does not always point to the same north point among the stars; its pointing traces out a circle in the heavens every 25,000 years.

Now, there will be times when the earth is at its extreme of aphelion or of perihelion, when one hemisphere will be most turned{vi-32} to the sun in its midsummer position and the other most turned away at its midwinter position. And as the precession of the equinoxes goes on, a time will come when the summer-winter position will come not at aphelion and perihelion, but at the half-way points between them. When the summer of one hemisphere happens at perihelion and the winter at aphelion, it will be clear that the summer of the other hemisphere will happen at aphelion and its winter at perihelion. One hemisphere will have a short hot summer and a very cold winter, and the other a long cold summer and a briefer warmish winter. But when the summer-winter positions come at the half-way point of the orbit, and it is the spring of one hemisphere and the autumn of the other that is at aphelion or perihelion, there will not be the same wide difference between the climate of the two hemispheres.

Here are three wavering systems of change all going on independently of each other; the precession of the equinoxes, the change in the obliquity of the equator to the orbit, and the changes in the eccentricity of the orbit. Each system tends by itself to produce periods of equability and periods of greater climatic contrast. And all these systems of change interplay with each other. When it happens that at the same time the orbit is most nearly circular, the equator is at its least inclination from the plane of the earth's orbit, and the spring and autumn are at perihelion and aphelion, then all these causes will be conspiring to make climate warm and uniform; there will be least difference of summer and winter. When, on the other hand, the orbit is in its most eccentric stage of deformation, when also the equator is most tilted up and when further the summer and winter are at aphelion and perihelion, then climates will be at their extremest and winter at its bitterest. There will be great accumulations of ice and snow in winter; the heat of the brief hot summer will be partly reflected back into space by the white snow, and it will be unequal to the task of melting all the winter's ice before the earth spins away once more towards its chilly aphelion. The earth will accumulate cold so long as this conspiracy of extreme conditions continues.

–

Diagram To Illustrate One Set of Causes, the Astronomical Variations, Which Make the Climate of the World Change Slowly but Continuously. It does not change in regular periods. It fluctuates through vast ages. As the world's climate changes, life must change too or perish.

So our earth's climate changes and wavers perpetually as these three systems of influence come together with a common tendency{v1-34} towards warmth or severity, or as they contradict and cancel each other.

We can trace in the Record of the Rocks an irregular series of changes due to the interplay of these influences; there have been great ages when the separate rhythms of these three systems kept them out of agreement and the atmosphere was temperate, ages of world-wide warmth, and other ages when they seemed to concentrate bitterly to their utmost extremity, to freeze out and inflict the utmost stresses and hardship upon life.

And in accordance we find from the record in the rocks that there have been long periods of expansion and multiplication when life flowed and abounded and varied, and harsh ages when there was a great weeding out and disappearance of species, genera, and classes, and the learning of stern lessons by all that survived. Such a propitious conjunction it must have been that gave the age of luxuriant low-grade growth of the coal-measures; such an adverse series of circumstances that chilled the closing æons of the Palæozoic time.

It is probable that the warm spells have been long relatively to the cold ages. Our world to-day seems to be emerging with fluctuations from a prolonged phase of adversity and extreme conditions. Half a million years ahead it may be a winterless world with trees and vegetation even in the polar circles. At present we have no certainty in such a forecast, but later on, as knowledge increases, it may be possible to reckon with more precision, so that our race will make its plans thousands of years ahead to meet the coming changes.

§ 2

Another entirely different cause of changes in the general climate of the earth may be due to variations in the heat of the sun. We do not yet understand what causes the heat of the sun or what sustains that undying fire. It is possible that in the past there have been periods of greater and lesser intensity. About that we know nothing; human experience has been too short; and so far we have been able to find no evidence on this matter in the geological record. On the whole, scientific men[vi-35] are inclined to believe that the sun has blazed with a general steadfastness throughout geological time. It may have been cooling slowly, but, speaking upon the scale of things astronomical, it has certainly not cooled very much.

§ 3

A third great group of causes influencing climate are to be found in the forces within the world itself. Throughout the long history of the earth there has been a continuous wearing down of the hills and mountains by frost and rain and a carrying out of their material to become sedimentary rocks under the seas. There has been a continuous process of wearing down the land and filling up the seas, by which the seas, as they became shallower, must have spread more and more over the land. The reverse process, a process of crumpling and upheaval, has also been in progress, but less regularly. The forces of upheaval have been spasmodic; the forces of wearing down continuous. For long ages there has been comparatively little volcanic upheaval, and then have come periods in which vast mountain chains have been thrust up and the whole outline of land and sea changed. Such a time was the opening stage of the Cainozoic period, in which the Alps, the Himalayas, and the Andes were all thrust up from the sea-level to far beyond their present elevations, and the main outlines of the existing geography of the world were drawn.

Now, a time of high mountains and deep seas would mean a larger dry land surface for the world, and a more restricted sea surface, and a time of low lands would mean a time of wider and shallower seas. High mountains precipitate moisture from the atmosphere and hold it out of circulation as snow and glaciers, while smaller oceans mean a lesser area for surface evaporation. Other things being equal, lowland stages of the world's history would be ages of more general atmospheric moisture than periods of relatively greater height of the mountains and greater depth of the seas. But even small increases in the amount of moisture in the air have a powerful influence upon the transmission of radiant heat through that air. The sun's heat will pass much_[vi-36] more freely through dry air than through moist air, and so a greater amount of heat would reach the land surfaces of the globe under the conditions of extremes of elevation and depth, than during the periods of relative lowness and shallowness. Dry phases in the history of the earth mean, therefore, hot days. But they also mean cold nights, because for the same reason that the heat comes abundantly to the earth, it will be abundantly radiated away. Moist phases mean, on the other hand, cooler days and warmer nights. The same principle applies to the seasons, and so a phase of great elevations and depressions of the surface would also be another contributory factor on the side of extreme climatic conditions.

And a stage of greater elevation and depression would intensify its extreme conditions by the gradual accumulation of ice caps upon the polar regions and upon the more elevated mountain masses. This accumulation would be at the expense of the sea, whose surface would thus be further shrunken in comparison with the land.

Here, then, is another set of varying influences that will play in with and help or check the influence of the astronomical variations stated in § 1 and § 2. There are other more localized forces at work into which we cannot go in any detail here, but which will be familiar to the student of the elements of physical geography; the influence of great ocean currents in carrying warmth from equatorial to more temperate latitudes; the interference of mountain chains with the moisture borne by prevalent winds and the like. As in the slow processes of nature these currents are deflected or the mountain chains worn down or displaced by fresh upheavals, the climate over great areas will be changed and all the conditions of life changed with it. Under the incessant slow variations of these astronomical, telluric, and geographical influences life has no rest. As its conditions change it must change or perish.

§ 4

And while we are enumerating the forces that change climate and the conditions of terrestrial life, we may perhaps look ahead a little and add a fourth set of influences, at first unimportant in the history of the world so far as the land surface is concerned,{v1-37} but becoming more important after the age of Reptiles, to which we shall proceed in our next chapter. These are the effects produced upon climate by life itself. Particularly great is the influence of vegetation, and especially that of forests. Every tree is continually transpiring water vapour into the air; the amount of water evaporated in summer by a lake surface is far less than the amount evaporated by the same area of beech forest. As in the later Mesozoic and the Cainozoic Age, great forests spread over the world, their action in keeping the air moist and mitigating and stabilizing climate by keeping the summer cool and the winter mild must have become more and more important. Moreover, forests accumulate and protect soil and so prepare the possibility of agricultural life.

Water-weeds again may accumulate to choke and deflect rivers, flood and convert great areas into marshes, and so lead to the destruction of forests or the replacement of grass-lands by boggy wildernesses.

Finally, with the appearance of human communities, came what is perhaps the most powerful of all living influences upon climate. By fire and plough and axe man alters his world. By destroying forests and by irrigation man has already affected the climate of great regions of the world's surface. The destruction of forests makes the seasons more extreme; this has happened, for instance, in the northeastern states of the United States of America. Moreover, the soil is no longer protected from the scour of rain, and is washed away, leaving only barren rock beneath. This has happened in Spain and Dalmatia and, some thousands of years earlier, in South Arabia. By irrigation, on the other hand, man restores the desert to life and mitigates climate. This process is going on in Northwest India and Australia. In the future, by making such operations worldwide and systematic, man may be able to control climate to an extent at which as yet we can only guess.{v1-38}

VI

THE AGE OF REPTILES

§ 1. *The Age of Lowland Life.* § 2. *Flying Dragons.* § 3. *The First Birds.* § 4. *An Age of Hardship and Death.* § 5. *The First Appearance of Fur and Feathers.*

1

W E know that for hundreds of thousands of years the wetness and warmth, the shallow lagoon conditions that made possible the vast accumulations of vegetable matter which, compressed and mummified,[14] are now coal, prevailed over most of the world. There were some cold intervals, it is true; but they did not last long enough to destroy the growths. Then that long age of luxuriant low-grade vegetation drew to its end, and for a time life on the earth seems to have undergone a period of world-wide bleakness.

When the story resumes again, we find life entering upon a fresh phase of richness and expansion. Vegetation has made great advances in the art of living out of water. While the Palæozoic plants of the coal-measures probably grew with swamp water flowing over their roots, the Mesozoic flora from its very outset included palm-like cycads and low-ground conifers that were distinctly land plants growing on soil above the water level. The lower levels of the Mesozoic land were no doubt covered by great fern brakes and shrubby bush and a kind of jungle growth of trees. But there existed as yet no grass, no small flowering plants, no turf nor greensward. Probably the Mesozoic was not an age of very brightly coloured vegetation. It must have had a flora green in the wet season and brown and purple in the dry.{vi-39} There were no gay flowers, no bright autumn tints before the fall of the leaf, because there was as yet no fall of the leaf. And beyond the lower levels the world was still barren, still unclothed, still exposed without any mitigation to the wear and tear of the wind and rain.

When one speaks of conifers in the Mesozoic the reader must not think of the pines and firs that clothe the high mountain slopes of our time. He must think of low-growing evergreens. The mountains were still as bare and lifeless as ever. The only colour effects among the mountains were the colour effects of naked rock, such colours as make the landscape of Colorado so marvellous to-day.

Amidst this spreading vegetation of the lower plains the reptiles were increasing mightily in multitude and variety. They were now in many cases absolutely land animals. There are numerous anatomical points of distinction between a reptile and an amphibian; they held good between such reptiles and amphibians as prevailed in the carboniferous time of the Upper Palæozoic; but the fundamental difference between reptiles and amphibia which matters in this history is that the amphibian must go back to the water to lay its eggs, and that in the early stages of its life it must live in and under water. The reptile, on the other hand, has cut out all the tadpole stages from its life cycle, or, to be more exact, its tadpole stages are got through before the young leave the egg case. The reptile has come out of the water altogether. Some had gone back to it again, just as the hippopotamus and the otter among mammals have gone back, but that is a further extension of the story to which we cannot give much attention in this *Outline*.

–

In the Palæozoic period, as we have said, life had not spread beyond the swampy river valleys and the borders of sea lagoons and the like; but in the Mesozoic, life was growing ever more accustomed to the thinner medium of the air, was sweeping boldly up over the plains and towards the hillsides. It is well for the student of human history and the human future to note that. If a disembodied intelligence with no knowledge of the future had come to earth and studied life during the early Palæozoic age, he might very reasonably have concluded that life was[vi-41] absolutely confined to the water, and that it could never spread over the land. It found a way. In the Later Palæozoic Period that visitant might have been equally sure that life could not go beyond the edge of a swamp. The Mesozoic Period would still have found him setting bounds to life far more limited than the bounds that are set to-day. And so to-day, though we mark how life and man are still limited to five miles of air and a depth of perhaps a mile or so of sea, we must not conclude from that present limitation that life, through man, may not presently spread out and up and down to a range of living as yet inconceivable.

The earliest known reptiles were beasts with great bellies and not very powerful legs, very like their kindred amphibia, wallowing as the crocodile wallows to this day; but in the Mesozoic they soon began to stand up and go stoutly on all fours, and several great sections of them began to balance themselves on tail and hind legs, rather as the kangaroos do now, in order to release the fore limbs for grasping food. The bones of one notable division of reptiles which retained a quadrupedal habit, a division of which many remains have been found in South African and Russian Early Mesozoic deposits, display a number of characters which approach those of the mammalian skeleton, and because of this resemblance to the mammals (beasts) this division is called the *Theriomorpha* (beastlike). Another division was the crocodile branch, and another developed towards the tortoises and turtles. The *Plesiosaurs* and *Ichthyosaurs* were two groups which have left no living representatives; they were huge reptiles returning to a whale-like life in the sea. *Pliosaurus*, one of the largest plesiosaurs, measured thirty feet from snout to tail tip—of which half was neck. The *Mosasaurs* were a third group of great porpoise-like marine lizards. But the largest and most diversified group of these Mesozoic reptiles was the group we have spoken of as kangaroo-like, the *Dinosaurs*, many of which attained enormous proportions. In bigness these greater *Dinosaurs* have never been exceeded, although the sea can still show in the whales creatures as great. Some of these, and the largest among them, were herbivorous animals; they browsed on the rushy vegetation and among the ferns and bushes, or they{vi-42} stood up and grasped trees with their fore legs while they devoured the foliage. Among the browsers, for example, were the *Diplodocus carnegii*, which measured eighty=four feet in length, and the *Atlantosaurus*. The *Gigantosaurus*, disinterred by a German expedition in 1912 from rocks in East Africa, was still more colossal. It measured well over a hundred feet! These greater{vi-43} monsters had legs, and they are usually figured as standing up on them; but it is very doubtful if they could have supported their weight in this way, out of water. Buoyed up by water or mud, they may have got along. Another noteworthy type we have figured is the *Triceratops*. There were also a number of great flesh-eaters who preyed upon these herbivores. Of these, *Tyrannosaurus* seems almost the last word in "frightfulness" among living things. Some species of this genus measured forty feet from snout to tail. Apparently it carried this vast body kangaroo fashion on its tail and hind legs. Probably it reared itself up. Some authorities even suppose that it leapt through the air. If so, it possessed muscles of a quite miraculous quality. A leaping elephant would be a far less astounding idea. Much more probably it waded half submerged in pursuit of the herbivorous river saurians.

§ 2

One special development of the dinosaurian type of reptile was a light, hopping, climbing group of creatures which developed a bat-like web between the fifth finger and the side of the body, which was used in gliding from tree to tree after the fashion of the flying squirrels. These bat-lizards were the *Pterodactyls*. They are often described as *flying*reptiles, and pictures are drawn of Mesozoic scenery in which they are seen soaring and swooping about. But their breastbone has no keel such as the breastbone of a bird has for the attachment of muscles strong enough for long-sustained flying. They must have flitted about like bats. They must have had a grotesque resemblance to heraldic dragons, and they played the part of bat-like birds in the Mesozoic jungles. But bird-like though they were, they were not birds nor the ancestors of birds. The structure of their wings was altogether different from that of birds. The structure of their wings was that of a hand with one long finger and a web; the wing of a bird is like an arm with feathers projecting from its hind edge. And these Pterodactyls had no feathers.

Far less prevalent at this time were certain other truly birdlike[vi-44] creatures, of which the earlier sorts also hopped and clambered and the later sorts skimmed and flew. These were at first—by all the standards of classification—Reptiles. They developed into true birds as they developed wings and as their reptilian scales became long and complicated, fronds rather than scales, and so at last, by much spreading and splitting, feathers. Feathers are the distinctive covering of birds, and they give a power of resisting heat and cold far greater than that of any other integumentary covering except perhaps the thickest fur. At a very early stage this novel covering of feathers, this new heatproof contrivance that life had chanced upon, enabled many species of birds to invade a province for which the pterodactyl was ill equipped. They took to sea fishing—if indeed they did not begin with it—and spread to the north and south polewards beyond the temperature limits set to the true reptiles. The earliest birds seem to have been carnivorous divers and water birds. To this day some of the most primitive bird forms are found among the sea birds of the Arctic and Antarctic seas, and it is among these sea birds that zoologists still find lingering traces of teeth, which have otherwise vanished completely from the beak of the bird.

The earliest known bird (the *Archæopteryx*) had no beak; it had a row of teeth in a jaw like a reptile's. It had three claws at the forward corner of its wing.

Its tail too was peculiar. All modern birds have their tail feathers set in a short compact bony rump; the *Archæopteryx* had a long bony tail with a row of feathers along each side.

§ 4

This great period of Mesozoic life, this second volume of the book of life, is indeed an amazing story of reptilian life proliferating and developing. But the most striking thing of all the story remains to be told. Right up to the latest Mesozoic Rocks we find all these reptilian orders we have enumerated still flourishing unchallenged. There is no hint of an enemy or competitor to them in the relics we find of their world. Then the record is broken. We do not know how long a time the break represents; many pages may be missing here, pages that may represent some{v1-45} great cataclysmal climatic change. When next we find abundant traces of the land plants and the land animals of the earth, this great multitude of reptile species had gone. For the most part they have left no descendants. They have been "wiped out." The pterodactyls have gone absolutely; of the plesiosaurs and ichthyosaurs none is alive; the mosasaurs have gone; of{v1-46} the lizards a few remain, the monitor of the Dutch East Indies is the largest; all the multitude and diversity of the dinosaurs have vanished. Only the crocodiles and the turtles and tortoises carry on in any quantity into Cainozoic times. The place of all these types in the picture that the Cainozoic fossils presently unfold to us is taken by other animals not closely related to the Mesozoic reptiles and certainly not descended from any of their ruling types. A new kind of life is in possession of the world.

This apparently abrupt ending up of the reptiles is, beyond all question, the most striking revolution in the whole history of the earth before the coming of mankind. It is probably connected with the close of a vast period of equable warm conditions and the onset of a new austerer age, in which the winters were bitterer and the summers brief but hot. The Mesozoic life, animal and vegetable alike, was adapted to warm conditions and capable of little resistance to cold. The new life, on the other hand, was before all things capable of resisting great changes of temperature.

Whatever it was that led to the extinction of the Mesozoic reptiles, it was probably some very far-reaching change indeed, for the life of the seas did at the same time undergo a similar catastrophic alteration. The crescendo and ending of the Reptiles on land was paralleled by the crescendo and ending of the Ammonites, a division of creatures like squids with coiled shells which swarmed in those ancient seas. All through the rocky record of this Mesozoic period there is a vast multitude and variety of these coiled shells; there are hundreds of species, and towards the end of the Mesozoic period they increased in diversity and produced exaggerated types. When the record resumes, these too have gone. So far as the reptiles are concerned, people may perhaps be inclined to argue that they were exterminated because the Mammals that replaced them competed with them, and were more fitted to survive; but nothing of the sort can be true of the Ammonites, because to this day their place has not been taken. Simply they are gone. Unknown conditions made it possible for them to live in the Mesozoic seas, and then some unknown change made life impossible for them. No genus of Ammonite survives to-day of all that vast variety,{vi-47} but there still exists one isolated genus very closely related to the Ammonites, the Pearly Nautilus. It is found, it is to be noted, in the warm waters of the Indian and Pacific oceans.[15]

And as for the Mammals competing with and ousting the less fit reptiles, a struggle of which people talk at times, there is not a scrap of evidence of any such direct competition. To judge by the Record of the Rocks as we know it to-day, there is much more reason for believing that first the reptiles in some inexplicable way perished, and then that later on, after a very hard time for all life upon the earth, the mammals, as conditions became more genial again, developed and spread to fill the vacant world.

Were there mammals in the Mesozoic period?

This is a question not yet to be answered precisely. Patiently and steadily the geologists gather fresh evidence and reason out completer conclusions. At any time some new deposit may reveal fossils that will illuminate this question. Certainly either mammals, or the ancestors of the mammals, must have lived throughout the Mesozoic period. In the very opening chapter of the Mesozoic volume of the Record there were those Theriomorphous Reptiles to which we have already alluded, and in the later Mesozoic a number of small jaw-bones are found, entirely mammalian in character. But there is not a scrap, not a bone, to suggest that there lived any Mesozoic Mammal which could look a dinosaur in the face. The Mesozoic mammals or mammal-like reptiles—for we do not know clearly which they were—seem to have been all obscure little beasts of the size of mice and rats, more like a down-trodden order of reptiles than a distinct class; probably they still laid eggs and were developing only slowly their distinctive covering of hair. They lived away from big waters, and perhaps in the desolate uplands, as marmots do now; probably they lived there beyond the pursuit of the carnivorous dinosaurs. Some perhaps went on all fours, some chiefly went on their hind legs and clambered with their fore limbs. They became fossils only so occasionally that chance[vi-48] has not yet revealed a single complete skeleton in the whole vast record of the Mesozoic rocks by which to check these guesses.

These little Theriomorphs, these ancestral mammals, developed hair. Hairs, like feathers, are long and elaborately specialized scales. Hair is perhaps the clue to the salvation of the early mammals. Leading lives upon the margin of existence,{vi-49} away from the marshes and the warmth, they developed an outer covering only second in its warmth-holding (or heat-resisting) powers to the down and feathers of the Arctic sea-birds. And so they held out through the age of hardship between the Mesozoic and Cainozoic ages, to which most of the true reptiles succumbed.

All the main characteristics of this flora and sea and land fauna that came to an end with the end of the Mesozoic age were such as were adapted to an equable climate and to shallow and swampy regions. But in the case of their Cainozoic successors, both hair and feathers gave *a power of resistance to variable temperatures* such as no reptile possessed, and with it they gave a range far greater than any animal had hitherto attained.

The range of life of the Lower Palæozoic Period was confined to warm water.

The range of life of the Upper Palæozoic Period was confined to warm water or to warm swamps and wet ground.

The range of life of the Mesozoic Period as we know it was confined to water and fairly low-lying valley regions under equable conditions.

Meanwhile in each of these periods there were types involuntarily extending the range of life beyond the limits prevailing in that period; and when ages of extreme conditions prevailed, it was these marginal types which survived to inherit the depopulated world.

That perhaps is the most general statement we can make about the story of the geological record; it is a story of widening range. Classes, genera, and species of animals appear and disappear, but the range widens. It widens always. Life has never had so great a range as it has to-day. Life to-day, in the form of man, goes higher in the air than it has ever done before; man's geographical range is from pole to pole, he goes under the water in submarines, he sounds the cold, lifeless darkness of the deepest seas, he burrows into virgin levels of the rocks, and in thought and knowledge he pierces to the centre of the earth and reaches out to the uttermost star. Yet in all the relics of the Mesozoic time we find no certain memorials of his ancestry. His ancestors, {v1-50} like the ancestors of all the kindred mammals, must have been creatures so rare, so obscure, and so remote that they have left scarcely a trace amidst the abundant vestiges of the monsters that wallowed rejoicing in the steamy air and lush vegetation of the Mesozoic lagoons, or crawled or hopped or fluttered over the great river plains of that time.[16]

VII

THE AGE OF MAMMALS

§ 1. *A New Age of Light.* § 2. *Tradition Comes into the World.* § 3. *An Age of Brain Growth.* § 4. *The World Grows Hard Again.* § 5. *Chronology of the Ice Age.*

§ 1

THE third great division of the geological record, the Cainozoic, opens with a world already physically very like the world we live in to-day. Probably the day was at first still perceptibly shorter, but the scenery had become very modern in its character. Climate was, of course, undergoing, age by age, its incessant and irregular variations; lands that are temperate to-day have passed, since the Cainozoic age began, through phases of great warmth, intense cold, and extreme dryness; but the landscape, if it altered, altered to nothing that cannot still be paralleled to-day in some part of the world or other. In the place of the cycads, sequoias, and strange conifers of the Mesozoic, the plant names that now appear in the lists of fossils include birch, beech, holly, tulip trees, ivy, sweet gum, bread-fruit trees. Flowers had developed concurrently with bees and butterflies. Palms were now very important. Such plants had already been in evidence in the later levels of the (American Cretaceous) Mesozoic, but now they dominated the scene altogether. Grass was becoming a great fact in the world. Certain grasses, too, had appeared in the later Mesozoic, but only with the Cainozoic period came grass plains and turf spreading wide over a world that was once barren stone.

The period opened with a long phase of considerable warmth; then the world cooled. And in the opening of this third part{vi-52} of the record, this Cainozoic period, a gigantic crumpling of the earth's crust and an upheaval of mountain ranges was in progress. The Alps, the Andes, the Himalayas, are all Cainozoic mountain ranges; the background of an early Cainozoic scene, to be typical, should display an active volcano or so. It must have been an age of great earthquakes.

Geologists make certain main divisions of the Cainozoic period, and it will be convenient to name them here and to indicate their climate. First comes the *Eocene* (dawn of recent life), an age of exceptional warmth in the world's history, subdivided into an older and newer Eocene; then the *Oligocene* (but little of recent life), in which the climate was still equable. The *Miocene* (with living species still in a minority) was the great age of mountain building, and the general temperature was falling. In the *Pliocene* (more living than extinct species), climate was very much at its present phase; but with the *Pleistocene* (a great majority of living species) there set in a long period of extreme conditions—it was the Great Ice Age. Glaciers spread from the poles towards the equator, until England to the Thames was covered in ice. Thereafter to our own time came a period of partial recovery.

§ 2

In the forests and following the grass over the Eocene plains there appeared for the first time a variety and abundance of mammals. Before we proceed to any description of these mammals, it may be well to note in general terms what a mammal is.

From the appearance of the vertebrated animals in the Lower Palæozoic Age, when the fish first swarmed out into the sea, there has been a steady progressive development of vertebrated creatures. A fish is a vertebrated animal that breathes by gills and can live only in water. An amphibian may be described as a fish that has added to its gill-breathing the power of breathing air with its swimming-bladder in adult life, and that has also developed limbs with five toes to them in place of the fins of a fish. A tadpole is for a time a fish; it becomes a land creature as it develops. A reptile is a further stage in this detachment from water; it is an amphibian that is no longer amphibious; it passes through its tadpole stage—its fish stage, that is—in an{vI-53} egg. From the beginning it must breathe in air; it can never breathe under water as a tadpole can do. Now, a modern mammal is really a sort of reptile that has developed a peculiarly effective protective covering, hair; and that also retains its eggs in the body until they hatch so that it brings forth living young[vi-54] (viviparous), and even after birth it cares for them and feeds them by its mammæ for a longer or shorter period. Some reptiles, some vipers for example, are viviparous, but none stand by their young as the real mammals do. Both the birds and the mammals, which escaped whatever destructive forces made an end to the Mesozoic reptiles, and which survived to dominate the Cainozoic world, have these two things in common: first, a far more effective protection against changes of temperature than any other variation of the reptile type ever produced; and, secondly, a peculiar care for their eggs, the bird by incubation and the mammal by retention, and a disposition to look after the young for a certain period after hatching or birth. There is by comparison the greatest carelessness about offspring in the reptile.

Hair was evidently the earliest distinction of the mammals from the rest of the reptiles. It is doubtful if the particular Theriodont reptiles who were developing hair in the early Mesozoic were viviparous. Two mammals survive to this day which not only do not suckle their young,[17] but which lay eggs, the *Ornithorhynchus* and the *Echidna*, and in the Eocene there were a number of allied forms. They are the survivors of what was probably a much larger number and variety of small egg-laying hairy creatures, hairy reptiles, hoppers, climbers, and runners, which included the Mesozoic ancestors of all existing mammals up to and including man.

Now we may put the essential facts about mammalian reproduction in another way. *The mammal is a family animal.* And the family habit involved the possibility of a new sort of continuity of experience in the world. Compare the completely closed-in life of an individual lizard with the life of even a quite lowly mammal of almost any kind. The former has no mental continuity with anything beyond itself; it is a little self-contained globe of experience that serves its purpose and ends; but the latter "picks up" from its mother, and "hands on" to[vI-55] its offspring. All the mammals, except for the two genera we have named, had already before the lower Eocene age arrived at this stage of pre-adult dependence and imitation. They were all more or less imitative in youth and capable of a certain modicum of education; they all, as a part of their development, received a certain amount of care and example and even direction from their mother. This is as true of the hyæna and rhinoceros as it is of the dog or man; the difference of educability is enormous, but the fact of protection and educability in the young stage is undeniable. So far as the vertebrated animals go, these new mammals, with their viviparous, young-protecting disposition, and these new birds, with their incubating, young-protecting disposition, introduce at the opening of the Cainozoic period a fresh thing into the expanding story of life, namely, social association, the addition to hard and inflexible instinct of *tradition*, and the nervous organization necessary to receive tradition.

All the innovations that come into the history of life begin very humbly. The supply of blood-vessels in the swimming-bladder of the mudfish in the lower Palæozoic torrent-river, that enabled it to pull through a season of drought, would have seemed at that time to that bodiless visitant to our planet we have already imagined, a very unimportant side fact in that ancient world of great sharks and plated fishes, sea-scorpions, and coral reefs and seaweed; but it opened the narrow way by which the land vertebrates arose to predominance. The mudfish would have seemed then a poor refugee from the too crowded and aggressive life of the sea. But once lungs were launched into the world, every line of descent that had lungs went on improving them. So, too, in the upper Palæozoic, the fact that some of the Amphibia were losing their "amphibiousness" by a retardation of hatching of their eggs, would have appeared a mere response to the distressful dangers that threatened the young tadpole. Yet that prepared the conquest of the dry land for the triumphant multitude of the Mesozoic reptiles. It opened a new direction towards a free and vigorous land-life along which all the reptilian animals moved. And this viviparous, young-tending training that the ancestral mammalia underwent during that age of inferiority and hardship for them, set going in the world a new continuity{vi-56} of perception, of which even man to-day only begins to appreciate the significance.

A number of types of mammal already appear in the Eocene. Some are differentiating in one direction, and some in another, some are perfecting themselves as herbivorous quadrupeds, some leap and climb among the trees, some turn back to the water to swim, but all types are unconsciously exploiting and developing the brain which is the instrument of this new power of acquisition and educability. In the Eocene rocks are found small early predecessors of the horse (Eohippus), tiny camels, pigs, early tapirs, early hedgehogs, monkeys and lemurs, opossums and carnivores. Now, all these were more or less ancestral to living forms, and all have brains relatively much smaller than their living representatives. There is, for instance, an early rhinoceros, *Titanotherium*, with a brain not one tenth the size of that of the existing rhinoceros. The latter is by no means a perfect type of the attentive and submissive student, but even so it is ten times more observant and teachable than its predecessor. This sort of thing is true of all the orders and families that survive until to-day. All the Cainozoic mammals were doing this one thing in common under the urgency of a common necessity; they were all growing brain. It was a parallel advance. In the same order or family to-day, the brain is usually from six to ten times what it was in the Eocene ancestor.

Grass was now spreading over the world, and with this extension arose some huge graminivorous brutes of which no representative survives to-day.

Such were the Uintatheres and the Titanotheres. And in pursuit of such beasts came great swarms of primitive dogs, some as big as bears, and the first cats, one in particular (*Smilodon*), a small fierce-looking creature with big knife-like canines, the first sabre-toothed tiger, which was to develop into greater things. American deposits in the Miocene display a great variety of camels, giraffe camels with long necks, gazelle camels, llamas, and true camels. North America, throughout most of the Cainozoic period, appears to have been in open and easy continuation with Asia, and when at last the glaciers[vi-57] of the Great Ice Age, and then the Bering Strait, came to separate the two great continental regions, the last camels were left in the old world and the llamas in the new.

In the Eocene the first ancestors of the elephants appear in northern Africa as snouted creatures; the elephant's trunk dawned on the world in the Miocene.

One group of creatures is of peculiar interest in a history that is mainly to be the story of mankind. We find fossils in the Eocene of monkeys and lemurs, but of one particular creature we have as yet not a single bone. It was half ape, half monkey; it clambered about the trees and ran, and probably ran well, on its hind legs upon the ground. It was small-brained by our present standards, but it had clever hands with which it handled fruits and beat nuts upon the rocks and perhaps caught up sticks and stones to smite its fellows. It was our ancestor.

Through millions of simian generations the spinning world circled about the sun; slowly its orbit, which may have been nearly circular during the equable days of the early Eocene, was drawn by the attraction of the circling outer planets into a more elliptical form. Its axis of rotation, which had always heeled over to the plane of its orbit, as the mast of a yacht under sail heels over to the level of the water, heeled over by imperceptible degrees a little more and a little more. And each year its summer point shifted a little further from perihelion round its path. These were small changes to happen to a one-inch ball, circling at a distance of 330 yards from a flaming sun nine feet across, in the course of a few million years. They were changes an immortal astronomer in Neptune, watching the earth from age to age, would have found almost imperceptible. But from the point of view of the surviving mammalian life of the Miocene, they mattered profoundly. Age by age the winters grew on the whole colder and harder and a few hours longer relatively to the summers in a thousand years; age by age the summers grew briefer. On an average the winter snow lay a little later in the spring in each century, and the glaciers in the northern mountains gained an inch this year, receded half an inch next, came on again a few inches....{v1-58}

The Record of the Rocks tells of the increasing chill. The Pliocene was a temperate time, and many of the warmth-loving plants and animals had gone.

Then, rather less deliberately, some feet or some inches every year, the ice came on.

An arctic fauna, musk ox, woolly mammoth, woolly rhinoceros, {vi-59} lemming, ushers in the Pleistocene. Over North America, and Europe and Asia alike, the ice advanced. For thousands of years it advanced, and then for thousands of years it receded, to advance again. Europe down to the Baltic shores, Britain down to the Thames, North America down to New England, and more centrally as far south as Ohio, lay for ages under the glaciers. Enormous volumes of water were withdrawn from the ocean and locked up in those stupendous ice caps so as to cause a world-wide change in the relative levels of land and sea. Vast areas were exposed that are now again sea bottom.

The world to-day is still coming slowly out of the last of four great waves of cold. It is not growing warmer steadily. There have been fluctuations. Remains of bog oaks, for example, which grew two or three thousand years ago, are found in Scotland at latitudes in which not even a stunted oak will grow at the present time. And it is amidst this crescendo and diminuendo of frost and snow that we first recognize forms that are like the forms of men. The Age of Mammals culminated in ice and hardship and man.

Guesses about the duration of the great age of cold are still vague, but in the Time diagram on page 60 we follow H. F. Osborn in accepting as our guides the estimates of Albrecht Penck[18] and C. A. Reeds.[19]

{v1-60}

Time Diagram of the Glacial Ages.
The reader should compare this diagram carefully with our first time diagram, Chapter II, § 2, p. 14. That diagram, if it were on the same scale as this one, would be between 41 and 410 feet long. The position of the Eoanthropus is very uncertain: it may be as early as the Pliocene

{v1-61}

BOOK II

THE MAKING OF MEN {v1-63}

VIII

THE ANCESTRY OF MAN[20]

§ 1. *Man Descended from a Walking Ape.* § 2. *First Traces of Man-like Creatures.* § 3. *The Heidelberg Sub-man.* § 4. *The Piltdown Sub-man.* § 5. *The Riddle of the Piltdown Remains.*

THE origin of man is still very obscure. It is commonly asserted that he is "descended" from some man-like ape such as the chimpanzee, the orang-utang, or the gorilla, but that of course is as reasonable as saying that I am "descended" from some Hottentot or Esquimaux as young or younger than myself. Others, alive to this objection, say that man is descended from the common ancestor of the chimpanzee, the orang-utang, and the gorilla. Some "anthropologists" have even indulged in a speculation whether mankind may not have a double or treble origin; the negro being descended from a gorilla-like ancestor, the Chinese from a chimpanzee-like ancestor, and so on. These are very fanciful ideas, to be mentioned only to be dismissed. It was formerly assumed that the human ancestor was "probably arboreal," but the current idea among those who are qualified to form an opinion seems to be that he was a "ground ape," and that the existing apes have developed in the arboreal direction.

Of course, if one puts the skeleton of a man and the skeleton of a gorilla side by side, their general resemblance is so great{v1-64} that it is easy to jump to the conclusion that the former is derived from such a type as the latter by a process of brain growth and general refinement. But if one examines closely into one or two differences, the gap widens. Particular stress has recently been laid upon the tread of the foot. Man walks on his toe and{v1-65} his heel; his great toe is his chief lever in walking, as the reader may see for himself if he examines his own footprints on the bathroom floor and notes where the pressure falls as the footprints become fainter. His great toe is the king of his toes.

Among all the apes and monkeys, the only group that have their great toes developed on anything like the same fashion as man are some of the lemurs. The baboon walks on a flat foot and all his toes, using his middle toe as his chief throw off, much as the bear does. And the three great apes all walk on the outer side of the foot in a very different manner from the walking of man.

Possible Appearance of the Sub-man Pithecanthropus. The face, jaws, and teeth are mere guess work (see text). The creature may have been much less human looking than this.

The great apes are forest dwellers; their walking even now is incidental; they are at their happiest among trees. They have very distinctive methods of climbing; they swing by the arms much more than the monkeys do, and do not, like the latter, take off with a spring from the feet. They have a specially developed climbing style of their own. But man walks so well and runs so swiftly as to suggest a very long ancestry upon the ground. Also, he does not climb well now; he climbs with caution and hesitation. His ancestors may have been running creatures for long ages. Moreover, it is to be noted that he does not swim naturally; he has to learn to swim, and that seems to point to a long-standing separation from rivers and lakes and the sea. Almost certainly that ancestor was a smaller and slighter creature than its human descendants. Conceivably the human ancestor{vl-66} at the opening of the Cainozoic period was a running ape, living chiefly on the ground, hiding among rocks rather than trees. It could still climb trees well and hold things between its great toe and its second toe (as the Japanese can to this day), but it was already coming down to the ground again from a still remoter, a Mesozoic arboreal ancestry. It is quite understandable that such a creature would very rarely die in water in such circumstances as to leave bones to become fossilized.

It must always be borne in mind that among its many other imperfections the Geological Record necessarily contains abundant traces only of water or marsh creatures or of creatures easily and frequently drowned. The same reasons that make any traces of the ancestors of the mammals rare and relatively unprocurable in the Mesozoic rocks, probably make the traces of possible human ancestors rare and relatively unprocurable in the Cainozoic rocks. Such knowledge as we have of the earliest men, for example, is almost entirely got from a few caves, into which they went and in which they left their traces. Until the hard Pleistocene times they lived and died in the open, and their bodies were consumed or decayed altogether.

But it is well to bear in mind also that the Record of the Rocks has still to be thoroughly examined. It has been studied only for a few generations, and by only a few men in each generation. Most men have been too busy making war, making profits out of their neighbours, toiling at work that machinery could do for them in a tenth of the time, or simply playing about, to give any attention to these more interesting things. There may be, there probably are, thousands of deposits still untouched containing countless fragments and vestiges of man and his progenitors. In Asia particularly, in India or the East Indies, there may be hidden the most illuminating clues. What we know to-day of early men is the merest scrap of what will presently be known.

The apes and monkeys already appear to have been differentiated at the beginning of the Cainozoic Age, and there are a number of Oligocene and Miocene apes whose relations to one another and to the human line have still to be made out. Among these we may mention *Dryopithecus* of the Miocene Age, with a very{v1-67} human-looking jaw. In the Siwalik Hills of northern India remains of some very interesting apes have been found, of which *Sivapithecus* and *Palæopithecus* were possibly related closely to the human ancestor. Possibly these animals already used implements. Charles Darwin represents baboons as opening nuts by breaking them with stones, using stakes to prize up rocks in the hunt for insects, and striking blows with sticks and stones.[21] The chimpanzee makes itself a sort of tree hut by intertwining branches. Stones apparently chipped for use have been found in strata of Oligocene Age at Boncelles in Belgium.

Possibly the implement-using disposition was already present in the Mesozoic ancestry from which we are descended.[22]

§ 2

Among the earliest evidences of some creature, either human or at least more man-like than any living ape upon earth, are a number of flints and stones very roughly chipped and shaped so as to be held in the hand. These were probably used as hand-axes. These early implements ("Eoliths") are often so crude and simple that there was for a long time a controversy whether they were to be regarded as natural or artificial productions.[23] The date of the earliest of them is put by geologists as Pliocene— that is to say, *before the First Glacial Age.* They occur also throughout the First Interglacial period. We know of no bones or other remains in Europe or America of the quasi-human beings of half a million years ago, who made and used these implements. They used them to hammer with, perhaps they used them to fight with, and perhaps they used bits of wood for similar purposes.[24]

But at Trinil, in Java, in strata which are said to correspond either to the later Pliocene or to the American and European First Ice Age, there have been found some scattered bones of a creature, such as the makers of these early implements may have been. The top of a skull, some teeth, and a thigh-bone have been found. The skull shows a brain-case about half-way in size between that of the chimpanzee and man, but the thigh-bone is that of a creature as well adapted to standing and running as a man, and as free, therefore, to use its hands. The creature was not a man, nor was it an arboreal ape like the chimpanzee. It was a walking ape. It has been named by naturalists *Pithecanthropus erectus* (the walking ape-man). We cannot say that it[v1-69] is a direct human ancestor, but we may guess that the creatures who scattered these first stone tools over the world must have been closely similar and kindred, and that our ancestor was a beast of like kind. This little trayful of bony fragments from Trinil is, at present, apart from stone implements, the oldest relic of early humanity, or of the close blood relations of early humanity, that is known.

While these early men or "sub-men" were running about Europe four or five hundred thousand years ago, there were mammoths, rhinoceroses, a huge hippopotamus, a giant beaver, and a bison and wild cattle in their world. There were also wild horses, and the sabre-toothed tiger still abounded. There are no traces of lions or true tigers at that time in Europe, but there were bears, otters, wolves, and a wild boar. It may be that the early sub-man sometimes played jackal to the sabre-toothed tiger, and finished up the bodies on which the latter had gorged itself.[25]

After this first glimpse of something at least sub-human in the record of geology, there is not another fragment of human or man-like bone yet known from that record for an interval of hundreds of thousands of years. It is not until we reach deposits which are stated to be of the Second Interglacial period, 200,000 years later, 200,000 or 250,000 years ago, that another little scrap of bone comes to hand. Then we find a jaw-bone.

This jaw-bone was found in a sandpit near Heidelberg, at a depth of eighty feet from the surface,[26] and it is not the jaw-bone of a man as we understand man, but it is man-like in every respect, except that it has absolutely no trace of a chin; it is more massive than a man's, and its narrowness behind could not, it is thought, have given the tongue sufficient play for articulate speech. It is not an ape's jaw-bone; the teeth are human. The owner of this jaw-bone has been variously named *Homo Heidelbergensis* and *Palæoanthropus Heidelbergensis*, according to the estimate formed of its humanity or sub-humanity by various authorities.{vi-70} He lived in a world not remotely unlike the world of the still earlier sub-man of the first implements; the deposits in which it is found show that there were elephants, horses, rhinoceroses, bison, a moose, and so forth with it in the world, but the sabre-toothed tiger was declining and the lion was spreading over Europe. The implements of this period (known as the Chellean period) are a very considerable advance upon those of the Pliocene Age. They are well made but *very much bigger* than any truly human implements. The Heidelberg man may have had a very big body and large forelimbs. He may have been a woolly strange-looking creature.

§ 4

We must turn over the Record for, it may be, another 100,000 years for the next remains of anything human or sub-human. Then in a deposit ascribed to the Third Interglacial period, which may have begun 100,000 years ago and lasted 50,000 years,[27] the smashed pieces of a whole skull turn up. The deposit is a gravel which may have been derived from the washing out of still earlier gravel strata and this skull fragment may be in reality as old as the First Glacial period. The bony remains discovered at Piltdown in Sussex display a creature still ascending only very gradually from the sub-human.

The first scraps of this skull were found in an excavation for road gravel in Sussex. Bit by bit other fragments of this skull were hunted out from the quarry heaps until most of it could be pieced together. It is a thick skull, thicker than that of any living race of men, and it has a brain capacity intermediate between that of Pithecanthropus and man. This creature has been named *Eoanthropus*, the dawn man. In the same gravel-pits were found teeth of rhinoceros, hippopotamus, and the leg-bone of a deer with marks upon it that may be cuts. A curious bat-shaped instrument of elephant bone has also been found.[28]

There was, moreover, a jaw-bone among these scattered remains, which was at first assumed naturally enough to belong to{vi-71} *Eoanthropus*, but which it was afterwards suggested was probably that of a chimpanzee. It is extraordinarily like that of a chimpanzee, but Dr. Keith, one of the greatest authorities in these questions, assigns it, after an exhaustive analysis in his *Antiquity of Man* (1915), to the skull with which it is found. It is, as a jaw-bone, far less human in character than the jaw of the much more ancient *Homo Heidelbergensis*, but the teeth are in some respects more like those of living men.

Diagram to Illustrate the Riddle of The Piltdown Sub-man.

Dr. Keith, swayed by the jaw-bone, does not think that *Eoanthropus*, in spite of its name, is a creature in the direct ancestry of man. Much less is it an intermediate form between the Heidelberg man and the Neanderthal man we shall presently describe. It was only related to the true ancestor of man as the orang is related to the chimpanzee. It was one of a number of sub-human running apes of more than ape-like intelligence, and if it was not on the line royal, it was at any rate a very close collateral.

After this glimpse of a skull, the Record for very many centuries gives nothing but flint implements, which improve steadily in quality. A very characteristic form is shaped like a sole, with one flat side stricken off at one blow and the other side worked. The archæologists, as the Record continues, are presently able to distinguish scrapers, borers, knives, darts, throwing stones, and the like. Progress is now more rapid; in a few centuries the shape of the hand-axe shows distinct and recognizable improvements. And then comes quite a number of remains. The Fourth(v1-72) Glacial Age is rising towards its maximum. Man is taking to caves and leaving vestiges there; at Krapina in Croatia, at Neanderthal near Düsseldorf, at Spy, human remains have been found, skulls and bones of a creature that is certainly a man. Somewhere about 50,000 years ago, if not earlier, appeared *Homo Neanderthalensis* (also called *Homo antiquus* and *Homo primigenius*), a quite passable human being. His thumb was not quite equal in flexibility and usefulness to a human thumb, he stooped forward, and could not hold his head erect, as all living men do, he was chinless and perhaps incapable of speech, there were curious differences about the enamel and the roots of his teeth from those of all living men, he was very thick-set, he was, indeed, not quite of the human species; but there is no dispute about his attribution to the genus *Homo*. He was certainly not descended from Eoanthropus, but his jaw-bone is so like the Heidelberg jaw-bone as to make it possible that the clumsier and heavier *Homo Heidelbergensis*, a thousand centuries before him, was of his blood and race.

Upon this question of the Piltdown jaw-bone, it may be of interest to quote here a letter to the writer from Sir Ray Lankester, discussing the question in a familiar and luminous manner. It will enable the reader to gauge the extent and quality of the evidence that we possess at present upon the nature of these early human and sub-human animals. Upon these fragile Piltdown fragments alone more than a hundred books, pamphlets, and papers have been written. These scraps of bone are guarded more carefully from theft and wilful damage than the most precious jewels, and in the museum cases one sees only carefully executed *fac-similes*.

"As to the Piltdown jaw-bone, the best study of it is that by Smith Woodward, who first described it and the canine found later. The jaw is imperfect in front, but has the broad, flat symphysis of the Apes. G. S. Miller, an American anthropologist, has made a very good comparison of it with a chimpanzee's jaw, and concludes that it is a chimpanzee's. (His monograph is in the *Am. Jour. of Phys. Anthrop.*, vol. i, no. 1.) The one{vı-73} point in the Piltdown jaw itself against chimpanzee identification is the smooth, flat, worn surface of the molars. This is a human character, and is due to lateral movement of the jaw, and hence rubbing down of the tubercles of the molars. This is not worth much. But the serious question is, are we to associate this jaw with the cranium found close by it? If so, it is certainly not chimpanzee nor close to the Apes, but decidedly hominid. Two other small fragments of crania and a few more teeth have been found in the gravel two miles from Piltdown, which agree with the Piltdown cranium in having superciliary ridges fairly strong for a human skull, but not anything like the great superciliary ridges of Apes. The fact one has to face is this; here you have an imperfect cranium, very thick-walled and of small cubical contents (1100 or so), but much larger in that respect than any ape's. A few yards distant from it in the same layer of gravel is found a jaw-bone having rather large pointed canines, a flat, broad symphysis, and other points about the inner face of the ramus and ridges which resemble those of the chimpanzee. Which is the more likely: (*a*) that these two novel fragments tending apewards from man were parts of the same individual; or (*b*), that the sweeping of the Wealden valley has brought there together a half-jaw and a broken cranium *both* more ape-like in character than any known human corresponding bits, and yet derived from two separate anthropoid beasts, one (the jaw) more simian, and the other (the cranium) much less so? As to the probabilities, we must remember that this patch of gravel at Piltdown, clearly and definitely, is a wash-up of remains of various later tertiary and post-tertiary deposits. It contains fragments of Miocene mastodon and rhinoceros teeth. These latter differ entirely in mineral character from the Eoanthropus jaw and the cranium. But (and this needs re-examination and *chemical* analysis) the Piltdown jaw and the Piltdown cranium do not seem to me to be quite alike in their mineral condition. The jaw is more deeply iron-stained, and I should say (but not confidently), harder than the cranium. Now, it is easy to attribute too much importance to that difference, since in a patch of iron-stained gravel, such as that at Piltdown, the soaking of water and iron salts into bones embedded may{vI-74} be much greater in one spot than in another only a yard off, or a few inches deeper!

"So I think we are stumped and baffled! The most prudent way is to keep the jaw and the cranium apart in all argument about them. On the other hand, on the principle that hypotheses are not to be multiplied beyond necessity, there is a case for regarding the two—jaw and cranium—as having been parts of one beast—or man."

To which Sir H. H. Johnston adds: "Against the chimpanzee hypothesis it must be borne in mind that so far no living chimpanzee or fossil chimpanzee-like remains have been found nearer England than north equatorial Africa or North-west India, and no remains of great apes at all nearer than Southern France and the upper Rhine—and those widely different from the *Eoanthropus* jaw.{vI-75}"

IX

THE NEANDERTHAL MEN, AN EXTINCT RACE

(The Early Palæolithic Age[29])

§ 1. *The World 50,000 Years Ago.* § 2. *The Daily Life of the First Men.* § 3. *The Last Palæolithic Men.*

§ 1

IN the time of the Third Interglacial period the outline of Europe and western Asia was very different from what it is to-day. Vast areas to the west and northwest which are now under the Atlantic waters were then dry land; the Irish Sea and the North Sea were river valleys. Over these northern areas there spread and receded and spread again a great ice cap such as covers central Greenland to-day (see Map, on page 77). This vast ice cap, which covered both polar regions of the earth, withdrew huge masses of water from the ocean, and the sea-level consequently fell, exposing great areas of land that are now submerged again. The Mediterranean area was probably a great valley below the general sea-level, containing two inland seas cut off from the general ocean. The climate of this Mediterranean basin was perhaps cold temperate, and the region of the Sahara to the south was not then a desert of baked rock and blown sand, but a well-watered and fertile country. Between the ice sheets to the north and the Alps and Mediterranean valley{v1-76} to the south stretched a bleak wilderness whose climate changed from harshness to a mild kindliness and then hardened again for the Fourth Glacial Age.

Across this wilderness, which is now the great plain of Europe, wandered a various fauna. At first there were hippopotami, rhinoceroses, mammoths, and elephants. The sabre-toothed tiger was diminishing towards extinction. Then, as the air chilled, the hippopotamus, and then other warmth-loving creatures, ceased to come so far north, and the sabre-toothed tiger disappeared altogether. The woolly mammoth, the woolly rhinoceros, the musk ox, the bison, the aurochs, and the reindeer became prevalent, and the temperate vegetation gave place to plants of a more arctic type. The glaciers spread southward to the maximum of the Fourth Glacial Age (about 50,000 years ago), and then receded again. In the earlier phase, the Third Interglacial period, a certain number of small family groups of men (*Homo Neanderthalensis*) and probably of sub-men (*Eoanthropus*) wandered over the land, leaving nothing but their flint implements to witness to their presence. They probably used a multitude and variety of wooden implements also; they had probably learnt much about the shapes of objects and the use of different shapes from wood, knowledge which they afterwards applied to stone; but none of this wooden material has survived; we can only speculate about its forms and uses. As the weather hardened to its maximum of severity, the Neanderthal men, already it would seem acquainted with the use of fire, began to seek shelter under rock ledges and in caves—and so leave remains behind them. Hitherto they had been accustomed to squat in the open about the fire, and near their water supply. But they were sufficiently intelligent to adapt themselves to the new and harder conditions. (As for the sub-men, they seem to have succumbed to the stresses of this Fourth Glacial Age altogether. At any rate, the rudest type of Palæolithic implements presently disappears.)

Not merely man was taking to the caves. This period also had a cave lion, a cave bear, and a cave hyæna. These creatures had to be driven out of the caves and kept out of the caves in which these early men wanted to squat and hide; and no doubt fire was an effective method of eviction and protection. Prob{vi-78}ably early men did not go deeply into the caves, because they had no means of lighting their recesses. They got in far enough to be out of the weather, and stored wood and food in odd corners. Perhaps they barricaded the cave mouths. Their only available light for going deeply into the caverns would be torches.

What did these Neanderthal men hunt? Their only possible weapons for killing such giant creatures as the mammoth or the cave bear, or even the reindeer, were spears of wood, wooden clubs, and those big pieces of flint they left behind them, the "Chellean" and "Mousterian" implements;[30] and probably their usual quarry was smaller game. But they did certainly eat the flesh of the big beasts when they had a chance, and perhaps they followed them when sick or when wounded by combats, or took advantage of them when they were bogged or in trouble with ice or water. (The Labrador Indians still kill the caribou with spears at awkward river crossings.) At Dewlish in Dorset, an artificial trench has been found which is supposed to have been a Palæolithic trap for elephants.[31] We know that the Neanderthalers partly ate their kill where it fell; but they brought back the big marrow bones to the cave to crack and eat at leisure, because few ribs and vertebræ are found in the caves, but great quantities of cracked and split long bones. They used skins to wrap about them, and the women probably dressed the skins.{v1-79}

We know also that they were right-handed like modern men, because the left side of the brain (which serves the right side of the body) is bigger than the right. But while the back parts of the brain which deal with sight and touch and the energy of the body are well developed, the front parts, which are connected with thought and speech, are comparatively small. It was as big a brain as ours, but different. This species of *Homo* had certainly a very different mentality from ours; its individuals were not merely simpler and lower than we are, they were on another line. It may be they did not speak at all, or very sparingly. They had nothing that we should call a language.

2

In Worthington Smith's *Man the Primeval Savage* there is a very vividly written description of early Palæolithic life, from which much of the following account is borrowed. In the original, Mr. Worthington Smith assumes a more extensive social life, a larger community, and a more definite division of labour among its members than is altogether justifiable in the face of such subsequent writings as J. J. Atkinson's memorable essay on Primal Law.[32] For the little tribe Mr. Worthington Smith described there has been substituted, therefore, a family group under the leadership of one Old Man, and the suggestions of Mr. Atkinson as to the behaviour of the Old Man have been worked into the sketch.

Mr. Worthington Smith describes a squatting-place near a stream, because primitive man, having no pots or other vessels, must needs have kept close to a water supply, and with some chalk cliffs adjacent from which flints could be got to work. The air was bleak, and the fire was of great importance, because fires once out were not easily relit in those days. When not required to blaze it was probably banked down with ashes. The most probable way in which fires were started was by hacking a bit of iron pyrites with a flint amidst dry dead leaves;

concretions of iron pyrites and flints are found together in England where the[vi-80] gault and chalk approach each other.[33] The little group of people would be squatting about amidst a litter of fern, moss, and such-like dry material. Some of the women and children would need to be continually gathering fuel to keep up the fires. It would be a tradition that had grown up. The young would imitate their elders in this task. Perhaps there would be rude wind shelters of boughs on one side of the encampment.

The Old Man, the father and master of the group, would perhaps be engaged in hammering flints beside the fire. The children would imitate him and learn to use the sharpened fragments. Probably some of the women would hunt good flints; they would fish them out of the chalk with sticks and bring them to the squatting-place.

There would be skins about. It seems probable that at a very early time primitive men took to using skins. Probably they were wrapped about the children, and used to lie upon when the ground was damp and cold. A woman would perhaps be preparing a skin. The inside of the skin would be well scraped free of superfluous flesh with trimmed flints, and then strained and pulled and pegged out flat on the grass, and dried in the rays of the sun.

–

Away from the fire other members of the family group prowl in search of food, but at night they all gather closely round the fire and build it up, for it is their protection against the wandering bear and such-like beasts of prey. The Old Man is the only fully adult male in the little group. There are women, boys and girls, but so soon as the boys are big enough to rouse the Old Man's jealousy, he will fall foul of them and either drive them off or kill them. Some girls may perhaps go off with these exiles, or two or three of these youths may keep together for a time, wandering until they come upon some other group, from which they may try to steal a mate. Then they would probably fall out among themselves. Some day, when he is forty years old perhaps or even older, and his teeth are worn down and his energy abating,{v1-82} some younger male will stand up to the Old Man and kill him and reign in his stead. There is probably short shrift for the old at the squatting-place. So soon as they grow weak and bad-tempered, trouble and death come upon them.

What did they eat at the squatting-place?

"Primeval man is commonly described as a hunter of the great hairy mammoth, of the bear, and the lion, but it is in the highest degree improbable that the human savage ever hunted animals much larger than the hare, the rabbit, and the rat. Man was probably the hunted rather than the hunter.

–

"The primeval savage was both herbivorous and carnivorous. He had for food hazel-nuts, beech-nuts, sweet chestnuts, earth-nuts, and acorns. He had crab-apples, wild pears, wild cherries, wild gooseberries, bullaces, sorbs, sloes, blackberries, yewberries, hips and haws, water-cress, fungi, the larger and softer leaf-buds, Nostoc (the vegetable substance called 'fallen stars' by country-folk), the fleshy, juicy, asparagus-like rhizomes or subterranean stems of the *Labiatæ* and like plants, as well as other delicacies of the vegetable kingdom. He had birds' eggs, young birds, and the honey and honeycomb of wild bees. He had newts, snails, and frogs—the two latter delicacies are still highly esteemed in Normandy and Brittany. He had fish, dead and alive, and fresh-water mussels; he could easily catch fish with his hands and paddle and dive for and trap them. By the seaside he would have fish,[vi-83]mollusca, and seaweed. He would have many of the larger birds and smaller mammals, which he could easily secure by throwing stones and sticks, or by setting simple snares. He would have the snake, the slow-worm, and the crayfish. He would have various grubs and insects, the large larvæ of beetles and various caterpillars. The taste for caterpillars still survives in China, where they are sold in dried bundles in the markets. A chief and highly nourishing object of food would doubtlessly be bones smashed up into a stiff and gritty paste.

"A fact of great importance is this—primeval man would not be particular about having his flesh food over-fresh. He would constantly find it in a dead state, and, if semi-putrid, he would relish it none the less—the taste for high or half-putrid game still survives. If driven by hunger and hard pressed, he would perhaps sometimes eat his weaker companions or unhealthy children who happened to be feeble or unsightly or burthensome. The larger animals in a weak and dying state would no doubt be much sought for; when these were not forthcoming, dead and half-rotten examples would be made to suffice. An unpleasant odour would not be objected to; it is not objected to now in many continental hotels.

"The savages sat huddled close together round their fire, with fruits, bones, and half-putrid flesh. We can imagine the old man and his women twitching the skin of their shoulders, brows, and muzzles as they were annoyed or bitten by flies or other insects. We can imagine the large human nostrils, indicative of keen scent, giving rapidly repeated sniffs at the foul meat before it was consumed; the bad odour of the meat, and the various other disgusting odours belonging to a haunt of savages, being not in the least disapproved.

"Man at that time was not a *degraded* animal, for he had never been higher; he was therefore an exalted animal, and, low as we esteem him now, he yet represented the highest stage of development of the animal kingdom of his time."

That is at least an acceptable sketch of a Neanderthal squatting-place. But before extinction overtook them, even the Neanderthalers learnt much and went far.

Whatever the older Palæolithic men did with their dead, there{vI-84} is reason to suppose that the later *Homo   Neanderthalensis* buried   some individuals at least with respect and ceremony. One of the best-known Neanderthal skeletons is that of a youth who apparently had been deliberately interred. He had been placed in a sleeping posture, head on the right fore-arm. The head lay on a number of flint fragments carefully piled together "pillow fashion." A big hand-axe lay near his head, and around him were numerous charred and split ox bones, as though there had been a feast or an offering.

To this appearance of burial during the later Neanderthal age we shall return when we are considering the ideas that were inside the heads of primitive men.

This sort of men may have wandered, squatted about their fires, and died in Europe for a period extending over 100,000 years, if we assume, that is, that the Heidelberg jaw-bone belongs to a member of the species, a period so vast that all the subsequent history of our race becomes a thing of yesterday. Along its own line this species of men was accumulating a dim tradition, and working out its limited possibilities. Its thick skull imprisoned its brain, and to the end it was low-browed and brutish.

§ 3

When the Dutch discovered Tasmania, they found a detached human race not very greatly advanced beyond this Lower Palæolithic stage. But over most of the world the Lower Palæolithic culture had developed into a more complicated and higher life twenty or thirty thousand years ago. The Tasmanians were not racially Neanderthalers;[34] their brain-cases, their neck-bones, their jaws and teeth, show that; they had no Neanderthal affinities; they were of the same species as ourselves. There can be little doubt that throughout the hundreds of centuries during which the scattered little groups of Neanderthal men were all that represented men in Europe, real men, of our own species, in some other part of the world, were working their way along parallel lines from much the same stage as the Neanderthalers ended at, and which the Tasmanians preserved, to a higher{v1-85} level of power and achievement. The Tasmanians, living under unstimulating conditions, remote from any other human competition or example, lagged behind the rest of the human brotherhood.[35]

About 200 centuries ago or earlier, real men of our own species, if not of our own race, came drifting into the European area.{v1-86}

X

THE LATER POSTGLACIAL PALÆOLITHIC MEN,
THE FIRST TRUE MEN

(Later Palæolithic Age)

§ 1. *The Coming of Men Like Ourselves.* §
2. *Subdivision of the Later Palæolithic.* § 3. *The Earliest True Men Were Splendid Savages.* §
4. *Hunters Give Place to Herdsmen.* § 5. *No Submen in America.*

§ 1

THE Neanderthal type of man prevailed in Europe at least for tens of thousands of years. For ages that make all history seem a thing of yesterday, these nearly human creatures prevailed. If the Heidelberg jaw was that of a Neanderthaler, and if there is no error in the estimate of the age of that jaw, then the Neanderthal Race lasted out for more than 200,000 years! Finally, between 40,000 and 25,000 years ago, as the Fourth Glacial Age softened towards more temperate conditions (see Map on p. 89), a different human type came upon the scene, and, it would seem, exterminated *Homo Neanderthalensis.*[36] This new type was probably developed in South Asia or North Africa, or in lands now submerged in the Mediterranean basin, and, as{v1-87} more remains are collected and evidence accumulates, men will learn more of their early stages. At present we can only guess where and how, through the slow ages, parallel with the Neanderthal cousin, these first *true men* arose out of some more ape-like progenitor. For hundreds of centuries they were acquiring skill of hand and limb, and power and bulk of brain, in that still unknown environment. They were already far above the Neanderthal level of achievement and intelligence, when first they come into our ken, and they had already split into two or more very distinctive races.

These new-comers did not migrate into Europe in the strict sense of the word, but rather, as century by century the climate ameliorated, they followed the food and plants to which they were accustomed, as those spread into the new realms that opened to them. The ice was receding, vegetation was increasing, big game of all sorts was becoming more abundant. Steppe-like conditions, conditions of pasture and shrub, were bringing with them vast herds of wild{v1-88} horse. Ethnologists (students of race) class these new human races in one same species as ourselves, and with all human races subsequent to them, under one common specific name of *Homo sapiens*. They had quite human brain-cases and hands. Their teeth and their necks were anatomically as ours are.

Now here again, with every desire to be plain and explicit with the reader, we have still to trouble him with qualified statements and notes of interrogation. There is now an enormous literature about these earliest true men, the men of the Later

Palæolithic Age, and it is still for the general reader a very confusing literature indeed. It is confusing because it is still confused at the source. We know of two distinct sorts of skeletal remains in this period, the first of these known as the Cro-Magnon race, and the second the Grimaldi race; but the great bulk of the human traces and appliances we find are either without human bones or with insufficient bones for us to define their associated physical type. There may have been many more distinct races than these two. There may have been intermediate types. In the grotto of Cro-Magnon it was that complete skeletons of one main type of these Newer Palæolithic men, these true men, were first found, and so it is that they are spoken of as Cro-Magnards.

–

These Cro-Magnards were a tall people with very broad faces, prominent noses, and, all things considered, astonishingly big brains. The brain capacity of the woman in the Cro-Magnon cave exceeded that of the average male to-day. Her head had been smashed by a heavy blow. There were also in the same cave with her the complete skeleton of an older man, nearly six feet high, the fragments of a child's skeleton, and the skeletons of two young men. There were also flint implements and perforated sea-shells, used no doubt as ornaments. Such is one sample of the earliest true men. But at the Grimaldi cave, near Mentone, were discovered two skeletons also of the Later Palæolithic period, but of a widely contrasted type, with negroid characteristics that point rather to the negroid type. There can be no doubt that we have to deal in this period with at least two, and probably more, highly divergent races of true men. They may have overlapped in time, or Cro-Magnards may have fol{vi-90}lowed the Grimaldi race, and either or both may have been contemporary with the late Neanderthal men. Various authorities have very strong opinions upon these points, but they are, at most, opinions. The whole story is further fogged at present by our inability to distinguish, in the absence of skeletons, which race has been at work in any particular case. In what follows{vi-91} the reader will ask of this or that particular statement, "Yes, but is this the Cro-Magnard or the Grimaldi man or some other that you are writing about?" To which in most cases the honest answer is, "As yet we do not know." Confessedly our account of the newer Palæolithic is a jumbled account. There are probably two or three concurrent and only roughly similar histories of these newer Palæolithic men as yet, inextricably mixed up together. Some authorities appear to favour the Cro-Magnards unduly and to dismiss the Grimaldi people with as little as possible of the record.

The appearance of these truly human postglacial Palæolithic peoples was certainly an enormous leap forward in the history of mankind. Both of these main races had a human fore-brain, a human hand, an intelligence very like our own. They dispossessed *Homo Neanderthalensis* from his caverns and his stone quarries. And they agreed with modern ethnologists, it would seem, in regarding him as a different species. Unlike most savage conquerors, who take the women of the defeated side for their own and interbreed with them, it would seem that the true men would have nothing to do with the Neanderthal race, women or men. There is no trace of any intermixture between the races, in spite of the fact that the newcomers, being also flint users, were establishing themselves in the very same spots that their predecessors had occupied. We know nothing of the appearance of the Neanderthal man, but this absence of intermixture seems to suggest an extreme hairiness, an ugliness, or a repulsive strangeness in his appearance over and above his low forehead, his beetle brows, his ape neck, and his inferior stature. Or he—and she—may have been too fierce to tame. Says Sir Harry Johnston, in a survey of the rise of modern man in his *Views and Reviews*: "The dim racial remembrance of such gorilla-like monsters, with cunning brains, shambling gait, hairy bodies, strong teeth, and possibly cannibalistic tendencies, may be the germ of the ogre in folklore...."

These true men of the Palæolithic Age, who replaced the Neanderthalers, were coming into a milder climate, and although they used the caves and shelters of their predecessors, they lived largely in the open. They were hunting peoples, and some or all of[v1-92] them appear to have hunted the mammoth and the wild horse as well as the reindeer, bison, and aurochs. They ate much horse. At a great open-air camp at Solutré, where they seem to have had animal gatherings for many centuries, it is estimated that there are the bones of 100,000 horses, besides reindeer, mammoth, and bison bones. They probably followed herds of horses, the little bearded ponies of that age, as these moved after pasture. They hung about on the flanks of the herd, and became very wise about its habits and dispositions. A large part of these men's lives must have been spent in watching animals.

Whether they tamed and domesticated the horse is still an open question. Perhaps they learnt to do so by degrees as the centuries passed. At any rate, we find late Palæolithic drawings of horses with marks about the heads that are strongly suggestive of bridles, and there exists a carving of a horse's head showing what is perhaps a rope of twisted skin or tendon. But even if they tamed the horse, it is still more doubtful whether they rode it or had much use for it when it was tamed. The horse they knew was a wild pony with a beard under its chin, not up to carrying a man for any distance. It is improbable that these men had yet learnt the rather unnatural use of animal's milk as food. If they tamed the horse at last, it was the only animal they seem to have tamed. They had no dogs, and they had little to do with any sort of domesticated sheep or cattle.

It greatly aids us to realize their common humanity that these earliest true men could draw. Both races, it would seem, drew astonishingly well. They were by all standards savages, but they were artistic savages. They drew better than any of their successors down to the beginnings of history. They drew and painted on the cliffs and cave walls that they had wrested from the Neanderthal men. And the surviving drawings come to the ethnologist, puzzling over bones and scraps, with the effect of a plain message shining through guesswork and darkness. They drew on bones and antlers; they carved little figures.

These late Palæolithic people not only drew remarkably well for our information, and with an increasing skill as the centuries passed, but they have also left us other information about their{v1-93} lives in their graves. They buried. They buried their dead, often with ornaments, weapons, and food; they used a lot of colour in the burial, and evidently painted the body. From that one may infer that they painted their bodies during life. Paint was a big fact in their lives. They were inveterate painters; they used black, brown, red, yellow, and white pigments, and the pigments they used endure to this day in the caves of France and Spain. Of all modern races, none have shown so pictorial a disposition; the nearest approach to it has been among the American Indians.

These drawings and paintings of the later Palæolithic people went on through a long period of time, and present wide fluctuations in artistic merit. We give here some early sketches, from which we learn of the interest taken by these early men in the bison, horse, ibex, cave bear, and reindeer. In its early stages the drawing is often primitive like the drawing of clever children; quadrupeds are usually drawn with one hindleg and one{vl-94} foreleg, as children draw them to this day. The legs on the other side were too much for the artist's technique. Possibly the first drawings began as children's drawings begin, out of idle scratchings. The savage scratched with a flint on a smooth rock surface, and was reminded of some line or gesture. But their solid carvings are at least as old as their first pictures. The earlier{vl-95} drawings betray a complete incapacity to group animals. As the centuries progressed, more skilful artists appeared. The representation of beasts became at last astonishingly vivid and like. But even at the crest of their artistic time they still drew in profile as children do; perspective and the foreshortening needed for back and front views were too much for them.[37] They rarely drew themselves. The vast majority of their drawings represent animals. The mammoth and the horse are among the commonest themes. Some of the people, whether Grimaldi people or Cro-Magnon people, also made little ivory and soapstone statuettes, and among these are some very fat female figures. These latter suggest the physique of Grimaldi rather than of Cro-Magnon artists. They are like Bushmen women. The human sculpture of the earlier times inclined to caricature, and generally such human figures as they represent are far below the animal studies in vigour and veracity.

Later on there was more grace and less coarseness in the human representations. One little ivory head discovered is that of a girl with an elaborate coiffure. These people at a later stage also scratched and engraved designs on ivory and bone. Some of the most interesting groups of figures are carved very curiously round bone, and especially round rods of deer bone, so that it is impossible to see the entire design all together. Figures have also been found modelled in clay, although no Palæolithic people made any use of pottery.

Many of the paintings are found in the depths of unlit caves. They are often difficult of access. The artists must have employed lamps to do their work, and shallow soapstone lamps in which fat could have been burnt have been found. Whether the seeing of these cavern paintings was in some way ceremonial or under what circumstances they were seen, we are now altogether at a loss to imagine.

§ 2

Archæologists distinguish at present three chief stages in the history of these newer Palæolithic men in Europe, and we must name these stages here. But it may be as well to note at the{v1-96} same time that it is a matter of the utmost difficulty to distinguish which of two deposits in different places is the older or newer. We may very well be dealing with the work of more or less contemporary and different races when we think we are dealing with successive ones. We are dealing, the reader must bear in mind, with little disconnected patches of material, a few score all together. The earliest stage usually distinguished by the experts is the *Aurignacian* (from the grotto of Aurignac); it is characterized by very well-made flint implements, and by a rapid development of art and more particularly of statuettes and wall paintings. The most esteemed of the painted caves is ascribed to the latter part of this the first of the three subdivisions of the newer Palæolithic. The second subdivision of this period is called the *Solutrian* (from Solutré), and is distinguished particularly by the quality and beauty of its stone implements; some of its razor-like blades are only equalled and not surpassed by the very best of the Neolithic work. They are of course unpolished, but the best specimens are as thin as steel blades and almost as sharp. Finally, it would seem, came the *Magdalenian* (from La Madeleine) stage, in which the horse and reindeer were dwindling in numbers and the red deer coming into Europe.[38] The stone implements are smaller, and there is a great quantity of bone harpoons, spearheads, needles, and the like. The hunters of the third and last stage of the later Palæolithic Age appear to have supplemented a diminishing food supply by fishing. The characteristic art of the period consists of deep reliefs done upon bone and line engraving upon bone. It is to this period that the designs drawn round bones belong, and it has been suggested that these designs upon round bones were used to print coloured designs upon leather. Some of the workmanship on bone was extraordinarily fine. Parkyn quotes from de Mortillet, about the Reindeer Age (Magdalenian) bone needles, that they "are much superior to those of later, even historical, times, down to the Renaissance. The Romans, for example, never had needles comparable to those of the Magdalenian epoch."

TIME DIAGRAM SHOWING THE ESTIMATED DURATION OF THE TRUE HUMAN PERIODS.
This time diagram again is on a larger scale than its predecessors. The time diagram on page 60, if it were on this scale, would be nearly 4 feet long, and the diagram of the whole geological time on page 14, between 500 and 5000 feet long (or perhaps even as much as 10,000 feet long).

It is quite impossible at present to guess at the relative lengths[VI-98] of these ages. We are not even positive about their relative relationship. Each lasted perhaps for four or five more thousand years, more than double the time from the Christian Era to our own day.

At last it would seem that circumstances began to turn altogether against these hunting Newer Palæolithic people who had flourished for so long in Europe. They disappeared. New kinds of men appeared in Europe, replacing them. These latter seem to have brought in bow and arrows; they had domesticated animals and cultivated the soil. A new way of living, the Neolithic way of living, spread over the European area; and the life of the Reindeer Age and of the races of Reindeer Men, the Later Palæolithic men, after a reign vastly greater than the time between ourselves and the very earliest beginnings of recorded history, passed off the European stage.

§ 3

There is a disposition on the part of many writers to exaggerate the intellectual and physical qualities of these later Palæolithic men and make a wonder of them.[39]Collectively considered, these people had remarkable gifts, but a little reflection will show they had almost as remarkable deficiencies. The tremendous advance they display upon their Neanderthalian predecessors and their special artistic gift must not blind us to their very obvious limitations. For all the quantity of their brains, the quality was narrow and special. They had vivid perceptions, an acute sense of animal form, they had the real artist's impulse to render; so far they were fully grown human beings. But that disposition to paint and draw is shown to-day by the Bushmen, by Californian Indians, and by Australian black fellows; it is not a mark of all-round high intellectual quality. The cumulative effect of their drawings and paintings is very great, but we must not make the mistake of crowding all these achievements together in our minds as though they had suddenly flashed out upon the world in a brief interval of time, or as though they were all the achievements of one people. These races of Reindeer Men{v1-99} were in undisturbed possession of western Europe for a period at least ten times as long as the interval between ourselves and the beginning of the

Christian Era, and through all that immense time they were free to develop and vary their life to its utmost possibilities. Their art constitutes their one claim to be accounted more than common savages.

They were in close contact with animals, but they never seemed to have got to terms with any animal unless it was the horse. They had no dogs. They had no properly domesticated animals at all. They watched and drew and killed and ate. They do not seem to have cooked their food. Perhaps they scorched and grilled it, but they could not have done much more, because they had no cooking implements. Although they had clay available, and although there are several Palæolithic clay figures on record, they had *no pottery*. Although they had a great variety of flint and bone implements, they never rose to the possibilities of using timber for permanent shelters or such-like structures. They never made hafted axes or the like that would enable them to deal with timber. There is a suggestion in some of the drawings of a fence of stakes in which a mammoth seems to be entangled. But here we may be dealing with superimposed scratchings. They had *no buildings*. It is not even certain that they had tents or huts. They may have had simple skin tents. Some of the drawings seem to suggest as much. It is doubtful if they knew of the bow. They left no good arrowheads behind them. Certain of their implements are said to be "arrow-straighteners" by distinguished authorities, but that is about as much evidence as we have of arrows. They may have used sharpened sticks as arrows. They had *no cultivation* of grain or vegetables of any sort. Their women were probably squaws, smaller than the men; the earlier statuettes represent them as grossly fat, almost as the Bushmen women are often fat to-day. (But this may not be true of the Cro-Magnards.)

They clothed themselves, it would seem, in skins, if they clothed themselves at all. These skins they prepared with skill and elaboration, and towards the end of the age they used bone needles, no doubt to sew these pelts. One may guess pretty safely that they painted these skins, and it has even been supposed,{vi-100} printed off designs upon them from bone cylinders. But their garments were mere wraps; there are no clasps or catches to be found. They do not seem to have used grass or such-like fibre for textiles. Their statuettes are naked. They were, in fact, except for a fur wrap in cold weather, naked painted savages.

These hunters lived on open steppes for two hundred centuries or so, ten times the length of the Christian era. They were, perhaps, overtaken by the growth of the European forests, as the climate became milder and damper. When the wild horse and the reindeer diminished in Europe, and a newer type of human culture, with a greater power over food supply, a greater tenacity of settlement, and probably a larger social organization, arose, the Reindeer Men had to learn fresh ways of living or disappear. How far they learnt and mingled their strain with the new European populations, and how far they went under we cannot yet guess. Opinions differ widely. Wright lays much stress on the "great hiatus" between the Palæolithic and Neolithic remains, while Osborn traces the likeness of the former in several living populations. In the region of the Doubs and of the Dordogne in France, many individuals are to be met with to this day with skulls of the "Cro-Magnon" type. Apparently the Grimaldi type of men has disappeared altogether from Europe. Whether the Cro-Magnon type of men mingled completely with the Neolithic peoples, or whether they remained distinct and held their own in favourable localities to the north and west, following the reindeer over Siberia and towards America, which at that time was continuous with Siberia, or whether they disappeared altogether from the world, is a matter that can be only speculated about at present. There is not enough evidence for a judgment. Possibly they mingled to a certain extent. There is little to prevent our believing that they survived without much intermixture for a long time in north Asia, that "pockets" of them remained here and there in Europe, that there is a streak of their blood in most European peoples to-day, and that there is a much stronger streak, if not a predominant strain, in the Mongolian and American races.[40]

{v1-101}

§ 4

It was about 12,000 or fewer years ago that, with the spread of forests and a great change of the fauna, the long prevalence of the hunting life in Europe drew to its end. Reindeer vanished.

Changing conditions frequently bring with them new diseases. There may have been prehistoric pestilences. For many centuries there may have been no men in Britain or Central Europe (Wright). For a time there were in Southern Europe drifting communities of some little known people who are called the Azilians.[41] They may have been transition generations; they may have been a different race. We do not know. Some authorities incline to the view that the Azilians were the first wave of a race which, as we shall see later, has played a great part in populating Europe, the dark-white or Mediterranean or Iberian race. These Azilian people have left behind them a multitude of pebbles, roughly daubed with markings of an unknown purport (see illus., p. 94). The use or significance of these Azilian pebbles is still a profound mystery. Was this some sort of token writing? Were they counters in some game? Did the Azilians play with these pebbles or tell a story with them, as imaginative children will do with bits of wood and stone nowadays? At present we are unable to cope with any of these questions.

We will not deal here with the other various peoples who left their scanty traces in the world during the close of the New Palæolithic period, the spread of the forests where formerly there had been steppes, and the wane of the hunters, some 10,000 or 12,000 years ago. We will go on to describe the new sort of human community that was now spreading over the northern hemisphere, whose appearance marks what is called the *Neolithic Age*. The map of the world was assuming something like its present outlines, the landscape and the flora and fauna were taking on their existing characteristics. The prevailing animals in the spreading woods of Europe were the royal stag, the great ox, and the bison; the mammoth and the musk ox had gone. The great ox, or aurochs, is now extinct, but it survived in the German forests{vl-102} up to the time of the Roman Empire. It was never domesticated.[42] It stood eleven feet high at the shoulder, as high as an elephant. There were still lions in the Balkan peninsula, and they remained there until about 1000 or 1200 B.C. The lions of Württemberg and South Germany in those days were twice the size of the modern lion. South Russia and Central Asia were thickly wooded then, and there were elephants in Mesopotamia and Syria, and a fauna in Algeria that was tropical African in character.

Hitherto men in Europe had never gone farther north than the Baltic Sea or the English midlands, but now Ireland, the Scandinavian peninsula, and perhaps Great Russia were becoming possible regions for human occupation. There are no Palæolithic remains in Sweden or Norway, nor in Ireland or Scotland. Man, when he entered these countries, was apparently already at the Neolithic stage of social development.

Nor is there any convincing evidence of man in America before the end of the Pleistocene.[43] The same relaxation of the climate that permitted the retreat of the reindeer hunters into Russia and Siberia, as the Neolithic tribes advanced, may have allowed them to wander across the land that is now cut by Bering Strait, and so reach the American continent. They spread thence southward, age by age. When they reached South America, they found the giant sloth (the *Megatherium*), the glyptodon, and many other extinct creatures, still flourishing. The glyptodon was a monstrous South American armadillo, and a human{v1-103} skeleton has been found by Roth buried beneath its huge tortoise-like shell.[44]

All the human remains in America, even the earliest, it is to be noted, are of an Amer-Indian character. In America there does not seem to have been any preceding races of sub-men. Man was fully man when he entered America. The old world was the nursery of the sub-races of mankind.{v1-104}

XI

NEOLITHIC MAN IN EUROPE[45]

§ 1. *The Age of Cultivation Begins.* § 2. *Where Did the Neolithic Culture Arise?* § 3. *Everyday Neolithic*

Life. § 4. How Did Sowing Begin? § 5. Primitive Trade. § 6. The Flooding of the Mediterranean Valley.

§ 1

THE Neolithic phase of human affairs began in Europe about 10,000 or 12,000 years ago. But probably men had reached the Neolithic stage elsewhere some thousands of years earlier.[46] Neolithic men came slowly into Europe from the south or south-east as the reindeer and the open steppes gave way to forest and modern European conditions.

The Neolithic stage in culture is characterized by: (1) the presence of polished stone implements, and in particular the stone *axe*, which was perforated so as to be the more effectually fastened to a wooden handle, and which was probably used rather for working wood than in conflict. There are also abundant arrow heads. The fact that some implements are polished does not preclude the presence of great quantities of implements of unpolished stone. But there are differences in the make between even the unpolished tools of the Neolithic and of the Palæolithic Period. (2) The beginning of a sort of agriculture, and the use of plants and seeds. But at first there are abundant evidences that hunting was still of great importance in the Neolithic Age.{vi-105} Neolithic man did not at first sit down to his agriculture. He took snatch crops. He settled later. (3) Pottery and proper cooking. The horse is no longer eaten. (4) Domesticated animals. The dog appears very early. The Neolithic man had domesticated cattle, sheep, goats, and pigs. He was a huntsman turned herdsman of the herds he once hunted.[47] (5) Plaiting and weaving.

These Neolithic people probably "migrated" into Europe, in the same way that the Reindeer Men had migrated before them; that is to say, generation by generation and century by century, as the climate changed, they spread after their accustomed food. They were not "nomads." Nomadism, like civilization, had still to be developed. At present we are quite unable to estimate how far the Neolithic peoples were new-comers and how far their arts were developed or acquired by the descendants of some of the hunters and fishers of the Later Palæolithic Age.

Whatever our conclusions in that matter, this much we may say with certainty; there is no great break, no further sweeping away of one kind of man and replacement by another kind between the appearance of the Neolithic way of living and our own time. There are invasions, conquests, extensive emigrations and intermixtures, but the races as a whole carry on and continue to adapt themselves to the areas into which they began to settle in the opening of the Neolithic Age. The Neolithic men of Europe were white men ancestral to the modern Europeans. They may have been of a darker complexion than many of their descendants; of that we cannot speak with certainty. But there is no real break in culture from their time onward until we reach the age of coal, steam, and power-driven machinery that began in the eighteenth century.

After a long time gold, the first known of the metals, appears among the bone ornaments with jet and amber. Irish Neolithic remains are particularly rich in gold. Then, perhaps 6000 or 7000 years ago in Europe, Neolithic people began to use copper in certain centres, making out of it implements of much the same pattern as their stone ones. They cast the copper in moulds{vi-106} made to the shape of the stone implements. Possibly they first found native copper and hammered it into shape.[48] Later—we will not venture upon figures—men had found out how to get copper from its ore. Perhaps, as Lord Avebury suggested, they discovered the secret of smelting by the chance putting of lumps of copper ore among the ordinary stones with which they built the fire pits they used for cooking. In China, Hungary, Cornwall, and elsewhere copper ore and tinstone occur in the same veins; it is a very common association, and so, rather through dirtiness than skill, the ancient smelters, it may be, hit upon the harder and better bronze, which is an alloy of copper and tin.[49] Bronze is not only harder than copper, but the mixture of tin and copper is more fusible and easier to reduce. The so-called "pure-copper" implements usually contain a small proportion of tin, and there are no tin implements known, nor very much evidence to show that early men knew of tin as a separate metal.[50][51] The plant of a prehistoric copper smelter has been found in Spain, and the material of bronze foundries in various localities. The method of smelting revealed by these finds carries out Lord Avebury's suggestion. In India, where zinc and copper ore occur together, brass (which is an alloy of the two metals) was similarly hit upon.

So slight was the change in fashions and methods produced by the appearance of bronze, that for a long time such bronze axes and so forth as were made were cast in moulds to the shape of the stone implements they were superseding.

Finally, perhaps as early as 3000 years ago in Europe, and even{v1-107} earlier in Asia Minor, men began to smelt iron. Once smelting was known to men, there is no great marvel in the finding of iron. They smelted iron by blowing up a charcoal fire, and wrought it by heating and hammering. They produced it at first in comparatively small pieces;[52] its appearance worked a gradual revolution{v1-108} in weapons and implements; but it did not suffice to change the general character of men's surroundings. Much the same daily life that was being led by the more settled Neolithic men 10,000 years ago was being led by peasants in out-of-the-way places all over Europe at the beginning of the eighteenth century.[53]

People talk of the Stone Age, the Bronze Age, and the Iron Age in Europe, but it is misleading to put these ages as if they were of equal importance in history. Much truer is it to say that there was:

(1) An *Early Palæolithic Age*, of vast duration; (2) a *Later Palæolithic Age*, that lasted not a tithe of the time; and (3) the Age of Cultivation, the age of the white men in Europe, which began 10,000 or at most 12,000 years ago, of which the Neolithic Period was the beginning, and which is still going on.

§ 2

We do not know yet the region in which the ancestors of the white and whitish Neolithic peoples worked their way up from the Palæolithic stage of human development. Probably it was somewhere about south-western Asia, or in some region now submerged beneath the Mediterranean Sea or the Indian Ocean, that, while the Neanderthal men still lived their hard lives in the bleak climate of a glaciated Europe, the ancestors of the white men developed the rude arts of *their* Later Palæolithic period. But they do not seem to have developed the artistic skill of their more northerly kindred, the European Later Palæolithic races. And through the hundred centuries or so while Reindeer Men were living under comparatively unprogressive conditions upon the steppes of France, Germany, and Spain, these more-favoured and progressive people to the south were mastering agriculture, learning to develop their appliances, taming the dog, domesticating cattle, and, as the climate to the north mitigated and the{v1-109} equatorial climate grew more tropical, spreading northward. All these early chapters of our story have yet to be disinterred. They will probably be found in Asia Minor, Persia, Arabia, India, or north Africa, or they lie beneath the Mediterranean waters. Twelve thousand years ago, or thereabouts—we are still too early for anything but the roughest chronology—Neolithic peoples were scattered all over Europe, north Africa, and Asia. They were peoples at about the level of many of the Polynesian islanders of the last century, and they were the most advanced peoples in the world.

§ 3

It will be of interest here to give a brief account of the life of the European Neolithic people before the appearance of metals. We get our light upon that life from various sources. They scattered their refuse about, and in some places (*e.g.* on the Danish coast) it accumulated in great heaps, known as the kitchen middens. They buried some of their people, but not the common herd, with great care and distinction, and made huge heaps of earth over their sepulchres; these heaps are the barrows or dolmens which contribute a feature to the European, Indian, and American scenery in many districts to this day. In connection with these mounds, or independently of them, they set up great stones (megaliths), either singly or in groups, of which Stonehenge in Wiltshire and Carnac in Brittany are among the best-known examples. In various places their villages are still traceable.

One fruitful source of knowledge about Neolithic life comes from Switzerland, and was first revealed by the very dry winter of 1854, when the water level of one of the lakes, sinking to an unheard-of lowness, revealed the foundations of prehistoric pile dwellings of the Neolithic and early Bronze Ages, built out over the water after the fashion of similar homes that exist to-day in Celebes and elsewhere. Not only were the timbers of those ancient platforms preserved, but a great multitude of wooden, bone, stone, and earthenware utensils and ornaments, remains of food and the like, were found in the peaty accumulations below them. Even pieces of net and garments have been recovered.[vi-110] Similar lake dwellings existed in Scotland, Ireland, and elsewhere—there are well-known remains at Glastonbury in Somersetshire; in Ireland lake dwellings were inhabited from prehistoric times up to the days when O'Neil of Tyrone was fighting against the English before the plantation of Scotch colonists to replace the Irish in Ulster in the reign of James I of England. These lake villages had considerable defensive value, and there was a sanitary advantage in living over flowing water.

Probably these Neolithic Swiss pile dwellings did not shelter the largest communities that existed in those days. They were the homes of small patriarchal groups. Elsewhere upon fertile plains and in more open country there were probably already much larger assemblies of homes than in those mountain valleys. There are traces of such a large community of families in Wiltshire in England, for example; the remains of the stone circle of Avebury near Silbury mound were once the "finest megalithic ruin in Europe."[54] It consisted of two circles of stones surrounded by a larger circle and a ditch, and covering all together twenty-eight and a half acres. From it two avenues of stones, each a mile and a half long, ran west and south on either side of Silbury Hill. Silbury Hill is the largest prehistoric artificial mound in England. The dimensions of this centre of a faith and a social life now forgotten altogether by men indicate the concerted efforts and interests of a very large number of people, widely scattered though they may have been over the west and south and centre of England. Possibly they assembled at some particular season of the year in a primitive sort of fair. The whole community "lent a hand" in building the mounds and hauling the stones. The Swiss pile-dwellers, on the contrary, seem to have lived in practically self-contained villages.

These lake-village people were considerably more advanced in methods and knowledge, and probably much later in time than the early Neolithic people who accumulated the shell mounds, known as kitchen middens, on the Danish and Scotch coasts. These kitchen midden folk may have been as early as 10,000{vi-112} B.C. or earlier; the lake dwellings were probably occupied continuously from 5000 or 4000 B.C. down almost to historic times. Those early kitchen-midden people were among the most barbaric of Neolithic peoples, their stone axes were rough, and they had no domesticated animal except the dog. The lake-dwellers, on the other hand, had, in addition to the dog, which was of a medium-sized breed, oxen, goats, and sheep. Later on, as they were approaching the Bronze Age, they got swine. The remains of cattle and goats prevail in their débris, and, having regard to the climate and country about them, it seems probable that these beasts were sheltered in the buildings upon the piles in winter, and that fodder was stored for them. Probably the beasts lived in the same houses with the people, as the men and beasts do now in Swiss chalets. The people in the houses possibly milked the cows and goats, and milk perhaps played as important a part in their economy as it does in that of the mountain Swiss of to-day. But of that we are not sure at present. Milk is not a natural food for adults; it must have seemed queer stuff to take at first; and it may have been only after much breeding that a continuous supply of milk was secured from cows and goats. Some people think that the use of milk, cheese, butter, and other milk products came later into human life when men became nomadic. The writer is, however, disposed to give the Neolithic men credit for having discovered milking. The milk, if they did use it (and, no doubt, in that case sour curdled milk also, but not well-made cheese and butter), they must have kept in earthenware pots, for they had pottery, though it was{vi-113} roughly hand-made pottery and not the shapely product of the potter's wheel. They eked out this food supply by hunting. They killed and ate red deer and roe deer, bison and wild boar. And they ate the fox, a rather high-flavoured meat, and not what any one would eat in a world of plenty. Oddly enough, they do not seem to have eaten the hare, although it was available as food. They are supposed to have avoided eating it, as some savages are said to avoid eating it to this day, because they feared that the flesh of so timid a creature might make them, by a sort of infection, cowardly.[55]

Of their agricultural methods we know very little. No ploughs and no hoes have been found. They were of wood and have perished. Neolithic men cultivated and ate wheat, barley, and millet, but they knew nothing of oats or rye. Their grain they roasted, ground between stones and stored in pots, to be eaten when needed. And they made exceedingly solid and heavy bread, because round flat slabs of it have been got out of these deposits. Apparently they had no yeast. If they had no yeast, then they had no fermented drink. One sort of barley that they had is the sort that was cultivated by the ancient Greeks, Romans, and Egyptians, and they also had an Egyptian variety of wheat, showing that their ancestors had brought or derived this cultivation from the south-east. The centre of diffusion of wheat was somewhere in the eastern Mediterranean region. A wild form is still found in the neighbourhood of Mt. Hermon (see footnote to Ch. XVI, § 1). When the lake dwellers sowed their little patches of wheat in Switzerland, they were already following the immemorial practice of mankind. The seed must have been brought age by age from that distant centre of diffusion. In the ancestral lands of the south-east men had already been sowing wheat perhaps for thousands of years.[56] Those lake dwellers also ate peas, and crab-apples—the only apples that then existed in the world. Cultivation and selection had not yet produced the apple of to-day.[vi-114]

They dressed chiefly in skins, but they also made a rough cloth of flax. Fragments of that flaxen cloth have been discovered. Their nets were made of flax; they had as yet no knowledge of hemp and hempen rope. With the coming of bronze, their pins and ornaments increased in number. There is reason to believe they set great store upon their hair, wearing it in large shocks with pins of bone and afterwards of metal. To judge from the absence of realistic carvings or engravings or paintings, they either did not decorate their garments or decorated them with plaids, spots, interlacing designs, or similar conventional ornament. Before the coming of bronze there is no evidence of stools or tables; the Neolithic people probably squatted on their clay floors. There were no cats in these lake dwellings; no mice or rats had yet adapted themselves to human dwellings; the cluck of the hen was not as yet added to the sounds of human life, nor the domestic egg to its diet.[57]

The chief tool and weapon of Neolithic man was his axe; his next the bow and arrow. His arrow heads were of flint, beautifully made, and he lashed them tightly to their shafts. Probably he prepared the ground for his sowing with a pole, or a pole upon which he had stuck a stag's horn. Fish he hooked or harpooned. These implements no doubt stood about in the interior of the house, from the walls of which hung his fowling-nets. On the floor, which was of clay or trodden cow-dung (after the fashion of hut floors in India to-day), stood pots and jars and woven baskets containing grain, milk, and such-like food. Some of the pots and pans hung by rope loops to the walls. At one end of the room, and helping to keep it warm in winter by their animal heat, stabled the beasts. The children took the cows and goats out to graze, and brought them in at night before the wolves and bears came prowling.{vl-115}

Hut urns, the first probably representing a lake-dwelling.... After Lubbock.

Since Neolithic man had the bow, he probably also had stringed instruments, for the rhythmic twanging of a bow-string seems almost inevitably to lead to that. He also had earthenware drums across which skins were stretched; perhaps also he made drums by stretching skins over hollow tree stems.[58] We do not know when man began to sing, but evidently he was making music, and since he had words, songs were no doubt being made. To begin with, perhaps, he just let his voice loose as one may hear Italian peasants now behind their ploughs singing songs without words. After dark in the winter he sat in his house and talked and sang and made implements by touch rather than sight. His lighting must have been poor, and chiefly firelight, but there was probably always some fire in the village, summer or winter. Fire was too troublesome to make for men to be willing to let it out readily. Sometimes a great disaster happened to those pile villages, the fire got free, and they were burnt out. The Swiss deposits contain clear evidence of such catastrophes.

All this we gather from the remains of the Swiss pile dwellings, and such was the character of the human life that spread over Europe, coming from the south and from the east with the forests as, 10,000 or 12,000 years ago, the reindeer and the Reindeer Men passed away. It is evident that we have here a way[vi-116] of life already separated by a great gap of thousands of years of invention from its original Palæolithic stage. The steps by which it rose from that condition we can only guess at. From being a hunter hovering upon the outskirts of flocks and herds of wild cattle and sheep, and from being a co-hunter with the dog, man by insensible degrees may have developed a sense of proprietorship in the beasts and struck up a friendship with his canine competitor. He learnt to turn the cattle when they wandered too far; he brought his better brain to bear to guide them to fresh pasture. He hemmed the beasts into valleys and enclosures where he could be sure to find them again. He fed them when they starved, and so slowly he tamed them. Perhaps his agriculture began with the storage of fodder. He reaped, no doubt, before he sowed. The Palæolithic ancestor away in that unknown land of origin to the south-east first supplemented the precarious meat supply of the hunter by eating roots and fruits and wild grains. Man storing graminiferous grasses for his cattle might easily come to beat out the grain for himself.

§ 4

How did man learn to sow in order that he might reap?

We may hesitate here to guess at the answer to that question. But a very great deal has been made of the fact that wherever sowing occurs among primitive people in any part of the world, it is accompanied by a human sacrifice or by some ceremony which may be interpreted as the mitigation and vestige of an ancient sacrificial custom. This is the theme of Sir J. G. Frazer's *Golden Bough*. From this it has been supposed that the first sowings were in connection with the burial of a human being, either through wild grain being put with the dead body as food or through the scattering of grain over the body. It may be argued that there is only one reason why man should have disturbed the surface of the earth before he took to agriculture, and that was to bury his dead; and in order to bury a dead body and make a mound over it, it was probably necessary for him to disturb the surface over a considerable area. Neolithic man's chief apparatus for mound-making consisted of picks of deer's horn and shovels of their shoulder-blades, and with this he would have{vi-117} found great difficulty in making a deep excavation. Nor do we find such excavations beside the barrows. Instead of going down into tough subsoil, the mound-makers probably scraped up some of the surface soil and carried it to the mound. All this seems probable, and it gives just that wide area of bared and turned-over earth upon which an eared grass, such as barley, millet, or primitive wheat, might have seeded and grown. Moreover, the mound-makers, being busy with the mound, would not have time to hunt meat, and if they were accustomed to store and eat wild grain, they would be likely to scatter grain, and the grain would be blown by the wind out of their rude vessels over the area they were disturbing. And if they were bringing up seed in any quantity in baskets and pots to bury with the corpse, some of it might easily blow and be scattered over the fresh earth. Returning later to the region of the mound, they would discover an exceptionally vigorous growth of food grain, and it would be a natural thing to associate it with the buried person, and regard it as a consequence of his death and burial. He had given them back the grain they gave him increased a hundredfold.

At any rate, there is apparently all over the world a traceable association in ancient ceremonial and in the minds of barbaric people between the death and burial of a person and the ploughing and sowing of grain. From this it is assumed that there was once a world-wide persuasion that it was necessary that some one should be buried before a crop could be sown, and that out of this persuasion arose a practice and tradition of human sacrifice at seedtime, which has produced profound effects in the religious development of the race. There may have been some idea of refreshing the earth by a blood draught or revivifying it with the life of the sacrificed person. We state these considerations here merely as suggestions that have been made of the way in which the association of seedtime and sacrifice arose. They are, at the best, speculations; they have a considerable vogue at the present time, and we have to note them, but we have neither the space nor the time here to examine them at length. The valuable accumulations of suggestions due to the industry and ingenuity of Sir J. G. Frazer still{vi-118} await a thorough critical examination, and to his works the reader must go for the indefatigable expansion of this idea.

§ 5

All these early beginnings must have taken place far back in time, and in regions of the world that have still to be effectively explored by the archæologists. They were probably going on in Asia or Africa, in what is now the bed of the Mediterranean, or in the region of the Indian Ocean, while the Reindeer man was developing his art in Europe. The Neolithic men who drifted over Europe and western Asia 12,000 or 10,000 years ago were long past these beginnings; they were already close, a few thousand years, to the dawn of written tradition and the remembered history of mankind. Without any very great shock or break, bronze came at last into human life, giving a great advantage in warfare to those tribes who first obtained it. Written history had already begun before weapons of iron came into Europe to supersede bronze.

Already in those days a sort of primitive trade had sprung up. Bronze and bronze weapons, and such rare and hard stones as jade, gold because of its plastic and ornamental possibilities, and skins and flax-net and cloth, were being swapped and stolen and passed from hand to hand over great stretches of country. Salt also was probably being traded. On a meat dietary men can live without salt, but grain-consuming people need it just as herbivorous animals need it. Hopf says that bitter tribal wars have been carried on by the desert tribes of the Soudan in recent years for the possession of the salt deposits between Fezzan and Murzuk. To begin with, barter, blackmail, tribute, and robbery by violence passed into each other by insensible degrees. Men got what they wanted by such means as they could.[59]

§ 6

So far we have been telling of a history without events, a history of ages and periods and stages in development. But before we[vi-119] conclude this portion of the human story, we must record what was probably an event of primary importance and at first perhaps of tragic importance to developing mankind, and that was the breaking in of the Atlantic waters to the great Mediterranean valley.

The reader must keep in mind that we are endeavouring to give him plain statements that he can take hold of comfortably. But both in the matter of our time charts and the three maps we have given of prehistoric geography there is necessarily much speculative matter. We have dated the last Glacial Age and the appearance of the true men as about 40,000 or 35,000 years ago. Please bear that "about" in mind. The truth may be 60,000 or 20,000. But it is no good saying "a very long time" or "ages" ago, because then the reader will not know whether we mean centuries or millions of years. And similarly in these maps we give, they represent not the truth, but something like the truth. The outline of the land was "some such outline." There were such seas and such land masses. But both Mr. Horrabin, who has drawn these maps, and I, who have incited him to do so, have preferred to err on the timid side.[60] We are not geologists enough to launch out into original research in these matters, and so we have stuck to the 40-fathom line and the recent deposits as our guides for our post-glacial map and for the map of 12,000 to 10,000 B.C. But in one matter we have gone beyond these guides. It is practically certain that at the end of the last Glacial Age the Mediterranean was a couple of land-locked sea basins, not connected—or only connected by a torrential overflow river. The eastern basin was the fresher; it was fed by the Nile, the "Adriatic" river, the "Red-Sea" river, and perhaps by a river that poured down amidst the mountains that are now the Greek Archipelago from the very much bigger Sea of Central Asia that then existed. Almost certainly human beings, and possibly even Neolithic men, wandered over that now lost Mediterranean valley.

The reasons for believing this are very good and plain. To this day the Mediterranean is a sea of evaporation. The rivers that flow into it do not make up for the evaporation from its{v1-120} surface. There is a constant current of water pouring into the Mediterranean from the Atlantic, and another current streaming in from the Bosphorus and Black Sea. For the Black Sea gets more water than it needs from the big rivers that flow into it; it is an overflowing sea, while the Mediterranean is a thirsty sea. From which it must be plain that when the Mediterranean was cut off both from the Atlantic Ocean and the Black Sea it must have been a shrinking sea with its waters sinking to a much lower level than those of the ocean outside. This is the case of the Caspian Sea to-day. Still more so is it the case with the Dead Sea.

But if this reasoning is sound, then where to-day roll the blue waters of the Mediterranean there must once have been great areas of land, and land with a very agreeable climate. This was probably the case during the last Glacial Age, and we do not know how near it was to our time when the change occurred that brought back the ocean waters into the Mediterranean basin. Certainly there must have been Grimaldi people, and perhaps even Azilian and Neolithic people going about in the valleys and forests of these regions that are now submerged. The Neolithic Dark Whites, the people of the Mediterranean race, may have gone far towards the beginnings of settlement and civilization in that great lost Mediterranean Valley.

Mr. W. B. Wright[61] gives us some very stimulating suggestions here. He suggests that in the Mediterranean basin there were two lakes, "one a fresh-water lake, in the eastern depression, which drained into the other in the western depression. It is interesting to think what must have happened when the ocean level rose once more as a result of the dissipation of the ice-sheets, and its waters began to pour over into the Mediterranean area. The inflow, small at first, must have ultimately increased to enormous dimensions, as the channel was slowly lowered by erosion and the ocean level slowly rose. If there were any unconsolidated materials on the sill of the Strait, the result must have been a genuine debacle, and if we consider the length of time which even an enormous torrent would take to fill such a basin as that of the Mediterranean, we must conclude{vi-121} that this result was likely to have been attained in any case. Now, this may seem all the wildest speculation, but it is not entirely so, for if we examine a submarine contour map of the Straits of Gibraltar, we find there is an enormous valley running up from the Mediterranean deep, right through the Straits, and trenching some distance out on to the Atlantic shelf. This valley or gorge is probably the work of the inflowing waters of the ocean at the termination of the period of interior drainage."

This refilling of the Mediterranean, which by the rough chronology we are employing in this book may have happened somewhen between 30,000 and 10,000 B.C., must have been one of the greatest single events in the pre-history of our race. If the later date is the truer, then, as the reader will see plainly enough after reading the next two chapters, the crude beginnings of civilization, the first lake dwellings and the first cultivation, were probably round that eastern Levantine Lake into which there flowed not only the Nile, but the two great rivers that are now the Adriatic and the Red Sea. Suddenly the ocean waters began to break through over the westward hills and to pour in upon these primitive peoples— the lake that had been their home and friend became their enemy; its waters rose and never abated; their settlements were submerged; the waters pursued them in their flight. Day by day and year by year the waters spread up the valleys and drove mankind before them. Many must have been surrounded and caught by the continually rising salt flood. It knew no check; it came faster and faster; it rose over the treetops, over the hills, until it had filled the whole basin of the present Mediterranean and until it lapped the mountain cliffs of Arabia and Africa. Far away, long before the dawn of history, this catastrophe occurred.{v1-122}

XII

EARLY THOUGHT[62]

§ 1. Primitive Philosophy. § 2. The Old Man in Religion. § 3. Fear and Hope in Religion. § 4. Stars and Seasons. § 5. Story-telling and Myth-making. § 6. Complex Origins of Religion.

§ 1

BEFORE we go on to tell how 6000 or 7000 years ago men began to gather into the first towns and to develop something more than the loose-knit tribes that had hitherto been their highest political association, something must be said about the things that were going on inside these brains of which we have traced the growth and development through a period of 500,000 years from the Pithecanthropus stage.

What was man thinking about himself and about the world in those remote days?

At first he thought very little about anything but immediate things. At first he was busy thinking such things as: "Here is a bear; what shall I do?" Or "There is a squirrel; how can I get it?" Until language had developed to some extent there could have been little thinking beyond the range of actual experience, for language is the instrument of thought as book-keeping is the instrument of business. It records and fixes and enables thought to get on to more and more complex ideas. It[vi-123] is the hand of the mind to hold and keep. Primordial man, before he could talk, probably saw very vividly, mimicked very cleverly, gestured, laughed, danced, and lived, without much speculation about whence he came or why he lived. He feared the dark, no doubt, and thunderstorms and big animals and queer things and whatever he dreamt about, and no doubt he did things to propitiate what he feared or to change his luck and please the imaginary powers in rock and beast and river. He made no clear distinction between animate and inanimate things; if a stick hurt him, he kicked it; if the river foamed and flooded, he thought it was hostile. His thought was probably very much at the level of a bright little contemporary boy of four or five. He had the same subtle unreasonableness of transition and the same limitations. But since he had little or no speech he would do little to pass on the fancies that came to him, and develop any tradition or concerted acts about them.

The drawings even of Late Palæolithic man do not suggest that he paid any attention to sun or moon or stars or trees. He was preoccupied only with animals and men. Probably he took day and night, sun and stars, trees and mountains, as being in the nature of things—as a child takes its meal times and its nursery staircase for granted. So far as we can judge, he drew no fantasies, no ghosts or anything of that sort. The Reindeer Men's drawings are fearless familiar things, with no hint about them of any religious or occult feelings. There is scarcely anything that we can suppose to be a religious or mystical symbol at all in his productions. No doubt he had a certain amount of what is called *fetishism* in his life; he did things we should now think unreasonable to produce desired ends, for that is all fetishism amounts to; it is only incorrect science based on guess-work or false analogy, and entirely different in its nature from religion. No doubt he was excited by his dreams, and his dreams mixed up at times in his mind with his waking impressions and puzzled him. Since he buried his dead, and since even the later Neanderthal men seem to have buried their dead, and apparently with food and weapons, it has been argued that he had a belief in a future life. But it is just as reasonable to suppose that early men buried their dead with food and weapons because they doubted if{vi-124} they were dead, which is not the same thing as believing them to have immortal spirits, and that their belief in their continuing vitality was reinforced by dreams of the departed. They may have ascribed a sort of were-wolf existence to the dead, and wished to propitiate them.

The Reindeer man, we feel, was too intelligent and too like ourselves not to have had some speech, but quite probably it was not very serviceable for anything beyond direct statement or matter of fact narrative. He lived in a larger community than the Neanderthaler, but how large we do not know. Except when game is swarming, hunting communities must not keep together in large bodies or they will starve. The Indians who depend upon the caribou in Labrador must be living under circumstances rather like those of the Reindeer men. They scatter in small family groups, as the caribou scatter in search of food; but when the deer collect for the seasonal migration, the Indians also collect. That is the time for trade and feasts and marriages. The simplest American Indian is 10,000 years more sophisticated than the Reindeer man, but probably that sort of gathering and dispersal was also the way of Reindeer men. At Solutré in France there are traces of a great camping and feasting-place. There was no doubt an exchange of news there, but one may doubt if there was anything like an exchange of ideas. One sees no scope in such a life for theology or philosophy or superstition or speculation. Fears, yes; but unsystematic fears; fancies and freaks of the imagination, but personal and transitory freaks and fancies.

Perhaps there was a certain power of suggestion in these encounters. A fear really felt needs few words for its transmission; a value set upon something may be very simply conveyed.

In these questions of primitive thought and religion, we must remember that the lowly and savage peoples of to-day probably throw very little light on the mental state of men before the days of fully developed language. Primordial man could have had little or no tradition before the development of speech. All savage and primitive peoples of to-day, on the contrary, are soaked in tradition—the tradition of thousands of generations. They may have weapons like their remote ancestors and methods

{125} like them, but what were slight and shallow impressions on the minds of their predecessors are now deep and intricate grooves worn throughout the intervening centuries generation by generation.

§ 2

Certain very fundamental things there may have been in men's minds long before the coming of speech. Chief among these must have been fear of the Old Man of the tribe. The young of the primitive squatting-place grew up under that fear. Objects associated with him were probably forbidden. Every one was forbidden to touch his spear or to sit in his place, just as to-day little boys must not touch father's pipe or sit in his chair. He was probably the master of all the women. The youths of the little community had to remember that. The idea of *something forbidden*, the idea of things being, as it is called, *tabu*, not to be touched, not to be looked at, may thus have got well into the human mind at a very early stage indeed. J. J. Atkinson, in an ingenious analysis of these primitive tabus which are found among savage peoples all over the world, the tabus that separate brother and sister, the tabus that make a man run and hide from his stepmother, traces them to such a fundamental cause as this.[63] Only by respecting this primal law could the young male hope to escape the Old Man's wrath. And the Old Man must have been an actor in many a primordial nightmare. A disposition to propitiate him even after he was dead is quite understandable. One was not sure that he *was* dead. He might only be asleep or shamming. Long after an Old Man was dead, when there was nothing to represent him but a mound and a megalith, the women would convey to their children how awful and wonderful he was. And being still a terror to his own little tribe, it was easy to go on to hoping that he would be a terror to other and hostile people. In his life he had fought for his tribe, even if he had bullied it. Why not when he was dead? One sees that the Old Man idea was an idea very natural to the primitive mind and capable of great development.[64]

{v1-126}

§ 3

Another idea probably arose early out of the mysterious visitation of infectious diseases, and that was the idea of uncleanness and of being accurst. From that, too, there may have come an idea of avoiding particular places and persons, and persons in particular phases of health. Here was the root of another set of tabus. Then man, from the very dawn of his mental life, may have had a feeling of the sinister about places and things. Animals, who dread traps, have that feeling. A tiger will abandon its usual jungle route at the sight of a few threads of cotton.[65] Like most young animals, young human beings are easily made fearful of this or that by their nurses and seniors. Here is another set of ideas, ideas of repulsion and avoidance, that sprang up almost inevitably in men.

As soon as speech began to develop, it must have got to work upon such fundamental feelings and begun to systematize them, and keep them in mind. By talking together men would reinforce each other's fears, and establish a common tradition of tabus of things forbidden and of things unclean. With the idea of uncleanness would come ideas of cleansing and of removing a curse. The cleansing would be conducted through the advice and with the aid of wise old men or wise old women, and in such cleansing would lie the germ of the earliest priestcraft and witchcraft.

Speech from the first would be a powerful supplement to the merely imitative education and to the education of cuffs and blows conducted by a speechless parent. Mothers would tell their young and scold their young. As speech developed, men would find they had experiences and persuasions that gave them or seemed to give them power. They would make secrets of these things. There is a double streak in the human mind, a streak of cunning secretiveness and a streak perhaps of later origin that makes us all anxious to tell and astonish and impress each other. Many people make secrets in order to have secrets to tell. These secrets of early men they would convey to younger, more impressionable people, more or less honestly and impressively in {vi-127} some process of initiation. Moreover, the pedagogic spirit overflows in the human mind; most people like "telling other people not to." Extensive arbitrary prohibitions for the boys, for the girls, for the women, also probably came very early into human history.

Then the idea of the sinister has for its correlative the idea of the propitious, and from that to the idea of making things propitious by ceremonies is an easy step.[66]

$§ 4$

Out of such ideas and a jumble of kindred ones grew the first quasi-religious elements in human life. With every development of speech it became possible to intensify and develop the tradition of tabus and restraints and ceremonies. There is not a savage or barbaric race to-day that is not held in a net of such tradition. And with the coming of the primitive herdsman there would be a considerable broadening out of all this sort of practice. Things hitherto unheeded would be found of importance in human affairs. Neolithic man was nomadic in a different spirit from the mere daylight drift after food of the primordial hunter. He was a herdsman, upon whose mind a sense of direction and the lie of the land had been forced. He watched his flock by night as well as by day. The sun by day and presently the stars by night helped to guide his migrations; he began to find after many ages that the stars are steadier guides than the sun. He would begin to note particular stars and star groups, and to distinguish any individual thing was, for primitive man, to believe it individualized and personal. He would begin to think of the chief stars as persons, very shining and dignified and trustworthy persons looking at him like bright eyes in the night. His primitive tillage strengthened his sense of the seasons. Particular stars ruled his heavens when seedtime was due. The beginnings of agriculture were in the sub-tropical zone, or even nearer the equator, where stars of the first magnitude shine with a splendour unknown in more temperate latitudes.{vi-128}

And Neolithic man was counting, and falling under the spell of numbers. There are savage languages that have no word for any number above five. Some peoples cannot go above two. But Neolithic man in the lands of his origin in Asia and Africa even more than in Europe was already counting his accumulating possessions. He was beginning to use tallies, and wondering at the triangularity of three and the squareness of four, and why some quantities like twelve were easy to divide in all sorts of ways, and others, like thirteen, impossible. Twelve became a noble, generous, and familiar number to him, and thirteen rather an outcast and disreputable one.

A CARVED STATUE ("MENHIR") OF THE NEOLITHIC PERIOD—A CONTRAST TO THE FREEDOM AND VIGOUR OF PALÆOLITHIC ART.

Probably man began reckoning time by the clock of the full and new moons. Moonlight is an important thing to herdsmen who no longer merely hunt their herds, but watch and guard them. Moonlight, too, was perhaps his time for love-making, as indeed it may have been for primordial man and the ground ape ancestor before him. But from the phases of the moon, as his tillage increased, man's attitude would go on to the greater cycle of the seasons. Primordial man probably only drifted before the winter as the days grew cold. Neolithic man knew surely that the winter would come, and stored his fodder and{vl-129} presently his grain. He had to fix a seedtime, a propitious seedtime, or his sowing was a failure. The earliest recorded reckoning is by moons and by generations of men. The former seems to be the case in the Book of Genesis, where, if one reads the great ages of the patriarchs who lived before the flood as lunar months instead of years, Methusaleh and the others are reduced to a credible length of life. But with agriculture began the difficult task of squaring the lunar month with the solar year; a task which has left its scars on our calendar to-day. Easter shifts uneasily from year to year, to the great discomfort of holiday-makers; it is now inconveniently early and now late in the season because of this ancient reference of time to the moon.

And when men began to move with set intention from place to place with their animal and other possessions, then they would begin to develop the idea of other places in which they were not, and to think of what might be in those other places. And in any valley where they lingered for a time, they would, remembering how they got there, ask, "How did this or that other thing get here?" They would begin to wonder what was beyond the mountains, and where the sun went when it set, and what was above the clouds.

The capacity for telling things increased with their vocabulary. The simple individual fancies, the unsystematic fetish tricks and fundamental tabus of Palæolithic man began to be handed on and made into a more consistent system. Men began to tell stories about themselves, about the tribe, about its tabus and why they had to be, about the world and the why for the world. A tribal mind came into existence, a tradition. Palæolithic man was certainly more of a free individualist, more of an artist, as well as more of a savage, than Neolithic man. Neolithic man was coming under prescription; he could be trained from his youth and told to do things and not to do things; he was not so free to form independent ideas of his own about things. He had thoughts given to him; he was under a new power of suggestion. And to have more words and to attend more to words is not simply to increase mental power; words themselves are powerful things and dangerous things. Palæolithic man's words, perhaps, were {vi-130} chiefly just names. He used them for what they were. But Neolithic man was thinking about these words, he was thinking about a number of things with a great deal of verbal confusion, and getting to some odd conclusions. In speech he had woven a net to bind his race together, but also it was a net about his feet. Man was binding himself into new and larger and more efficient combinations indeed, but at a price. One of the most notable things about the Neolithic Age is the total absence of that free direct artistic impulse which was the supreme quality of later Palæolithic man. We find much industry, much skill, polished implements, pottery with conventional designs, co-operation upon all sorts of things, but no evidence of personal creativeness.[67] Self-suppression is beginning for men. Man has entered upon the long and tortuous and difficult path towards a life for the common good, with all its sacrifice of personal impulse, which he is still treading to-day.

Certain things appear in the mythology of mankind again and again. Neolithic man was enormously impressed by serpents—and he no longer took the sun for granted. Nearly everywhere that Neolithic culture went, there went a disposition to associate the sun and the serpent in decoration and worship. This primitive serpent worship spread ultimately far beyond the regions where the snake is of serious practical importance in human life.

§ 6

With the beginnings of agriculture a fresh set of ideas arose in men's minds. We have already indicated how easily and naturally men may have come to associate the idea of sowing with a burial. Sir J. G. Frazer has pursued the development of this association in the human mind, linking up with it the conception of special sacrificial persons who are killed at seedtime, the conception of a specially purified class of people to kill these sacrifices, the first priests, and the conception of a *sacrament*, a ceremonial[VI-131] feast in which the tribe eats portions of the body of the victim in order to share in the sacrificial benefits.

Out of all these factors, out of the Old Man tradition, out of the desire to escape infection and uncleanness, out of the desire for power and success through magic, out of the sacrificial tradition of seedtime, and out of a number of like beliefs and mental experiments and misconceptions, a complex something was growing up in the lives of men which was beginning to bind them together mentally and emotionally in a common life and action. This something we may call *religion* (Lat. *religare*, to bind[68]). It was not a simple or logical something, it was a tangle of ideas about commanding beings and spirits, about gods, about all sorts of "musts" and "must-nots." Like all other human matters, religion has grown. It must be clear from what has gone before that primitive man—much less his ancestral apes and his ancestral Mesozoic mammals—could have had no idea of God or Religion; only very slowly did his brain and his powers of comprehension become capable of such general conceptions. Religion is something that has grown up with and through human association, and God has been and is still being discovered by man.

This book is not a theological book, and it is not for us to embark upon theological discussion; but it is a part, a necessary and central part, of the history of man to describe the dawn and development of his religious ideas and their influence upon his activities. All these factors we have noted must have contributed to this development, and various writers have laid most stress upon one or other of them. Sir J. G. Frazer we have already noted as the leading student of the derivation of sacraments from magic sacrifices. Grant Allen, in his *Evolution of the Idea of God*, laid stress chiefly on the posthumous worship of the "Old Man." Sir E. B. Tylor (*Primitive Culture*) gave his attention mainly to the disposition of primitive man to ascribe a soul to every object animate and inanimate. Mr. A. E. Crawley, in *The Tree of Life*, has called attention to other centres of impulse and emotion, and particularly to sex as a source of deep excitement. The thing we have to bear in mind is that Neolithic[vi-132] man was still mentally undeveloped, he could be confused and illogical to a degree quite impossible to an educated modern person. Conflicting and contradictory ideas could lie in his mind without challenging one another; now one thing ruled his thoughts[vi-133] intensely and vividly and now another; his fears, his acts, were still disconnected as children's are.

TIME DIAGRAM SHOWING THE GENERAL DURATION OF THE NEOLITHIC PERIOD IN WHICH EARLY THOUGHT DEVELOPED.

Confusedly under the stimulus of the need and possibility of co-operation and a combined life, Neolithic mankind was feeling out for guidance and knowledge. Men were becoming aware that personally they needed protection and direction, cleansing from impurity, power beyond their own strength. Confusedly in response to that demand,

bold men, wise men, shrewd and{vl-134} cunning men
were arising to become magicians, priests, chiefs,
and kings. They are not to be thought of as cheats or
usurpers of power, nor the rest of mankind as their
dupes. All men are mixed in their motives; a hundred
things move men to seek ascendancy over other
men, but not all such motives are base or bad. The
magicians usually believed more or less in their own
magic, the priests in their ceremonies, the chiefs in
their right. The history of mankind henceforth is a
history of more or less blind endeavours to conceive
a common purpose in relation to which all men may
live happily, and to create and develop a common
consciousness and a common stock of knowledge
which may serve and illuminate that purpose. In a
vast variety of forms this appearance of kings and
priests and magic men was happening all over the
world under Neolithic conditions. Everywhere
mankind was seeking where knowledge and mastery
and magic power might reside; everywhere
individual men were willing, honestly or dishonestly,
to rule, to direct, or to be the magic beings who
would reconcile the confusions of the community.

In many ways the simplicity, directness, and
detachment of a later Palæolithic rock-painter appeal
more to modern sympathies than does the state of
mind of these Neolithic men, full of the fear of some
ancient Old Man who had developed into a tribal
God, obsessed by ideas of sacrificial propitiation and
magic murder. No doubt the reindeer hunter was a
ruthless hunter and a combative and passionate
creature, but he killed for reasons we can still

understand; Neolithic man, under the sway of talk and a confused thought process, killed on theory, he killed for monstrous and now incredible ideas, he killed those he loved through fear and under direction. Those Neolithic men not only made human sacrifices at seedtime; there is every reason to suppose they sacrificed wives and slaves at the burial of their chieftains; they killed men, women, and children whenever they were under adversity and thought the gods were athirst. They practised infanticide.[69] All these things passed on into the Bronze Age.

Hitherto a social consciousness had been asleep and not even{VI-135} dreaming in human history. Before it awakened it produced nightmares.

Away beyond the dawn of history, 3000 or 4000 years ago, one thinks of the Wiltshire uplands in the twilight of a midsummer day's morning. The torches pale in the growing light. One has a dim apprehension of a procession through the avenue of stone, of priests, perhaps fantastically dressed with skins and horns and horrible painted masks—not the robed and bearded dignitaries our artists represent the Druids to have been—of chiefs in skins adorned with necklaces of teeth and bearing spears and axes, their great heads of hair held up with pins of bone, of women in skins or flaxen robes, of a great peering crowd of shock-headed men and naked children. They have assembled from many distant places; the ground between the avenues and Silbury Hill is dotted with their encampments. A certain festive cheerfulness prevails. And amidst the throng march the appointed human victims, submissive, helpless, staring towards the distant smoking altar at which they are to die—that the harvests may be good and the tribe increase.... To that had life progressed 3000 or 4000 years ago from its starting-place in the slime of the tidal beaches.{v1-136}

XIII

THE RACES OF MANKIND

§1. Is Mankind Still Differentiating? §2. The Main Races of Mankind. §3. Was There an Alpine Race? §4. The Brunet Peoples. §5. How Existing Races may be Related to Each Other.

§ 1

IT is necessary now to discuss plainly what is meant by a phrase, used often very carelessly, "The Races of Mankind."

It must be evident from what has already been explained in Chapter III that man, so widely spread and subjected therefore to great differences of climate, consuming very different food in different regions, attacked by different enemies, must always have been undergoing considerable local modification and differentiation. Man, like every other species of living thing, has constantly been tending to differentiate into several species; wherever a body of men has been cut off, in islands or oceans or by deserts or mountains, from the rest of humanity, it must have begun very soon to develop special characteristics, specially adapted to the local conditions. But, on the other hand, man is usually a wandering and enterprising animal, for whom there exist few insurmountable barriers. Men imitate men, fight and conquer them, interbreed, one people with another. Concurrently for thousands of years there have been two sets of forces at work, one tending to separate men into a multitude of local varieties, and another to remix and blend these varieties together before a separate species has been established.

These two sets of forces may have fluctuated in this relative effect in the past. Palæolithic man, for instance, may have been more of a wanderer, he may have drifted about over a much{vi-137} greater area, than later Neolithic man; he was less fixed to any sort of home or lair, he was tied by fewer possessions. Being a hunter, he was obliged to follow the migrations of his ordinary quarry. A few bad seasons may have shifted him hundreds of miles. He may therefore have mixed very widely and developed few varieties over the greater part of the world.

The appearance of agriculture tended to tie those communities of mankind that took it up to the region in which it was most conveniently carried on, and so to favour differentiation. Mixing or differentiation is not dependent upon a higher or lower stage of civilization; many savage tribes wander now for hundreds of miles; many English villagers in the eighteenth century, on the other hand, had never been more than eight or ten miles from their villages, neither they nor their fathers nor grandfathers before them. Hunting peoples often have enormous range. The Labrador country, for instance, is inhabited by a few thousand Indians,[70] who follow the one great herd of caribou as it wanders yearly north and then south again in pursuit of food. This mere handful of people covers a territory as large as France. Nomad peoples also range very widely. Some Kalmuck tribes are said to travel nearly a thousand miles between summer and winter pasture.

It carries out this suggestion, that Palæolithic man ranged widely and was distributed, thinly indeed but uniformly, throughout the world, that the Palæolithic remains we find are everywhere astonishingly uniform. To quote Sir John Evans,[71] "The implements in distant lands are so identical in form and character with the British specimens that they might have been manufactured by the same hands.... On the banks of the Nile, many hundreds of feet above its present level, implements of the European types have been discovered; while in Somaliland, in an ancient river-valley at a great elevation above the sea, Sir H. W. Seton-Karr has collected a large number of implements formed of flint and quartzite, which, judging from their form and character, might have been dug out of the drift-deposits of the Somme and the Seine, the Thames or the ancient Solent.{vi-138}"

Phases of spreading and intermixture have probably alternated with phases of settlement and specialization in the history of mankind. But up to a few hundred years ago it is probable that since the days of the Palæolithic Age at least mankind has on the whole been differentiating. The species has differentiated in that period into a very great number of varieties, many of which have reblended with others, which have spread and undergone further differentiation or become extinct. Wherever there has been a strongly marked local difference of conditions and a check upon intermixture, there one is almost obliged to assume a variety of mankind must have appeared. Of such local varieties there must have been a great multitude.

In one remote corner of the world, Tasmania, a little cut-off population of people remained in the early Palæolithic stage until the discovery of that island by the Dutch in 1642. They are now, unhappily, extinct. The last Tasmanian died in 1877. They may have been cut off from the rest of mankind for 15,000 or 20,000 or 25,000 years.

But among the numerous obstacles and interruptions to intermixture there have been certain main barriers, such as the Atlantic Ocean, the highlands, once higher, and the now vanished seas of central Asia and the like, which have cut off great groups of varieties from other great groups of varieties over long periods of time. These separated groups of varieties developed very early certain broad resemblances and differences. Most of the varieties of men in eastern Asia and America, but not all, have now this in common, that they have yellowish buff skins, straight black hair, and often high cheek-bones. Most of the native peoples of Africa south of the Sahara, but not all, have black or blackish skins, flat noses, thick lips, and frizzy hair. In north and western Europe a great number of peoples have fair hair, blue eyes, and ruddy complexions; and about the Mediterranean there is a prevalence of white-skinned peoples with dark eyes and black hair. The black hair of many of these dark whites is straight, but never so strong and waveless as the hair of the yellow peoples. It is straighter in the east than in the west. In southern India we find brownish and darker peoples with straight black hair, and these as we pass eastward give place to more distinctly yellow peoples.[v1-139] In scattered islands and in Papua and New Guinea we find another series of black and brownish peoples of a more lowly type with frizzy hair.

But it must be borne in mind that these are very loose-fitting generalizations. Some of the areas and isolated pockets of mankind in the Asiatic area may have been under conditions more like those in the European area; some of the African areas are of a more Asiatic and less distinctively African type. We find a wavy-haired, fairish, hairy-skinned race, the Ainu, in Japan. They are more like the Europeans in their facial type than the surrounding yellow Japanese. They may be a drifted patch of the whites or they may be a quite distinct people. We find primitive black people in the Andaman Islands far away from Australia and far away from Africa.

There is a streak of very negroid blood traceable in south Persia and some parts of India. These are the "Asiatic" negroids. There is little or no proof that all[vi-140] black people, the Australians, the Asiatic negroids and the negroes, derive from one origin, but only that they have lived for vast periods under similar conditions. We must not assume that human beings in the eastern Asiatic area were all differentiating in one direction and all the human beings in Africa in another. There were great currents of tendency, it is true, but there were also backwaters, eddies, admixtures, readmixtures, and leakages from one main area to the other. A coloured map of the world to show the races would not present just four great areas of colour; it would have to be dabbed over with a multitude of tints and intermediate shades, simple here, mixed and overlapping there.

In the early Neolithic Period in Europe—it may be 10,000 or 12,000 years ago or so—man was differentiating all over the world, and he had already differentiated into a number of varieties, but he has never differentiated into different *species*. A "species," we must remember, in biological language is distinguished from a "variety" by the fact that varieties can interbreed, while species either do not do so or produce offspring which, like mules, are sterile. All mankind can interbreed freely, can learn to understand the same speech, can adapt itself to co-operation. And in the present age, man is probably no longer undergoing differentiation at all. Readmixture is now a far stronger force than differentiation. Men mingle more and more. Mankind from the view of a biologist is an animal species in a state of arrested differentiation and possible readmixture.

§ 2

It is only in the last fifty or sixty years that the varieties of men came to be regarded in this light, as a tangle of differentiations recently arrested or still in progress. Before that time students of mankind, influenced, consciously or unconsciously, by the story of Noah and the Ark and his three sons, Shem, Ham, and Japhet, were inclined to classify men into three or four great races, and they were disposed to regard these races as having always been separate things, descended from originally separate ancestors. They ignored the great possibilities of blended races and of special local isolations and variations. The classification{v1-141} has varied considerably, but there has been rather too much readiness to assume that mankind *must* be completely divisible into three or four main groups. Ethnologists (students of race) have fallen into grievous disputes about a multitude of minor peoples, as to whether they were of this or that primary race or "mixed," or strayed early forms, or what not. But all races are more or less mixed. There are, no doubt, four main groups, but each is a miscellany, and there are little groups that will not go into any of the four main divisions.

Subject to these reservations, when it is clearly understood that when we speak of these main divisions we mean not simple and pure races, but groups of races, then they have a certain convenience in discussion. Over the European and Mediterranean area and western Asia there are, and have been for many thousand years, white peoples, usually called the CAUCASIANS,[72] subdivided into two or three subdivisions, the northern blonds, an alleged intermediate race about which many authorities are doubtful, and the southern dark whites; over eastern Asia and America a second group of races prevails, the MONGOLIANS, generally with yellow skins, straight black hair, and sturdy bodies; over Africa the NEGROES, and in the region of Australia and New Guinea the black, primitive AUSTRALOIDS. These are convenient terms, provided the student bears in mind that they are not exactly defined terms. They represent only the common characteristics of certain main groups of races; they leave out a number of little peoples who belong properly to none of these[vi-142]divisions, and they disregard the perpetual mixing where the main groups overlap.

§ 3

Mongolian Types

Whether the "Caucasian" race is to be divided into two or three main subdivisions depends upon the classificatory value to be attached to certain differences in the skeleton and particularly to the shape of the skull. The student in his further reading will meet with constant references to round-skulled (Brachycephalic) and long-skulled peoples (Dolichocephalic). No skull looked at from above is completely round, but some skulls (the dolichocephalic) are much more oblong than others; when the width of a skull is four-fifths or more of its length from back to front, that skull is called brachycephalic; when the width is less than four-fifths of the length, the skull is dolichocephalic. While some ethnologists regard the difference between brachycephaly and dolichocephaly as a difference of quite primary importance, another school—which the writer must confess has entirely captured his convictions—dismisses this as a mere secondary distinction. It seems probable that the skull shapes of a people may under special circumstances vary in comparatively{vI-I43} few generations.[73]

We do not know what influences alter the shape of the skull, just as we do not know why people of British descent in the Darling region of Australia ("Cornstalks") grow exceptionally tall, or why in New England their jaw-bones seem to become slighter and their teeth in consequence rather crowded. Even in Neolithic times dolichocephalic and brachycephalic skulls are found in the same group of remains and often buried together, and that is true of most peoples to-day. Some peoples, such as the mountain people of central Europe, have more brachycephalic individuals per cent. than others; some, as the Scandinavians, are more prevalently[vi-144] dolichocephalic. In Neolithic Britain and in Scandinavia the earliest barrows (= tomb mounds) are long grave-shaped barrows and the late ones round, and the skulls found in the former are usually dolichocephalic and in the latter most frequently brachycephalic. This points perhaps to a succession of races in western Europe in the Neolithic Period (see Chapter XLV), but it may also point to changes of diet, habit, or climate.

Caucasian Types

But it is this study of skull shapes which has led many ethnologists to divide the Caucasian race, not, as it was divided by Huxley, into two, the northern *blonds* and the Mediterranean and North African *dark whites* or brunets, but into three. They split his blonds into two classes. They distinguish a northern European type, blond and dolichocephalic, the Nordic; a Mediterranean or Iberian race, Huxley's dark whites,[vi-146] which is dark-haired and dolichocephalic, and between these two they descry this third race, their brachycephalic race, the Alpine race. The opposite school would treat the alleged Alpine race simply as a number of local brachycephalic varieties of Nordic or Iberian peoples. The Iberian peoples were the Neolithic people of the long barrows, and seem at first to have pervaded most of Europe and western Asia.

This Mediterranean or Iberian race certainly had a wider range in early times, and was a less specialized and distinctive race than the Nordic. It is very hard to define its southward boundaries from the Negro, or to mark off its early traces in central Asia from those of early Dravidians or Mongolians. Wilfred Scawen Blunt[74] says that Huxley "had long suspected a common origin of the Egyptians and the Dravidians of India, perhaps a long belt of brown-skinned men from India to Spain in very early days." Across France and Great Britain these dark-white Iberian or Mediterranean people were ousted by a round-barrow-making "Alpine" or Alpine-Nordic race, and the dawn of history in Europe sees them being pressed westward and southward everywhere by the expansion of the fairer northern peoples.

It is possible that this "belt" of Huxley's of dark-white and brown-skinned men, this race of brunet-brown folk, ultimately spread even farther than India; that they reached to the shores of the Pacific, and that they were everywhere the original possessors of the Neolithic culture and the beginners of what we call civilization. The Nordic and the Mongolian peoples may have been but north-western and north-eastern branches from this more fundamental stem. Or the Nordic race may have been a branch, while the Mongolian, like the Negro, may have been another equal and distinct stem with which the brunet-browns met and mingled in South

China. Or the Nordic peoples also may have developed separately from a palæolithic stage.

At some period in human history (see Elliot Smith's *Migrations of Early Culture*) there seems to have been a special type of{vl-147} Neolithic culture widely distributed in the world which had a group of features so curious and so unlikely to have been independently developed in different regions of the earth, as to compel us to believe that it was in effect one culture. It reached through all the regions inhabited by the brunet Mediterranean race, and beyond through India, Further India, up the Pacific coast of China, and it spread at last across the Pacific and to Mexico and Peru. It was a coastal culture not reaching deeply inland. (Here again we cover the ground of Huxley's "belt of brown-skinned men," and extend it far to the east across the stepping-stones of Polynesia. There are, we may note, some very striking resemblances between early Japanese pottery and so forth and similar Peruvian productions.) This peculiar development of the Neolithic culture, which, Elliot Smith called the *heliolithic*[75] culture, included many or all of the following odd practices: (1) circumcision, (2) the very queer custom of sending the *father* to bed when a child is born, known as the *couvade*, (3) the practice of massage, (4) the making of mummies, (5) megalithic monuments[76] (*e.g.* Stonehenge), (6) artificial deformation of the heads of the young by bandages, (7) tattooing, (8) religious association of the sun and the serpent, and (9) the use of the symbol known as the swastika (see figure) for good luck.

This odd little symbol spins gaily round the world; it seems incredible that men would have invented and made a pet of it twice over. Elliot Smith traces these practices in a sort of constellation all over this great Mediterranean-Indian Ocean-Pacific area. Where one occurs, most of the others occur. They link Brittany with Borneo and Peru. But this constellation of practices does not crop up in the primitive homes of Nordic or Mongolian peoples, nor does it extend southward much beyond equatorial Africa. For thousands of years, from 15,000 to 1000 B.C., such a{v1-148} heliolithic Neolithic culture and its brownish possessors may have been oozing round the world through the warmer regions of the world, drifting by canoes often across wide stretches of sea. And its region of origin may have been, as Elliot Smith suggests, the Mediterranean and North-African region. It must have been spreading up the Pacific Coast and across the island stepping-stones to America, long after it had passed on into other developments in its areas of origin. Many of the peoples of the East Indies, Melanesia and Polynesia were still in this heliolithic stage of development when they were discovered by European navigators in the eighteenth century. The first civilizations in Egypt and the Euphrates-Tigris valley probably developed directly out of this widespread culture.[77] We will discuss later whether the Chinese civilization had a different origin. The Semitic nomads of the Arabian desert seem also to have had a heliolithic stage.

It may clear up the necessarily rather confused discussion of this chapter to give a summary of the views expressed here in a diagram. This, on page 149, should be compared later with the language diagram on page 155.

We have put the Australoids as a Negroid branch, but many authorities would set back the Australoid stem closer to the Tasmanian, and there may even be sound reasons for transferring both Australoids and Tasmanians as separate branches to the left of the "Later Palæolithic Races." To avoid crowding we have omitted the Hairy Ainu. They may be the last vestiges of an ancient primitive Pre-Nordic Pre-Mongolian strain from which the Nordic races are descended.{vI-149}

{vI-150}

XIV

THE LANGUAGES OF MANKIND

§ 1. No one Primitive Language. § 2. The Aryan Languages. § 3. The Semitic Languages. § 4. The Hamitic Languages. § 5. The Ural Altaic Languages. § 6. The Chinese Languages. § 7. Other Language Groups. § 8. Submerged and Lost Languages. § 9. How Languages may be Related.

IT is improbable that there was ever such a thing as a common human language. We know nothing of the language of Palæolithic man; we do not even know whether Palæolithic man talked freely.

We know that Palæolithic man had a keen sense of form and attitude, because of his drawings; and it has been suggested that he communicated his ideas very largely by gesture. Probably such words as the earlier men used were mainly cries of alarm or passion or names for concrete things, and in many cases they were probably imitative sounds made by or associated with the things named.[78]

The first languages were probably small collections of such words; they consisted of interjections and nouns. Probably the nouns were said in different intonations to convey different meanings. If Palæolithic man had a word for "horse" or "bear," he probably showed by tone or gesture whether he meant "bear is coming," "bear is going," "bear is to be hunted," "dead bear,{vi-151}" "bear has been here," "bear did this," and so on. Only very slowly did the human mind develop methods of indicating action and relationship in a formal manner. Modern languages contain many thousands of words, but the earlier languages could have consisted only of a few hundred. It is said that even modern European peasants can get along with something less than a thousand words, and it is quite conceivable that so late as the Early Neolithic Period that was the limit of the available vocabulary. Probably men did not indulge in those days in conversation or description. For narrative purposes they danced and acted rather than told. They had no method of counting beyond a method of indicating two by a dual number, and some way of expressing many. The growth of speech was at first a very slow process indeed, and grammatical forms and the expression of abstract ideas may have come very late in human history, perhaps only 400 or 500 generations ago.

§ 2

The students of languages (philologists) tell us that they are unable to trace with certainty any common features in all the languages of mankind. They cannot even find any elements common to all the Caucasian languages. They find over great areas groups of languages which have similar root words and similar ways of expressing the same idea, but then they find in other areas languages which appear to be dissimilar down to their fundamental structure, which express action and relation by entirely dissimilar devices, and have an altogether different grammatical scheme.[79] One great group of languages, for example, now covers nearly all Europe and stretches out to India; it includes English, French, German, Spanish, Italian, Greek, Russian, Armenian, Persian, and various Indian tongues. It is called the Indo-European or ARYAN family. The same fundamental roots, the same grammatical ideas, are traceable through all this family. Compare, for example, English *father, mother*, Gothic *fadar, moutar*, German *vater, mutter*, Latin *pater, mater*, Greek *pater, meter*, French *père, mère*, Armenian *hair, mair*,[vi-152] Sanscrit *pitar, matar*, etc., etc. In a similar manner the Aryan languages ring the changes on a great number of fundamental words, *f* in the Germanic languages becoming *p* in Latin, and so on. They follow a law of variation called Grimm's Law. These languages are not different things, they are variations of one thing. The people who use these languages think in the same way.

At one time in the remote past, in the Neolithic Age, that is to say 6000[80] years or more ago, there may have been one simple original speech from which all these Aryan languages have differentiated. Somewhere between central Europe and western Asia there must have wandered a number of tribes sufficiently intermingled to develop and use one tongue. It is convenient here to call them the Aryan peoples. Sir H. H. Johnston has called them "Aryan Russians." They belonged mostly to the Caucasian group of races and to the blond and northern subdivision of the group, to the Nordic race that is.

Here one must sound a note of warning. There was a time when the philologists were disposed to confuse languages and races, and to suppose that people who once all spoke the same tongue must be all of the same blood. That, however, is not the case, as the reader will understand if he will think of the negroes of the United States who now all speak English, or of the Irish, who—except for purposes of political demonstration—no longer speak the old Erse language but English, or of the Cornish people, who have lost their ancient Keltic speech. But what a common language does do, is to show that a common intercourse has existed, and the possibility of intermixture; and if it does not point to a common origin, it points at least to a common future.

But even this original Aryan language, which was a spoken speech perhaps 4000 or 3000 B.C., was by no means a *primordial* language or the language of a savage race. Its speakers were in or past the Neolithic stage of civilization. It had grammatical forms and verbal devices of some complexity. The vanished methods of expression of the later Palæolithic peoples, of the Azilians, or of the early Neolithic kitchen-midden people for[vi-153] instance, were probably much cruder than the most elementary form of Aryan.

Probably the Aryan group of languages became distinct in a wide region of which the Danube, Dnieper, Don, and Volga were the main rivers, a region that extended eastward beyond the Ural mountains north of the Caspian Sea. The area over which the Aryan speakers roamed probably did not for a long time reach to the Atlantic or to the south of the Black Sea beyond Asia Minor. There was no effectual separation of Europe from Asia then at the Bosphorus.[81] The Danube flowed eastward to a great sea that extended across the Volga region of south-eastern Russia right into Turkestan, and included the Black, Caspian, and Aral Seas of to-day. Perhaps it sent out arms to the Arctic Ocean. It must have been a pretty effective barrier between the Aryan speakers and the people in north-eastern Asia. South of this sea stretched a continuous shore from the Balkans to Afghanistan.[82] North-west of it a region of swamps and lagoons reached to the Baltic.

§ 3

Next to Aryan, philologists distinguish another group of languages which seem to have been made quite separately from the Aryan languages, the Semitic. Hebrew and Arabic are kindred, but they seem to have even a different set of root words from the Aryan tongues; they express their ideas of relationship in a different way; the fundamental ideas of their grammars are generally different. They were in all probability made by human communities quite out of touch with the Aryans, separately and independently. Hebrew, Arabic, Abyssinian, ancient Assyrian, ancient Phœnician, and a number of associated tongues are put together, therefore, as being derived from a second primary language, which is called the SEMITIC. In the very beginnings of recorded history we find Aryan-speaking peoples and Semitic-speaking peoples carrying on the liveliest intercourse of war and trade round and about the eastern end of the Mediterranean, but the fundamental differences of the primary{vi-154} Aryan and primary Semitic languages oblige us to believe that in early Neolithic times, before the historical period, there must for thousands of years have been an almost complete separation of the Aryan-speaking and the Semitic-speaking peoples. The latter seem to have lived either in south Arabia or in north-east Africa. In the opening centuries of the Neolithic Age the original Aryan speakers and the original Semitic speakers were probably living, so to speak, in different worlds, with a minimum of intercourse. Racially, it would seem, they had a remote common origin; both Aryan speakers and Semites are classed as Caucasians; but while the original Aryan speakers seem to have been of Nordic race, the original Semites were rather of the Mediterranean type.

§ 4

Philologists speak with less unanimity of a third group of languages, the HAMITIC, which some declare to be distinct from, and others allied to, the Semitic. The weight of opinion inclines now towards the idea of some primordial connection of these two groups. The Hamitic group is certainly a much wider and more various language group than the Semitic or the Aryan, and the Semitic tongues are more of a family, have more of a common likeness, than the Aryan. The Semitic languages may have arisen as some specialized proto-Hamitic group, just as the birds arose from a special group of reptiles (Chap. IV). It is a tempting speculation, but one for which there is really no basis of justifying fact, to suppose that the rude primordial ancestor group of the Aryan tongues branched off from the proto-Hamitic speech forms at some still earlier date than the separation and specialization of Semitic. The Hamitic speakers to-day, like the Semitic speakers, are mainly of the Mediterranean Caucasian race. Among the Hamitic languages are the ancient Egyptian and Coptic, the Berber languages (of the mountain people of north Africa, the Masked Tuaregs, and other such peoples), and what are called the Ethiopic group of African languages in eastern Africa, including the speech of the Gallas and the Somalis. The general grouping of these various tongues suggests that they originated over some great area to the west, as the primitive Semitic[v1-156] may have arisen to the east of the Red Sea divide. That divide was probably much more effective in Pleistocene times; the sea extended across to the west of the Isthmus of Suez, and a great part of lower Egypt was under water. Long before the dawn of history, however, Asia and Africa had joined at Suez, and these two language systems were in contact in that region. And if Asia and Africa were separated then at Suez, they may, on the other hand, have been joined by way of Arabia and Abyssinia.

These Hamitic languages may have radiated from a centre on the African coast of the Mediterranean, and they may have extended over the then existing land connections very widely into western Europe.

All these three great groups of languages, it may be noted, the Aryan, Semitic, and Hamitic, have one feature in common which they do not share with any other language, and that is grammatical gender; but whether that has much weight as evidence of a remote common origin of Aryan, Semitic, and Hamitic, is a question for the philologist rather than for the general student. It does not affect the clear evidence of a very long and very ancient prehistoric separation of the speakers of these three diverse groups of tongues.

The bulk of the Semitic and Hamitic-speaking peoples are put by ethnologists with the Aryans among the Caucasian group of races. They are "white." The Semitic and Nordic "races" have a much more distinctive physiognomy; they seem, like their characteristic languages, to be more marked and specialized than the Hamitic-speaking peoples.

§ 5

Across to the north-east of the Aryan and Semitic areas there must once have spread a further distinct language system which is now represented by a group of languages known as the TURANIAN, or URAL-ALTAIC group. This included the Lappish of Lapland and the Samoyed speech of Siberia, the Finnish language, Magyar, Turkish or Tartar, Manchu and Mongol; it has not as a group been so exhaustively studied by European philologists, and there is insufficient evidence yet whether it does or does not include the Korean and Japanese languages. (A Japanese{vi-157} writer, Mr. K. Hirai, has attempted to show that Japanese and Aryan may have had a common parent tongue.[83])

§ 6

A fifth region of language formation was south-eastern Asia, where there still prevails a group of languages consisting of monosyllables without any inflections, in which the tone used in uttering a word determines its meaning. This may be called the Chinese or MONOSYLLABIC group, and it includes Chinese, Burmese, Siamese, and Tibetan. The difference between any of these Chinese tongues and the more western languages is profound. In the Pekinese form of Chinese there are only about 420 primary monosyllables, and consequently each of these has to do duty for a great number of things, and the different meanings are indicated either by the context or by saying the word in a distinctive tone. The relations of these words to each other are expressed by quite different methods from the Aryan methods; Chinese grammar is a thing different in nature from English grammar; it is a separate and different invention. Many writers declare there is no Chinese grammar at all, and that is true if we mean by grammar anything in the European sense of inflections and concords. Consequently any such thing as a literal translation from Chinese into English is an impossibility. The very method of the thought is different.[84] Their philosophy remains still largely a sealed book to the European on this account, and vice versa, because of the different nature of the expressions.

In addition the following other great language families are distinguished by the philologist. All the American-Indian languages,[vi-158] which vary widely among themselves, are separable from any Old World group. Here we may lump them together not so much as a family as a miscellany.[85] There is one great group of languages in Africa, from a little way north of the equator to its southern extremity, the BANTU, and in addition a complex of other languages across the centre of the continent about which we will not trouble here.[86] There are also two probably separate groups, the DRAVIDIAN in South India, and the MALAY-POLYNESIAN stretched over Polynesia, and also now including Indian tongues.

Now it seems reasonable to conclude from these fundamental differences that about the time when men were passing from the Palæolithic to Neolithic conditions, and beginning to form rather larger communities than the family herd, when they were beginning to tell each other long stories and argue and exchange ideas, human beings were distributed about the world in a number of areas which communicated very little with each other. They were separated by oceans, seas, thick forests, deserts or mountains from one another. There may have been in that remote time, it may be 10,000 years ago or more, Aryan, Semitic, Hamitic, Turanian, American, and Chinese-speaking tribes and families, wandering over their several areas of hunting and pasture, all at very much the same stage of culture, and each developing its linguistic instrument in its own way. Probably each of these original tribes was not more numerous altogether than the Indians in Hudson Bay Territory to-day. Agriculture was barely beginning, and until agriculture made a denser population possible men may have been almost as rare as the great apes have always been.

In addition to these early Neolithic tribes, there must have been various varieties of still more primitive forest folk in Africa and in India. Central Africa, from the Upper Nile, was{vl-159} then a vast forest, impenetrable to ordinary human life, a forest of which the Congo forests of to-day are the last shrunken remains.

Possibly the spread of men of a race higher than primitive Australoids into the East Indies,[87] and the development of the languages of the Malay-Polynesian type came later in time than the origination of these other language groups.

The language divisions of the philologist do tally, it is manifest, in a broad sort of way with the main race classes of the ethnologist, and they carry out the same idea of age-long separations between great divisions of mankind. In the Glacial Age, ice, or at least a climate too severe for the free spreading of peoples, extended from the north pole into central Europe and across Russia and Siberia to the great tablelands of central Asia. After the last Glacial Age, this cold north mitigated its severities very slowly, and was for long without any other population than the wandering hunters who spread eastward and across Bering Strait. North and central Europe and Asia did not become sufficiently temperate for agriculture until quite recent times, times that is within the limit of 12,000 or possibly even 10,000 years, and a dense forest period intervened between the age of the hunter and the agricultural clearings.

This forest period was also a very wet period. It has been called the Pluvial or Lacustrine Age, the rain or pond period. It has to be remembered that the outlines of the land of the world have changed greatly even in the last hundred centuries. Across European Russia, from the Baltic to the Caspian Sea, as the ice receded there certainly spread much water and many impassable swamps; the Caspian Sea and the Sea of Aral and parts of the Desert of Turkestan, are the vestiges of a great extent of sea that reached far up to the Volga valley and sent an arm westward to join the Black Sea. Mountain barriers much higher than they are now, and the arm of the sea that is now the region of the Indus, completed the separation of the early Caucasian races from the Mongolians and the Dravidians, and made the broad racial differentiation of those groups possible.{v1-160}

Again the blown-sand Desert of Sahara—it is not a dried-up sea, but a wind desert, and was once fertile and rich in life—becoming more and more dry and sandy, cut the Caucasians off from the sparse primitive Negro population in the central forest region of Africa.

The Persian Gulf extended very far to the north of its present head, and combined with the Syrian desert to cut off the Semitic peoples from the eastern areas, while on the other hand the south of Arabia, much more fertile than it is to-day, may have reached across what is now the Gulf of Aden towards Abyssinia and Somaliland. The Mediterranean and Red Sea were probably still joined at Suez. The Himalayas and the higher and vaster massif of central Asia and the northward extension of the Bay of Bengal up to the present Ganges valley divided off the Dravidians from the Mongolians, the canoe was the chief link between Dravidian and Southern Mongol, and the Gobi system of seas and lakes which presently became the Gobi desert, and the great system of mountain chains which follow one another across Asia from the center to the north-east, split the Mongolian races into the Chinese and the Ural-Altaic language groups.

Bering Strait, when this came into existence, before or after the Pluvial Period, isolated the Amer-Indians.

These ancient separations must have remained effectual well into Neolithic times. The barriers between Africa, Asia, and Europe were lowered or bridged by that time, but mixing had not gone far. The practical separation of the west from Dravidian India and China continued indeed down almost into historical times; but the Semite, the Hamite, and the Aryan were already in close contact and vigorous reaction again in the very dawn of history.

We are not suggesting here, be it noted, that these ancient separations were absolute separations, but that they were effectual enough at least to prevent any great intermixture of blood or any great intermixture of speech in those days of man's social beginnings. There was, nevertheless, some amount of meeting and exchange even then, some drift of knowledge that spread the crude patterns and use of various implements, and the seeds of a primitive agriculture about the world.{vi-161}

§ 8

The fundamental tongues of these nine main language groups we have noted were not by any means all the human speech beginnings of the Neolithic Age. There may have been other, and possibly many other, ineffective centres of speech which were afterwards overrun by the speakers of still surviving tongues, and of elementary languages which faded out. We find strange little patches of speech still in the world which do not seem to be connected with any other language about them. Sometimes, however, an exhaustive inquiry seems to affiliate these disconnected patches, seems to open out to us tantalizing glimpses of some simpler, wider, and more fundamental and universal form of human speech. One language group that has been keenly discussed is the Basque group of dialects. The Basques live now on the north and south slopes of the Pyrenees; they number perhaps 600,000 altogether in Europe, and to this day they are a very sturdy and independent-spirited people. Their language, as it exists to-day, is a fully developed one. But it is developed upon lines absolutely different from those of the Aryan languages about it. Basque newspapers have been published in the Argentine and in the United States to supply groups of prosperous emigrants. The earliest "French" settlers in Canada were Basque, and Basque names are frequent among the French Canadians to this day. Ancient remains point to a much wider distribution of the Basque speech and people over Spain. For a long time this Basque language was a profound perplexity to scholars, and its structural character led to the suggestion that it might be related to some Amer-Indian tongue. A. H. Keane, in *Man Past and Present*, assembles reasons for linking it—though remotely—with the Berber language of North Africa, and through the Berber with the general body of Hamitic languages, but this relationship is questioned by other philologists. They find Basque more akin to certain similarly stranded vestiges of speech found in the Caucasian Mountains, and they are disposed to regard it as a last surviving member, much changed and specialized, of a once very widely extended group of pre-Hamitic languages, otherwise extinct, spoken chiefly by peoples[v1-162] of that brunet Mediterranean race (round-barrow men) which once occupied most of western and southern Europe and western Asia, and which may have been very closely related to the Dravidians of India and the peoples with a heliolithic culture who spread eastward thence through the East Indies to Polynesia and beyond.

It is quite possible that over western and southern Europe language groups extended 10,000 years ago that have completely vanished before Aryan tongues. Later on we shall note, in passing, the possibility of three lost language groups represented by (1) Ancient Cretan, Lydian, and the like (though these may have belonged, says Sir H. H. Johnston, to the "Basque-Caucasian-Dravidian (!) group"), (2) Sumerian, and (3) Elamite. The suggestion has been made—it is a mere guess—that ancient Sumerian may have been a linking language between the early Basque-Caucasian and early Mongolian groups. If this is true, then we have in this "Basque-Caucasian-Dravidian-Sumerian-proto-Mongolian" group a still more ancient and more ancestral system of speech than the fundamental Hamitic.

The Hottentot language is said to have affinities with the Hamitic tongues, from which it is separated by the whole breadth of Bantu-speaking central Africa. A Hottentot-like language with Bushman affinities is still spoken in equatorial east Africa, and this strengthens the idea that the whole of east Africa was once Hamitic-speaking. The Bantu languages and peoples spread, in comparatively recent times, from some center of origin in west central Africa and cut off the Hottentots from the other Hamitic peoples. But it is at least equally probable that the Hottentot is a separate language group.

Among other remote and isolated little patches of language are the Papuan speech of New Guinea and the native Australian. The now extinct Tasmanian language is little known. What we know of it is in support of what we have guessed about the comparative speechlessness of Palæolithic man.

We may quote a passage from Hutchinson's *Living Races of Mankind* upon this matter:—

"The language of the natives is irretrievably lost, only imperfect indication of its structure and a small proportion of its{vi-163} words having been preserved. In the absence of sibilants and some other features, their dialects resembled the Australian, but were of ruder, of less developed structure, and so imperfect that, according to Joseph Milligan, our best authority on the subject, they observed no settled order or arrangement of words in the construction of their sentences, but conveyed in a supplementary fashion by tone, manner, and gesture those modifications of meaning which we express by mood, tense, number, etc. Abstract terms were rare; for every variety of gum-tree or wattle-tree there was a name, but no word for 'tree' in general, nor for qualities such as hard, soft, warm, cold, long, short, round, etc. Anything hard was 'like a stone,' anything round 'like the moon,' and so on, usually suiting the action to the word and confirming by some sign the meaning to be understood."

§ 9

In reading this chapter it is well to remember how laborious and difficult are the tasks of comparative philology, and how necessary it is to understand the qualifications and limitations that are to be put{v1-164} upon its conclusions. The Aryan group of languages is much better understood than any other, for the simple reason that it has been more familiar and accessible to European science. The other groups have been less thoroughly investigated, because so far they have not been studied exhaustively by men accustomed to use them, and whose minds are set in the key of their structure. Even the Semitic languages have been approached at a disadvantage because few Jews think in Hebrew. But a time is fast approaching when Japanese, Chinese, Arabic, and Indian philologists will come to the rescue in these matters, and good reason may be found for revising much that has been said above about the native American, Ural-Altaic, primitive Chinese, and Polynesian groups of tongues.{v1-165}

BOOK III

THE DAWN OF HISTORY {v1-167}

XV

THE ARYAN-SPEAKING PEOPLES IN PREHISTORIC TIMES

§ 1. *The Spreading of the Aryan-Speakers.* § 2. *Primitive Aryan Life.* § 3. *Early Aryan Daily Life.*

W E have spoken of the Aryan language as probably arising in the region of the Danube and South Russia and spreading from that region of origin. We say "probably," because it is by no means certainly proved that that was the centre; there have been vast discussions upon this point and wide divergences of opinion. We give the prevalent view. As it spread widely, Aryan began to differentiate into a number of subordinate languages. To the west and south it encountered the Basque language, which was then widely spread in Spain, and also possibly various Hamitic Mediterranean languages.

The Neolithic Mediterranean race, the Iberian race, was distributed over Great Britain, Ireland, France, Spain, north Africa, south Italy, and, in a more civilized state, Greece and Asia Minor. It was probably closely related to the Egyptian. To judge by its European vestiges it was a rather small human type, generally with an oval face and a long head. It buried its chiefs and important people in megalithic chambers—*i.e.* made of big stones—covered over by great mounds of earth; and these mounds of earth, being much longer than they are broad, are spoken of as the long barrows. These people sheltered at times in caves, and also buried some of their dead therein; and from the traces of charred, broken, and cut human bones, including the bones of children, it is inferred that they were cannibals. These short dark Iberian tribes (and the Basques also if they were a different race) were thrust back westward, and conquered and enslaved by slowly advancing waves of a taller and fairer Aryan-speaking people, coming southward and westward through central Europe, who are spoken of as the Kelts. Only the Basque resisted the conquering Aryan speech. Gradually these Keltic-speakers made their way to the Atlantic, and all that now remains of the Iberians is mixed into the Keltic population. How far the Keltic invasion affected the Irish population is a matter of debate at the present time; the Kelts may have been a mere caste of conquerors who imposed their language on a larger subject population. It is even doubtful if the north of England is more Aryan than pre-Keltic in blood. There is a sort of short dark Welshman, and certain types of Irishmen, who are Iberians by race. The modern Portuguese are also largely of Iberian blood.

The Kelts spoke a language, Keltic,[88] which was also in its turn to differentiate into the language of Gaul, Welsh, Breton, Scotch and Irish Gaelic, and other tongues. They buried the ashes of their chiefs and important people in round barrows. While these Nordic Kelts were spreading westward, other Nordic Aryan peoples were pressing down upon the dark white Mediterranean race in the Italian and Greek peninsulas, and developing the Latin and Greek groups of tongues. Certain other Aryan tribes were drifting towards the Baltic and across into Scandinavia, speaking varieties of the Aryan which became ancient Norse—the parent of Swedish,

Danish, Norwegian, and Icelandic—Gothic, and Low and High German.

While the primitive Aryan speech was thus spreading and breaking up into daughter languages to the west, it was also spreading and breaking up to the east. North of the Carpathians and the Black Sea, Aryan-speaking tribes were increasing and spreading and using a distinctive dialect called Slavonian, from which came Russian, Serbian, Polish, Bulgarian, and other tongues; other variations of Aryan distributed over Asia Minor and Persia[v1-169] were also being individualized as Armenian and Indo-Iranian, the parent of Sanscrit and Persian. In this book we have used the word Aryan for all this family of languages, but the term Indo-European is sometimes used for the entire family, and "Aryan" itself restricted in a narrower sense to the Indo-Iranian speech.[89] This Indo-Iranian speech was destined to split later into a number of languages, including Persian and Sanscrit, the latter being the language of certain tribes of fair-complexioned Aryan speakers who pushed eastward into India somewhen between 3000 and 1000 B.C. and conquered dark Dravidian peoples who were then in possession of that land.

§ 2

What sort of life did these prehistoric Aryans lead, these Nordic Aryans who were the chief ancestors of most Europeans and most white Americans and European colonists of to-day, as well as of the Armenians,[90] Persians, and high-caste Hindus?

In answering that question we are able to resort to a new source of knowledge in addition to the dug-up remains and vestiges upon which we have had to rely in the case of Palæolithic man. We have language. By careful study of the Aryan languages it has been found possible to deduce a number of conclusions about the life of these Aryan peoples 5000 or 4000 years ago. All these languages have a common resemblance, as each, as we have already explained, rings the changes upon a number of common roots. When we find the same root word running through all or most of these tongues, it seems reasonable to conclude that the thing that root word signifies must have been known to the common ancestors. Of course, if they have *exactly the same word* in their languages, this may not be the case; it may be the new{vi-170} name of a new thing or of a new idea that has spread over the world quite recently. "Gas," for instance is a word that was made by Van Helmont, a Dutch chemist, about 1625, and has spread into most civilized tongues, and "tobacco" again is an American-Indian word which followed the introduction of smoking almost everywhere. But if the same word turns up in a number of languages, and *if it follows the characteristic modifications of each language*, we may feel sure that it has been in that language, and a part of that language, since the beginning, suffering the same changes with the rest of it. We know, for example, that the words for waggon and wheel run in this fashion through the Aryan tongues, and so we are able to conclude that the primitive Aryans, the more purely Nordic Aryans, had waggons, though it would seem from the absence of any common roots for spokes, rim, or axle that their wheels were not wheelwright's wheels with spokes, but made of the trunks of trees shaped out with an axe between the ends.

These primitive waggons were drawn by oxen. The early Aryans did not ride or drive horses; they had very little to do with horses. The Reindeer men were a horse-people, but the Neolithic Aryans were a cow-people. They ate beef, not horse; and after many ages they began this use of draught cattle. They reckoned wealth by cows. They wandered, following pasture, and "trekking" their goods, as the South African Boers do, in ox-waggons, though of course their waggons were much clumsier than any to be found in the world to-day. They probably ranged over very wide areas. They were migratory, but not in the strict sense of the word "nomadic"; they moved in a slower, clumsier fashion than did the later, more specialized nomadic peoples. They were forest and parkland people without horses. They were developing a migratory life out of the more settled "forest clearing" life of the earlier Neolithic period. Changes of climate which were replacing forest by pasture, and the accidental burning of forests by fire may have assisted this development.

When these early "Aryans" came to big rivers or open water, they built boats, at first hollow tree trunks and then skin-covered frameworks of lighter wood. Before history began there was already some Aryan canoe-traffic across the English Channel[vi-171] and in the Baltic, and also among the Greek islands. But the Aryans, as we shall see later, were probably not the first peoples to take to the sea.

We have already described the sort of home the primitive Aryan occupied and his household life, so far as the remains of the Swiss pile-dwellings enable us to describe these things. Mostly his houses were of too flimsy a sort, probably of wattle and mud, to have survived, and possibly he left them and trekked on for very slight reasons. The Aryan peoples burnt their dead, a custom they still preserve in India, but their predecessors, the long-barrow people, the Iberians, buried their dead in a sitting position. In some ancient Aryan burial mounds (round barrows) the urns containing the ashes of the departed are shaped like houses, and these represent rounded huts with thatched roofs. See Fig. p. 57.

The grazing of the primitive Aryan was far more important to him than his agriculture. At first he cultivated with a rough wooden hoe; then, after he had found out the use of cattle for draught purposes, he began real ploughing with oxen, using at first a suitably bent tree bough as his plough. His first cultivation before that came about must have been rather in the form of garden patches near the house buildings than of fields. Most of the land his tribe occupied was common land on which the cattle grazed together.

He never used stone for building house walls until upon the very verge of history. He used stone for hearths (*e.g.* at Glastonbury) and sometimes stone sub-structures. He did, however, make a sort of stone house in the centre of the great mounds in which he buried his illustrious dead. He may have learnt this custom from his Iberian neighbours and predecessors. It was these dark whites of the heliolithic culture, and not the primitive Aryans, who were responsible for such primitive temples as Stonehenge or Carnac in Brittany.

His social life was growing. Man was now living in clans and tribal communities. These clans and communities clashed; they took each other's grazing land, they sought to rob each other; there began a new thing in human life, *war*. For war is not a primeval thing; it has not been in this world for more than{vi-172} 20,000 years. To this day very primitive peoples, such as the Australian black-fellows, do not understand war. The Palæolithic Age was an age of fights and murder, no doubt, but not of the organized collective fighting of numbers of men.[91] But now men could talk together and group themselves under leaders, and they found a need of centres where they could come together with their cattle in time of raids and danger. They began to make camps with walls of earth and palisades, many of which are still to be traced in the history-worn contours of the European scenery. The leaders under whom men fought in war were often the same men as the sacrificial purifiers who were their early priests.

The knowledge of bronze spread late in Europe. Neolithic man had been making his slow advances age by age for 7000 or 8000 years before the metals came. By that time his social life had developed so that there were men of various occupations and men and women of different ranks in the community. There were men who worked wood and leather, potters and carvers. The women span and wove and embroidered. There were chiefs and families that were distinguished as leaderly and noble; and man varied the monotony of his herding and wandering, he consecrated undertakings and celebrated triumphs, held funeral assemblies, and distinguished the traditional seasons of the year, by *feasts*. His meats we have already glanced at; but somewhen between 10,000 B.C. and the broadening separation of the Aryan peoples towards 2000 or 1000 B.C., mankind discovered fermentation, and began to brew intoxicating drinks. He made these of honey, of barley, and, as the Aryan tribes spread southward, of the grape. And he got merry and drunken. Whether he first used yeast to make his bread light or to ferment his drink we do not know.

At his feasts there were individuals with a gift for "playing the fool," who did so no doubt to win the laughter of their friends,[92]{vi-173} but there was also another sort of men, of great importance in their time, and still more important to the historian, certain singers of songs and stories, the bards or rhapsodists. These *bards* existed among all the Aryan-speaking peoples; they were a consequence of and a further factor in that development of spoken language which was the chief of all the human advances made in Neolithic times. They chanted or recited stories of the past, or stories of the living chief and his people; they told other stories that they invented; they memorized jokes and catches. They found and seized upon and improved the rhythms, rhymes, alliterations, and such-like possibilities latent in language; they probably did much to elaborate and fix grammatical forms. They were the first great artists of the ear, as the later Aurignacian rock painters were the first great artists of the eye and hand. No doubt they used much gesture; probably they learnt appropriate gestures when they learnt their songs; but the order and sweetness and power of language was their primary concern.

And they mark a new step forward in the power and range of the human mind. They sustained and developed in men's minds a sense of a greater something than themselves, the tribe, and of a life that extended back into the past. They not only recalled old hatreds and battles, they recalled old alliances and a common inheritance. The feats of dead heroes lived again. A new thought came into men's minds, the desire to be remembered. Men began to live in thought before they were born and after they were dead.

Like most human things, this bardic tradition grew first slowly and then more rapidly. By the time bronze was coming into Europe there was not an Aryan people that had not a profession and training of bards. In their hands language became as beautiful as it is ever likely to be. These bards were living books, man-histories, guardians and makers of a new and more powerful tradition in human life. Every

Aryan people had its long poetical records thus handed down, its sagas (Teutonic), its epics (Greek), its vedas (Old Sanscrit). The earliest Aryan people were essentially a people of the voice. The recitation seems to have {vi-174}predominated even in those ceremonial and dramatic dances and that "dressing-up" which among most human races have also served for the transmission of tradition.[93]

At that time there was no writing, and when first the art of writing crept into Europe, as we shall tell later, it must have seemed far too slow, clumsy, and lifeless a method of record for men to trouble very much about writing down these glowing and beautiful treasures of the memory. Writing was at first kept for accounts and matters of fact. The bards and rhapsodists flourished for long after the introduction of writing. They survived, indeed, in Europe as the minstrels into the Middle Ages.

Unhappily their tradition had not the fixity of a written record. They amended and reconstructed, they had their fashions and their phases of negligence. Accordingly we have now only the very much altered and revised vestiges of that spoken literature of prehistoric times. One of the most interesting and informing of these prehistoric compositions of the Aryans survives in the Greek *Iliad*. An early form of *Iliad* was probably recited by 1000 B.C., but it was not written down until perhaps 700 or 600 B.C. Many men must have had to do with it as authors and improvers, but later Greek tradition attributed it to a blind bard named Homer, to whom also is ascribed the *Odyssey*, a composition of a very different spirit and outlook. To be a bard was naturally a blind man's occupation.[94] The Slavs called all bards *sliepac*, which was also their word for a blind man. The original recited[vi-175] version of the *Iliad* was older than that of the *Odyssey*. "The *Iliad* as a complete poem is older than the *Odyssey*, though the material of the *Odyssey*, being largely undatable folk-lore, is older than any of the historical material in the *Iliad*."[95] Both epics were probably written over and rewritten by some poet of a later date, in much the same manner that Lord Tennyson, the poet laureate of Queen Victoria, in his *Idylls of the King*, wrote over the *Morte d'Arthur* (which was itself a writing over by Sir Thomas Malory, *circ.* 1450, of pre-existing legends), making the speeches and sentiments and the characters more in accordance with those of his own time. But the events of the *Iliad* and the *Odyssey*, the way of living they describe, the spirit of the acts recorded, belong to the closing centuries of the prehistoric age. These sagas, epics, and vedas do supply, in addition to archæology and philology, a third source of information about those vanished times.

Here, for example, is the concluding passage of the *Iliad*, describing very exactly the making of a prehistoric barrow. (We have taken here Chapman's rhymed translation, correcting certain words with the help of the prose version of Lang, Leaf, and Myers.)

" ... Thus oxen, mules, in waggons straight they put,
Went forth, and an unmeasur'd pile of sylvan matter cut;
Nine days employ'd in carriage, but when the tenth morn shin'd

On wretched mortals, then they brought the bravest of his kind
Forth to be burned. Troy swam in tears. Upon the pile's most height
They laid the body, and gave fire. All day it burn'd, all night.
But when th' eleventh morn let on earth her rosy fingers shine,
The people flock'd about the pile, and first with gleaming wine
Quench'd all the flames. His brothers then, and friends, the snowy bones,
Gather'd into an urn of gold, still pouring out their moans.
Then wrapt they in soft purple veils the rich urn, digg'd a pit,
Grav'd it, built up the grave with stones, and quickly piled on it
A barrow....
... The barrow heap'd once, all the town
In Jove-nurs'd Priam's Court partook a sumptuous fun'ral feast,
And so horse-taming Hector's rites gave up his soul to rest."

There remains also an old English saga, *Beowulf*, made long before the English had crossed from Germany into England, which{vi-176} winds up with a similar burial. The preparation of a pyre is first described. It is hung round with shields and coats of mail. The body is brought and the pyre fired, and then for ten days the warriors built a mighty mound to be seen afar by the traveller on sea or land. *Beowulf*, which is at least a thousand years later than the *Iliad*, is also interesting because one of the main adventures in it is the looting of the treasures of a barrow already ancient in those days.

§ 3

The Greek epics reveal the early Greeks with no knowledge of iron, without writing, and before any Greek-founded cities existed in the land into which they had evidently come quite recently as conquerors. They were spreading southward from the Aryan region of origin. They seem to have been a fair people, newcomers in Greece, newcomers to a land that had been held hitherto by a darker people, people who are now supposed to have belonged to a dark white "aboriginal" race, a "Mediterranean" people allied to those Iberians whom the Kelts pressed westward, and to the Hamitic white people of North Africa.

Combat between Menelaus & Hector (in the Iliad)
From a platter ascribed to the end of the seventh century in the British Museum. This is probably the earliest known vase bearing a Greek inscription. Greek writing was just beginning. Note the Swastika.

Let us, at the risk of a slight repetition, be perfectly clear upon one point. The *Iliad* does not give us the primitive neolithic life of that Aryan region of origin; it gives us that life already well on the move towards a new state of affairs. The primitive neolithic way of living, with its tame and domesticated animals, its pottery and cooking, and its patches of rude cultivation, we have sketched in Chapter XI. We have already discussed in § 4 of[vi-177]Chapter XIII the probability of a widespread *heliolithic* culture, a sort of sub-civilization, very like the Polynesian and Indonesian life of a hundred years ago, an elaboration of the earlier Neolithic stage. Between 15,000 and 6000 B.C. the neolithic way of living had spread with the forests and abundant vegetation of the Pluvial Period, over the greater part of the old world, from the Niger to the Hwang-ho and from Ireland to the south of India. Now, as the climate of great portions of the earth was swinging towards drier and more open conditions again, the primitive neolithic life was developing along two divergent directions. One was leading to a more wandering life, towards at last a constantly migratory life between summer and winter pasture, which is called NOMADISM; the other, in certain sunlit river valleys, was towards a water-treasuring life of irrigation, in which men gathered into the first towns and made the first CIVILIZATION. The nature and development of civilization we shall consider more fully in the next chapter, but here we have to note that the Greeks, as the *Iliad* presents them, are neither simple neolithic nomads, innocent of civilization, nor are they civilized men. They are primitive nomads in an excited state, because they have just come upon civilization, and regard it as an opportunity for war and loot.[96] So far they are exceptional and not representative. But our interest in them in this chapter is not in their distinctively Greek and predatory aspect, but in what they reveal of the ordinary northward life from which they are coming.

These early Greeks of the *Iliad* are sturdy fighters, but without discipline—their battles are a confusion of single combats. They have horses, but no cavalry; they use the horse, which is a comparatively recent addition to Aryan resources, to drag a rude fighting chariot into battle. The horse is still novel enough to be something of a terror in itself. For ordinary draught purposes, as{vi-178} in the quotation from the *Iliad* we have just made, oxen were employed.

The only priests of these Aryans are the keepers of shrines and sacred places. There are chiefs, who are heads of families and who also perform sacrifices, but there does not seem to be much mystery or sacramental feeling in their religion. When the Greeks go to war, these heads and elders meet in council and appoint a king, whose powers are very loosely defined. There are no laws, but only customs; and no exact standards of conduct.

The social life of the early Greeks centred about the households of these leading men. There were no doubt huts for herds and the like, and outlying farm buildings; but the hall of the chief was a comprehensive centre, to which everyone went to feast, to hear the bards, to take part in games and exercises. The primitive craftsmen were gathered there. About it were cowsheds and stabling and such-like offices. Unimportant people slept about anywhere as retainers did in the mediæval castles and as people still do in Indian households. Except for quite personal possessions, there was still an air of patriarchal communism about the tribe. The tribe, or the chief as the head of the tribe, owned the grazing lands; forest and rivers were the wild.

The Aryan civilization seems, and indeed all early communities seem, to have been without the little separate households that make up the mass of the population in western Europe or America to-day. The tribe was a big family; the nation a group of tribal families; a household often contained hundreds of people. Human society began, just as herds and droves begin among animals, by the family delaying its breaking up. Nowadays the lions in East Africa are apparently becoming social animals in this way,{vl-179} by the young keeping with the mother after they are fully grown, and hunting in a group. Hitherto the lion has been much more of a solitary beast. If men and women do not cling to their families nowadays as much as they did, it is because the state and the community now supply safety and help and facilities that were once only possible in the family group.

In the Hindu community of to-day these great households of the earlier stages of human society are still to be found. Mr. Bhupendranath Basu has recently described a typical Hindu household.[97] It is an Aryan household refined and made gentle by thousands of years of civilization, but its social structure is the same as that of the households of which the Aryan epics tell.

"The joint family system," he said, "has descended to us from time immemorial, the Aryan patriarchal system of old still holding sway in India. The structure, though ancient, remains full of life. The joint family is a co-operative corporation, in which men and women have a well-defined place. At the head of the corporation is the senior member of the family, generally the eldest male member, but in his absence the senior female member often assumes control." (Cp. Penelope in the *Odyssey*.)

"All able-bodied members must contribute their labour and earnings, whether of personal skill or agriculture and trade, to the common stock; weaker members, widows, orphans, and destitute relations, all must be maintained and supported; sons, nephews, brothers, cousins, all must be treated equally, for any undue preference is apt to break up the family. We have no word for cousins—they are either brothers or sisters, and we do not know what are cousins two degrees removed. The children of a first cousin are your nephews and nieces, just the same as the children of your brothers and sisters. A man can no more marry a cousin, however removed, than he can marry his own sister, except in certain parts of Madras, where a man may marry his maternal uncle's daughter. The family affections, the family ties, are always very strong, and therefore the maintenance of an equal standard among so many members is not so difficult as it may appear at first sight. Moreover, life is very simple. Until recently shoes were not in{vi-180} general use at home, but sandals without any leather fastenings. I have known of a well-to-do middle-class family of several brothers and cousins who had two or three pairs of leather shoes between them, these shoes being only used when they had occasion to go out, and the same practice is still followed in the case of the more expensive garments, like shawls, which last for generations, and with their age are treated with loving care, as having been used by ancestors of revered memory.

"The joint family remains together sometimes for several generations, until it becomes too unwieldy, when it breaks up into smaller families, and you thus see whole villages peopled by members of the same clan. I have said that the family is a co-operative society, and it may be likened to a small state, and is kept in its place by strong discipline based on love and obedience. You see nearly every day the younger members coming to the head of the family and taking the dust of his feet as a token of benediction; whenever they go on an enterprise, they take his leave and carry his blessing.... There are many bonds which bind the family together—the bonds of sympathy, of common pleasures, of common sorrows; when a death occurs, all the members go into mourning; when there is a birth or a wedding, the whole family rejoices. Then above all is the family deity, some image of Vishnu, the preserver; his place is in a separate room, generally known as the room of God, or in well-to-do families in a temple attached to the house, where the family performs its daily worship. There is a sense of personal attachment between this image of the deity and the family, for the image generally comes down from past generations, often miraculously acquired by a pious ancestor at some remote time.... With the household gods is intimately associated the family priest.... The Hindu priest is a part of the family life of his flock, between whom and himself the tie has existed for many generations. The priest is not generally a man of much learning; he knows, however, the traditions of his faith.... He is not a very heavy burden, for he is satisfied with little—a few handfuls of rice, a few home-grown bananas or vegetables, a little unrefined sugar made in the village, and sometimes a few pieces of copper are all that is needed.... A picture of our family life would be incomplete without the household servants. A female[vi-181] servant is known as the 'jhi,' or daughter, in Bengal—she is like the daughter of the house; she calls the master and the mistress father and mother, and the young men and women of the family brothers and sisters. She participates in the life of the family; she goes to the holy places along with her mistress, for she could not go alone, and generally she spends her life with the family of her adoption; her children are looked after by the family. The treatment of men servants is very similar. These servants, men and women, are generally people of the humbler castes, but a sense of personal attachment grows up between them and the members of the family, and as they get on in years they are affectionately called by the younger members elder brothers, uncles, aunts, etc.... In a well-to-do house there is always a resident teacher, who instructs the children of the family as well as other boys of the village; there is no expensive school building, but room is found in some veranda or shed in the courtyard for the children and their teacher, and into this school low-caste boys are freely admitted. These indigenous schools were not of a very high order, but they supplied an agency of instruction for the masses which was probably not available in many other countries....

"With Hindu life is bound up its traditional duty of hospitality. It is the duty of a householder to offer a meal to any stranger who may come before midday and ask for one; the mistress of the house does not sit down to her meal until every member is fed, and, as sometimes her food is all that is left, she does not take her meal until well after midday lest a hungry stranger should come and claim one." ...

We have been tempted to quote Mr. Basu at some length, because here we do get to something like a living understanding of the type of household which has prevailed in human communities since Neolithic days, which still prevails to-day in India, China, and the Far East, but which in the west is rapidly giving ground before a state and municipal organization of education and a large-scale industrialism within which an amount of individual detachment and freedom is possible, such as these great households never knew....{v1-182}

But let us return now to the history preserved for us in the Aryan epics.

The Sanscrit epics tell a very similar story to that underlying the *Iliad*, the story of a fair, beef-eating people—only later did they become vegetarians—coming down from Persia into the plain of North India and conquering their way slowly towards the Indus. From the Indus they spread over India, but as they spread they acquired much from the dark Dravidians they conquered, and they seem to have lost their bardic tradition. The vedas, says Mr. Basu, were transmitted chiefly in the households by the women....

The oral literature of the Keltic peoples who pressed westward has not been preserved so completely as that of the Greeks or Indians; it was written down many centuries later, and so, like the barbaric, primitive English *Beowulf,* has lost any clear evidence of a period of migration into the lands of an antecedent people. If the pre-Aryans figure in it at all, it is as the fairy folk of the Irish stories. Ireland, most cut off of all the Keltic-speaking communities, retained to the latest date its primitive life; and the *Táin,* the Irish *Iliad,* describes a cattle-keeping life in which war chariots are still used, and war dogs also, and the heads of the slain are carried off slung round the horses' necks. The *Táin* is the story of a cattle raid. Here too the same social order appears as in the *Iliad;* the chiefs sit and feast in great halls, they build halls for themselves, there is singing and story-telling by the bards and drinking and intoxication.[98] Priests are not very much in evidence, but there is a sort of medicine man who deals in spells and prophecy.{vi-183}

XVI

THE FIRST CIVILIZATIONS

§ 1. *Early Cities and Early Nomads.* § 2A. *The Riddle of the Sumerians.* § 2B. *The Empire of Sargon the First.* § 2C. *The Empire of Hammurabi.* § 2D. *The Assyrians and their Empire.* § 2E. *The Chaldean Empire.* § 3. *The Early History of Egypt.* § 4. *The Early Civilization of India.* § 5. *The Early History of China.* § 6. *While the Civilizations were Growing.*

W HEN the Aryan way of speech and life was beginning to spread to the east and west of the region in which it began, and breaking up as it spread into a number of languages and nations, considerable communities of much more civilized men were already in existence in Egypt and in Mesopotamia, and probably also in China and in (still purely Dravidian) India. Our story has overshot itself in its account of the Aryans and of their slow progress from early Neolithic conditions to the heroic barbarism of the Bronze Age. We must now go back. Such a pre-Keltic gathering as we sketched at Avebury would have happened about 2000 B.C., and the building of the barrow for Hector as the *Iliad* describes it, 1300 B.C. or even later. It is perhaps natural for a European writer writing primarily for English-reading students to overrun his subject in this way. No great harm is done if the student does clearly grasp that there has been an overlap.

Here then we take up the main thread of human history again. We must hark back to 6000 B.C. or even earlier. But although we shall go back so far, the people we shall describe are people already in some respects beyond the Neolithic Aryans of three{vi-184} thousand years later, more particularly in their social organization and their material welfare. While in Central Europe and Central Asia the primitive Neolithic way of life was becoming more migratory and developing into nomadism, in the great river valleys it is becoming more settled and localized. It is still doubtful whether we are to consider Mesopotamia or Egypt the earlier scene of the two parallel beginnings of settled communities living in towns. By 4000 B.C., in both these regions of the earth, such communities existed, and had been going on for a very considerable time. The excavations of the American expedition[99] at Nippur have unearthed evidence of a city community existing there at least as early as 5000 B.C., and probably as early as 6000 B.C., an earlier date than anything we know of in Egypt. De Candolle asserts that it is only in the Euphrates-Tigris district that wheat has ever been found growing wild.[100] It may be that from Mesopotamia as a centre the cultivation of wheat spread over the entire eastern hemisphere. Or it may be that wheat grew wild in some regions now submerged. There may have been a wild wheat region in what is now the sea bottom of the eastern Mediterranean. But cultivation is not civilization; the growing of wheat had spread from the Atlantic to the Pacific with the distribution of the Neolithic culture by perhaps 10,000 or 9000 B.C., before the beginnings of civilization. Civilization is something more than the occasional seasonal growing of wheat. It is the settlement of men upon an area continuously cultivated and possessed, who live in buildings continuously inhabited with a common rule and a common city or citadel. For a long time civilization may quite possibly have developed in Mesopotamia without any relations with the parallel beginnings in Egypt. The two settlements may have been quite independent, arising separately out of the widely diffused Heliolithic Neolithic culture. Or they may have had a common origin in the region of the Mediterranean, the Red Sea, and southern Arabia.{vl-185}

{vl-186}

The first condition necessary to a real settling down of Neolithic men, as distinguished from a mere temporary settlement among abundant food, was of course a trustworthy all-the-year-round supply of water, fodder for the animals, food for themselves, and building material for their homes. There had to be everything they could need at any season, and no want that would tempt them to wander further. This was a possible state of affairs, no doubt, in many European and Asiatic valleys; and in many such valleys, as in the case of the Swiss lake-dwellings, men settled from a very early date indeed; but nowhere, of any countries now known to us, were these favourable conditions found upon such a scale, and nowhere did they hold good so surely year in and year out as in Egypt and in the country between the upper waters of the Euphrates and Tigris and the Persian Gulf.[101] Here was a constant water supply under enduring sunlight; trustworthy harvests year by year; in Mesopotamia wheat yielded, says Herodotus, two hundredfold to the sower; Pliny says that it was cut twice and afterwards yielded good fodder for sheep; there were abundant palms and many sorts of fruits; and as for building material, in Egypt there was clay and easily worked stone, and in

Mesopotamia a clay that becomes a brick in the sunshine. In such countries men would cease to wander and settle down almost unawares; they would multiply and discover themselves numerous and by their numbers safe from any casual assailant. They multiplied, producing a denser human population than the earth had ever known before; their houses became more substantial, wild beasts were exterminated over great areas, the security of life increased so that ordinary men went about in the towns and fields without encumbering themselves with weapons, and, among themselves at least, they became peaceful peoples. Men took root as man had never taken root before.

But in the less fertile and more seasonal lands outside these favoured areas, there developed on the other hand a thinner, more{vl-187} active population of peoples, the primitive nomadic peoples. In contrast with the settled folk, the agriculturists, these nomads lived freely and dangerously. They were in comparison lean and hungry men. Their herding was still blended with hunting; they fought constantly for their pastures against hostile families. The discoveries in the elaboration of implements and the use of metals made by the settled peoples spread to them and improved their weapons. They followed the settled folk from Neolithic phase to Bronze phase. It is possible that, in the case of iron, the first users were nomadic. They became more warlike with better arms, and more capable of rapid movements with the improvement of their transport. One must not think of a nomadic stage as a predecessor of a settled stage in human affairs. To begin with, man was a slow drifter, following food. Then one sort of men began to settle down, and another sort became more distinctly nomadic. The settled sort began to rely more and more upon grain for food; the nomad began to make a greater use of milk for food. He bred his cows for milk. The two ways of life specialized in opposite directions. It was inevitable that nomad folk and the settled folk should clash, that the nomads should seem hard barbarians to the settled peoples, and the settled peoples soft and effeminate and very good plunder to the nomad peoples. Along the fringes of the developing civilizations there must have been a constant raiding and bickering between hardy nomad tribes and mountain tribes and the more numerous and less warlike peoples in the towns and villages.

For the most part this was a mere raiding of the borders. The settled folk had the weight of numbers on their side; the herdsmen might raid and loot, but they could not stay. That sort of mutual friction might go on for many generations. But ever and again we find some leader or some tribe amidst the disorder of free and independent nomads, powerful enough to force a sort of unity upon its kindred tribes, and then woe betide the nearest civilization. Down pour the united nomads on the unwarlike, unarmed plains, and there ensues a war of conquest. Instead of carrying off the booty, the conquerors settle down on the conquered land, which becomes all booty for them; the villagers and townsmen are reduced to servitude and tribute-paying, they become{vi-188} hewers of wood and drawers of water, and the leaders of the nomads become kings and princes, masters and aristocrats. They too settle down, they learn many of the arts and refinements of the conquered, they cease to be lean and hungry, but for many generations they retain traces of their old nomadic habits, they hunt and indulge in open-air sports, they drive and race chariots, they regard work, especially agricultural work, as the lot of an inferior race and class.

This in a thousand variations has been one of the main stories in history for the last seventy centuries or more. In the first history that we can clearly decipher we find already in all the civilized regions a distinction between a non-working ruler class and the working mass of the population. And we find too that after some generations, the aristocrat, having settled down, begins to respect the arts and refinements and law-abidingness of settlement, and to lose something of his original hardihood. He intermarries, he patches up a sort of toleration between conqueror and conquered; he exchanges religious ideas and learns the lessons upon which soil and climate insist. He becomes a part of the civilization he has captured. And as he does so, events gather towards a fresh invasion by the free adventurers of the outer world.[102]

This alternation of settlement, conquest, refinement, fresh conquest, refinement, is particularly to be noted in the region of the Euphrates and Tigris, which lay open in every direction to great areas which are not arid enough to be complete deserts, but which were not fertile enough to support civilized populations. Perhaps the earliest people to form real cities in this part of the world, or indeed in any part of the world, were a people of mysterious origin[vi-189] called the Sumerians. They were neither Semites nor Aryans, and whence they came we do not know. Whether they were dark whites of Iberian or Dravidian affinities is less certainly to be denied.[103] They used a kind of writing which they scratched upon clay, and their language has been deciphered.[104] It was a language more like the unclassified Caucasic language groups than any others that now exist. These languages may be connected with Basque, and may represent what was once a widespread group extending from Spain and western Europe to eastern India, and reaching[vi-190] southwards to Central Africa. These people shaved their heads and wore simple tunic-like garments of wool. They settled first on the lower courses of the great river and not very far from the Persian Gulf, which in those days ran up for a hundred and thirty miles[105] and more beyond its present head. They fertilized their fields by letting water run through irrigation trenches, and they gradually became very skilful hydraulic engineers;

they had cattle, asses, sheep, and goats, but no horses; their collections of mud huts grew into towns, and their religion raised up towerlike temple buildings.

Clay, dried in the sun, was a very great fact in the lives of these people. This lower country of the Euphrates-Tigris valleys had little or no stone. They built of brick, they made pottery and earthenware images, and they drew and presently wrote upon thin tile-like cakes of clay. They do not seem to have had paper or to have used parchment. Their books and memoranda, even their letters, were potsherds.

At Nippur they built a great tower of brick to their chief god, El-lil (Enlil), the memory of which is supposed to be preserved in the story of the Tower of Babel. They seem to have been divided up into city states, which warred among themselves and maintained for many centuries their military capacity. Their soldiers carried long spears and shields, and fought in close formation. Sumerians conquered Sumerians. Sumeria remained unconquered by any stranger race for a very long period of time indeed. They developed their civilization, their writing, and their shipping, through a period that may be twice as long as the whole period from the Christian era to the present time.

The first of all known empires was that founded by the high priest of the god of the Sumerian city of Erech. It reached, says an inscription at Nippur, from the Lower (Persian Gulf) to the Upper (Mediterranean or Red?) Sea. Among the mud heaps of the Euphrates-Tigris valley the record of that vast period of history, that first half of the Age of Cultivation, is buried. There flourished the first temples and the first priest-rulers that we know of among mankind.{VI-191}

§ 2B

Upon the western edge of this country appeared nomadic tribes of Semitic-speaking peoples who traded, raided, and fought with the Sumerians for many generations. Then arose at last a great leader among these Semites, Sargon (2750 B.C.),[106] who united them, and not only conquered the Sumerians, but extended his rule from beyond the Persian Gulf on the east to the Mediterranean on the west. His own people were called the Akkadians and his empire is called the Sumerian Akkadian Empire. It endured for over two hundred years.

But though the Semites conquered and gave a king to the Sumerian cities, it was the Sumerian civilization which prevailed over the simpler Semitic culture. The newcomers learnt the Sumerian writing (the "cuneiform" writing) and the Sumerian language; they set up no Semitic writing of their own. The Sumerian language became for these barbarians the language of knowledge and power, as Latin was the language of knowledge and power among the barbaric peoples of the middle ages in Europe. This Sumerian learning had a very great vitality. It was destined to survive through a long series of conquests and changes that now began in the valley of the two rivers.

§ 2C

As the people of the Sumerian Akkadian Empire lost their political and military vigour, fresh inundations of a warlike people began from the east, the Elamites,[107] while from the west came the Semitic Amorites, pinching the Sumerian Akkadian Empire between them. The Amorites settled in what was at first a small up-river town, named Babylon; and after a hundred years of warfare became masters of all Mesopotamia under a great king, Hammurabi (2100 B.C.), who founded the first Babylonian Empire.

Again came peace and security and a decline in aggressive{vI-192} prowess, and in another hundred years fresh nomads from the east were invading Babylonia, bringing with them the horse and the war chariot, and setting up their own king in Babylon....

§2D

Higher up the Tigris, above the clay lands and with easy supplies of workable stone, a Semitic people, the Assyrians, while the Sumerians were still unconquered by the Semites, were settling about a number of cities of which Assur and Nineveh were the chief. Their peculiar physiognomy, the long nose and thick lips, was very like that of the commoner type of Polish Jew to-day. They wore great beards and ringletted long hair, tall caps and long robes. They were constantly engaged in mutual raiding with the Hittites to the west; they were conquered by Sargon I and became free again; a certain Tushratta, King of Mitanni, to the north-west, captured and held their capital, Nineveh, for a time; they intrigued with Egypt against Babylon and were in the pay of Egypt; they developed the military art to a very high pitch, and became mighty raiders and exacters of tribute; and at last, adopting the horse and the war chariot, they settled accounts for a time with the Hittites, and then, under Tiglath Pileser I, conquered Babylon for themselves (about 1100 B.C.[108]). But their hold on the lower, older, and more civilized land was not secure, and Nineveh, the stone city, as distinguished from Babylon, the brick city, remained their capital. For many centuries power swayed between Nineveh and Babylon, and sometimes it was an Assyrian and sometimes a Babylonian who claimed to be "king of the world."

For four centuries Assyria was restrained from expansion towards Egypt by a fresh northward thrust and settlement of another group of Semitic peoples, the Arameans, whose chief city was Damascus, and whose descendants are the Syrians of to-day. (There is, we may note, no connection whatever between the words Assyrian and Syrian. It is an accidental similarity.) Across these Syrians the Assyrian kings fought for power and expansion south-westward. In 745 B.C. arose another Tiglath Pileser,{v1-193} Tiglath Pileser III, the Tiglath Pileser of the Bible.[109] He not only directed the transfer of the Israelites to Media (the "Lost Ten Tribes" whose ultimate fate has exercised so many curious minds), but he conquered and ruled Babylon, so founding what historians know as the New Assyrian Empire. His son, Shalmaneser IV,[110] died during the siege of Samaria, and was succeeded by a usurper, who, no doubt to flatter Babylonian susceptibilities, took the ancient Akkadian Sumerian name of Sargon, Sargon II. He seems to have armed the Assyrian forces for the first time with iron weapons. It was probably Sargon II who actually carried out the deportation of the Ten Tribes.

Such shiftings about of population became a very distinctive part of the political methods of the Assyrian new empire. Whole nations who were difficult to control in their native country would be shifted en *masse* to unaccustomed regions and amidst strange neighbours, where their only hope of survival would lie in obedience to the supreme power.

Sargon's son, Sennacherib, led the Assyrian hosts to the borders of Egypt. There Sennacherib's army was smitten by a pestilence, a disaster described in the nineteenth chapter of the Second Book of Kings.

"And it came to pass that night, that the angel of the Lord went out, and smote in the camp of the Assyrians an hundred fourscore and five thousand; and when they arose early in the morning, behold, they were all dead corpses. So Sennacherib king of

Assyria departed, and went and returned, and dwelt at Nineveh."[111]

{v1-194}

Sennacherib's grandson, Assurbanipal (called by the Greeks Sardanapalus), did succeed in conquering and for a time holding lower Egypt.

§2E

The Assyrian Empire lasted only a hundred and fifty years after Sargon II. Fresh nomadic Semites coming from the south-east, the Chaldeans, assisted by two Aryan peoples from the north, the Medes and Persians, combined against it, and took Nineveh in 606 B.C.

The Chaldean Empire, with its capital at Babylon (Second Babylonian Empire), lasted under Nebuchadnezzar the Great (Nebuchadnezzar II) and his successors until 539 B.C., when it collapsed before the attack of Cyrus, the founder of the Persian power....

So the story goes on. In 330 B.C., as we shall tell later in some detail, a Greek conqueror, Alexander the Great, is looking on the murdered body of the last of the Persian rulers.

The story of the Tigris and Euphrates civilizations, of which we have given as yet only the bare outline, is a story of conquest following after conquest, and each conquest replaces old rulers and ruling classes by new; races like the Sumerian and the Elamite are swallowed up, their languages vanish, they interbreed and are lost, the Assyrian melts away into Chaldean and Syrian, the Hittites become Aryanized and lose distinction, the Semites who swallowed up the Sumerians give place to Aryan rulers, Medes and Persians appear in the place of the Elamites, the Aryan Persian language dominates the empire until the Aryan Greek ousts it from official life. Meanwhile the plough does its work year by year, the harvests are gathered, the builders build as they are told, the tradesmen work and acquire fresh devices; the knowledge of writing spreads, novel things, the horse and wheeled vehicles and iron, are introduced and become part of the permanent inheritance of mankind; the volume of trade upon sea and desert increases, men's ideas widen, and knowledge grows. There are set-backs, massacres, pestilence; but the story is, on the whole, one of enlargement. For four thousand years this new thing, civilization, which had set its root into the soil of the two rivers, grew{vi-195} as a tree grows; now losing a limb, now stripped by a storm, but always growing and resuming its growth. After four thousand years the warriors and conquerors were still going to and fro over this growing thing they did not understand, but men had now (330 B.C.) got iron, horses, writing and computation, money, a greater variety of foods and textiles, a wider knowledge of their world.

The time that elapsed between the empire of Sargon I and the conquest of Babylon by Alexander the Great was as long, be it noted, at the least estimate, as the time from Alexander the Great to the present day. And before the time of Sargon, men had been settled in the Sumerian land, living in towns, worshipping in temples, following an orderly Neolithic agricultural life in an organized community for at least as long again. "Eridu, Lagash, Ur, Uruk, Larsa, have already an immemorial past when first they appear in history."[112]

One of the most difficult things for both the writer and student of history is to sustain the sense of these time intervals and prevent these ages becoming shortened by perspective in his imagination. Half the duration of human civilization and the keys to all its chief institutions are to be found *before* Sargon I. Moreover, the reader cannot too often compare the scale of the dates in these latter fuller pages of man's history with the succession of countless generations to which the time diagrams given on pages 14, 60, and 89 bear witness.

§ 3

The story of the Nile valley from the dawn of its traceable history until the time of Alexander the Great is not very dissimilar from that of Babylonia; but while Babylonia lay open on every side to invasion, Egypt was protected by desert to the west and by desert and sea to the east, while to the south she had only negro peoples. Consequently her history is less broken by the invasions of strange races than is the history of Assyria and Babylon, and until towards the eighth century B.C., when she fell under an Ethiopian dynasty, whenever a conqueror did come into her story, he came in from Asia by way of the Isthmus of Suez.{v1-196}

The Stone Age remains in Egypt are of very uncertain date; there are Palæolithic and then Neolithic remains. It is not certain whether the Neolithic pastoral people who left those remains were the direct ancestors of the later Egyptians. In many respects they differed entirely from their successors. They buried their dead, but before they buried them they cut up the bodies and apparently ate portions of the flesh. They seem to have done this out of a feeling of reverence for the departed; the dead were "eaten with honour" according to the phrase of Mr. Flinders Petrie. It may have been that the survivors hoped to retain thereby some vestige of the strength and virtue that had died. Traces of similar savage customs have been found in the long barrows that were scattered over western Europe before the spreading of the Aryan peoples, and they have pervaded negro Africa, where they are only dying out at the present time.

About 5000 B.C., or earlier, the traces of these primitive peoples cease, and the true Egyptians appear on the scene. The former people were hut builders and at a comparatively low stage of Neolithic culture, the latter were already a civilized Neolithic people; they used brick and wood buildings instead of their predecessors' hovels, and they were working stone. Very soon they passed into the Bronze Age. They possessed a system of picture writing almost as developed as the contemporary writing of the Sumerians, but quite different in character. Possibly there was an irruption from southern Arabia by way of Aden, of a fresh people, who came into upper Egypt and descended slowly towards the delta of the Nile. Dr. Wallis Budge writes of them as "conquerors from the East." But their gods and{vl-198}their ways, like their picture writing, were very different indeed from the Sumerian. One of the earliest known figures of a deity is that of a hippopotamus goddess, and so very distinctively African.[113]

The clay of the Nile is not so fine and plastic as the Sumerian clay, and the Egyptians made no use of it for writing. But they early resorted to strips of the papyrus reed fastened together, from whose name comes our word "paper."

The broad outline of the history of Egypt is simpler than the history of Mesopotamia. It has long been the custom to divide the rulers of Egypt into a succession of Dynasties, and in speaking of the periods of Egyptian history it is usual to speak of the first, fourth, fourteenth, and so on, Dynasty. The Egyptians were ultimately conquered by the Persians after their establishment in Babylon, and when finally Egypt fell to Alexander the Great in 332 B.C., it was Dynasty XXXI that came to an end. In that long history of over 4000 years, a much longer period than that between the career of Alexander the Great and the present day, certain broad phases of development may be noted here. There was a phase known as the "old kingdom," which culminated in the IVth Dynasty; this Dynasty marks a period of wealth and splendour, and its monarchs were obsessed by such a passion for making monuments for themselves as no men have ever before or since had a chance to display and gratify. It was Cheops[114] and Chephren and Mycerinus of this IVth Dynasty who raised the vast piles of the great and the second and the third pyramids at Gizeh. These unmeaning[115] sepulchral piles, of an almost incredible vastness,{v1-199}[116] erected in an age when engineering science had scarcely begun, exhausted the resources of Egypt through three long reigns, and left her wasted as if by a war.

The story of Egypt from the IVth to the XVth Dynasty is a story of conflicts between alternative capitals and competing religions, of separations into several kingdoms and reunions. It is, so to speak, an internal history. Here we can name only one of that long series of Pharaohs, Pepi II, who reigned ninety years, the longest reign in history, and left a great abundance of inscriptions and buildings. At last there happened to Egypt what happened so frequently to the civilizations of Mesopotamia. Egypt was conquered by nomadic Semites, who founded a "shepherd" dynasty, the Hyksos (XVIth), which was finally expelled by native Egyptians. This invasion probably happened while that first Babylonian Empire which Hammurabi founded was flourishing, but the exact correspondences of dates between early Egypt and Babylonia are still very doubtful. Only after a long period of servitude did a popular uprising expel these foreigners again.

After the war of liberation (circa 1600 B.C.) there followed a period of great prosperity in Egypt, *the New Empire.* Egypt became a great and united military state, and pushed her expeditions at last as far as the Euphrates, and so the age-long struggle between the Egyptian and Babylonian-Assyrian power began.

For a time Egypt was the ascendant power. Thothmes III[117] {vi-200}and his son Amenophis III (XVIIIth Dynasty) ruled from Ethiopia to the Euphrates in the fifteenth century B.C.For various reasons these names stand out with unusual distinctness in the Egyptian record. They were great builders, and left many monuments and inscriptions. Amenophis III founded Luxor, and added greatly to Karnak. At Tel-el-Amarna a mass of letters has been found, the royal correspondence with Babylonian and Hittite and other monarchs, including that Tushratta who took Nineveh, throwing a flood of light upon the political and social affairs of this particular age. Of Amenophis IV we shall have more to tell later, but of one, the most extraordinary and able of Egyptian monarchs, Queen Hatasu, the aunt and stepmother of Thotmes III, we have no space to tell. She is represented upon her monuments in masculine garb, and with a long beard as a symbol of wisdom.

Thereafter there was a brief Syrian conquest of Egypt, a series, of changing dynasties, among which we may note the XIXth, which included Rameses II, a great builder of temples, who reigned seventy-seven years (about 1317 to 1250 B.C.), and who is supposed by some to have been the Pharaoh of Moses, and the XXIInd, which included Shishak, who plundered Solomon's temple (circa 930 B.C.). An Ethiopian conqueror from the Upper Nile founded the XXVth Dynasty, a foreign dynasty, which went down (670 B.C.) before the new Assyrian Empire created by Tiglath Pileser III, Sargon II, and Sennacherib, of which we have already made mention.

The days of any Egyptian predominance over foreign nations were drawing to an end. For a time under Psammetichus I of the XXVIth Dynasty (664-610 B.C.) native rule was restored, and Necho II recovered for a time the old Egyptian possessions in Syria up to the Euphrates while the Medes and Chaldeans were attacking Nineveh. From those gains Necho II was routed out again after the fall of Nineveh and the Assyrians by Nebuchadnezzar II, the great Chaldean king, the Nebuchadnezzar of the Bible. The Jews, who had been the allies of Necho II, were taken into captivity by Nebuchadnezzar to Babylon.

When, in the sixth century B.C., Chaldea fell to the Persians, Egypt followed suit, a rebellion later made Egypt independent once more for sixty years, and in 332 B.C. she welcomed Alexander{v1-201} the Great as her conqueror, to be ruled thereafter by foreigners, first by Greeks, then by Romans, then in succession by Arabs, Turks, and British, until the present day.

Such briefly is the history of Egypt from its beginnings; a history first of isolation and then of increasing entanglement with the affairs of other nations, as increasing facilities of communication drew the peoples of the world into closer and closer interaction.

§ 4

The history we need to tell here of India is simpler even than this brief record of Egypt. Somewhere about the time of Hammurabi or later, a branch of the Aryan-speaking people who then occupied North Persia and Afghanistan, pushed down the northwest passes into India. They conquered their way until they prevailed over all the darker populations of North India, and spread their rule or influence over the whole peninsula. They never achieved any unity in India; their history is a history of warring kings and republics. The Persian empire, in the days of its expansion after the capture of Babylon, pushed its boundaries beyond the Indus, and later Alexander the Great marched as far as the border of the desert that separates the Punjab from the Ganges valley. But with this bare statement we will for a time leave the history of India.

§ 5

Meanwhile, as this triple system of White Man civilization developed in India and in the lands about the meeting-places of Asia, Africa, and Europe, another and quite distinct civilization was developing and spreading out from the then fertile but now dry and desolate valley of the Tarim and from the slopes of the Kuen-lun mountains in two directions, down the course of the Hwang-ho, and into the valley of the Yang-tse-kiang. We know practically nothing as yet of the archæology of China, we do not know anything of the Stone Age in that part of the world, and at present our ideas of this early civilization are derived from the still very imperfectly explored Chinese literature. It has evidently been from the first and throughout a Mongolian civilization. Until{vi-203} after the time of Alexander the Great there are few traces of any Aryan or Semitic, much less of Hamitic influence. All such influences were still in another world, separated by mountains, deserts, and wild nomadic tribes until that time. The Chinese seem to have made their civilization spontaneously and unassisted. Some recent writers suppose indeed a connection with ancient Sumeria. Of course both China and Sumeria arose on the basis of the almost world-wide early Neolithic culture, but the Tarim valley and the lower Euphrates are separated by such vast obstacles of mountain and desert as to forbid the idea of any migration or interchange of peoples who had once settled down.

But though the civilization of China is wholly Mongolian (as we have defined Mongolian), it does not follow that the northern roots are the only ones from which it grew. If it grew first in the Tarim valley, then unlike all other civilizations (including the Mexican and Peruvian) it did not grow out of the heliolithic culture. We Europeans know very little as yet of the ethnology and pre-history of southern China. There the Chinese mingle with such kindred peoples as the Siamese and Burmese, and seem to bridge over towards the darker Dravidian peoples and towards the Malays. It is quite clear from the Chinese records that there were southern as well as northern beginnings of a civilization, and that the Chinese civilization that comes into history 2000 years B.C. is the result of a long process of conflicts, minglings, and interchanges between a southern and a northern culture of which the southern may have been the earlier. The southern Chinese perhaps played the rôle towards the northern Chinese that the Hamites or Sumerians played to the Aryan and Semitic peoples in the west, or that the settled Dravidians played towards the Aryans in India. They may have been the first agriculturists and the first temple builders. But so little is known as yet of this attractive chapter in pre-history, that we cannot dwell upon it further here.

The chief foreigners mentioned in the early annals of China were a Ural-Altaic people on the north-east frontier, the Huns, against whom certain of the earlier emperors made war.

Chinese history is still very imperfectly known to European students, and our accounts of the early records are particularly{v1-204} unsatisfactory. About 2700 to 2400 B.C. reigned five emperors, who seem to have been almost incredibly exemplary beings.

There follows upon these first five emperors a series of dynasties, of which the accounts become more and more exact and convincing as they become more recent. China has to tell a long history of border warfare and of graver struggles between the settled and nomad peoples. To begin with, China, like Sumer and like Egypt, was a land of city states. The government was at first a government of numerous kings; they became loosely feudal under an emperor, as the Egyptians did; and then later, as with the Egyptians, came a centralizing empire. Shang (1750 to 1125 B.C.) and Chow (1125 to 250 B.C.) are named as being the two great dynasties of the feudal period. Bronze vessels of these earlier dynasties, beautiful, splendid, and with a distinctive style of their own, still exist, and there can be no doubt of the existence of a high state of culture even before the days of Shang.

It is perhaps a sense of symmetry that made the later historians of Egypt and China talk of the earlier phases of their national history as being under dynasties comparable to the dynasties of the later empires, and of such early "Emperors" as Menes (in Egypt) or the First Five Emperors (in China). The early dynasties exercised far less centralized powers than the later ones. Such unity as China possessed under the Shang dynasty was a religious rather than an effective political union. The "Son of Heaven" offered sacrifices for all the Chinese. There was a common script, a common civilization, and a common enemy in the Huns of the north-western borders.

The last of the Shang Dynasty was a cruel and foolish monarch who burnt himself alive (1125 B.C.) in his palace after a decisive defeat by Wu Wang, the founder of the Chow Dynasty. Wu Wang seems to have been helped by allies from among the south-western tribes as well as by a popular revolt.

For a time China remained loosely united under the Chow emperors, as loosely united as was Christendom under the popes in the Middle Ages; the Chow emperors had become the traditional high priests of the land in the place of the Shang Dynasty and claimed a sort of overlordship in Chinese affairs, but gradually the loose ties of usage and sentiment that held the empire together lost their{vi-205} hold upon men's minds. Hunnish peoples to the north and west took on the Chinese civilization without acquiring a sense of its unity. Feudal princes began to regard themselves as independent. Mr. Liang-Chi-Chao,[118] one of the Chinese representatives at the Paris Conference of 1919, states that between the eighth and fourth centuries B.C. "there were in the Hwang-ho and Yang-tse valleys no less than five or six thousand small states with about a dozen powerful states dominating over them." The land was subjected to perpetual warfare ("Age of Confusion"). In the sixth century B.C. the great powers in conflict were Ts'i and Ts'in, which were northern Hwang-ho states, and Ch'u, which was a vigorous, aggressive power in the Yang-tse valley. A confederation against Ch'u laid the foundation for a league that kept the peace for a hundred years; the league subdued and incorporated Ch'u and made a general treaty of disarmament. It became the foundation of a new pacific empire.

The knowledge of iron entered China at some unknown date, but iron weapons began to be commonly used only about 500 B.C., that is to say two or three hundred years or more after this had become customary in Assyria, Egypt, and Europe. Iron was probably introduced from the north into China by the Huns.

The last rulers of the Chow Dynasty were ousted by the kings of Ts'in, the latter seized upon the sacred sacrificial bronze tripods, and so were able to take over the imperial duty of offering sacrifices to Heaven. In this manner was the Ts'in Dynasty established. It ruled with far more vigour and effect than any previous family. The reign of Shi-Hwang-ti (meaning "first universal emperor") of this dynasty is usually taken to mark the end of feudal and divided China. He seems to have played the unifying rôle in the east that Alexander the Great might have played in the west, but he lived longer, and the unity he made (or restored) was comparatively permanent, while the empire of Alexander the Great fell to pieces, as we shall tell, at his death. Shi-Hwang-ti, among other feats in the direction of common effort, organized the building of the Great Wall of China against the Huns. A civil war followed close upon his reign, and ended in the establishment of the Han{v1-206} Dynasty. Under this Han Dynasty the empire grew greatly beyond its original two river valleys, the Huns were effectively restrained, and the Chinese penetrated westward until they began to learn at last of civilized races and civilizations other than their own.

By 100 B.C. the Chinese had heard of India, their power had spread across Tibet and into Western Turkestan, and they were trading by camel caravans with Persia and the western world. So much for the present must suffice for our account of China. We shall return to the distinctive characters of its civilization later.

§ 6

And in these thousands of years during which man was making his way step by step from the barbarism of the heliolithic culture to civilization at these old-world centres, what was happening in the rest of the world? To the north of these centres, from the Rhine to the Pacific, the Nordic and Mongolian peoples, as we have told, were also learning the use of metals; but while the civilizations were settling down these men of the great plains were becoming migratory and developing from a slow wandering life towards a complete seasonal nomadism. To the south of the civilized zone, in central and southern Africa, the negro was making a slower progress, and that, it would seem, under the stimulus of invasion by whiter tribes from the Mediterranean regions, bringing with them in succession cultivation and the use of metals. These white men came to the black by two routes: across the Sahara to the west as Berbers and Tuaregs and the like, to mix with the negro and create such quasi-white races as the Fulas; and also by way of the Nile, where the Baganda (= Gandafolk) of Uganda, for example, may possibly be of remote white origin. The African forests were denser then, and spread eastward and northward from the Upper Nile.

The islands of the East Indies, three thousand years ago, were probably still only inhabited here and there by stranded patches of Palæolithic Australoids, who had wandered thither in those immemorial ages when there was a nearly complete land bridge by way of the East Indies to Australia. The islands of Oceania were uninhabited. The spreading of the heliolithic peoples by {v1-207} sea-going canoes into the islands of the Pacific came much later in the history of man, at earliest a thousand years B.C. Still later did they reach Madagascar. The beauty of New Zealand also was as yet wasted upon mankind; its highest living creatures were a great ostrich-like bird, the moa, now extinct, and the little kiwi which has feathers like coarse hair and the merest rudiment of wings.

In North America a group of Mongoloid tribes were now cut off altogether from the old world. They were spreading slowly southward, hunting the innumerable bison of the plains. They had still to learn for themselves the secrets of a separate agriculture based on maize, and in South America to tame the lama to their service and so build up in Mexico and Peru two civilizations roughly parallel in their nature to that of Sumer, but different in many respects, and later by six or seven thousand years....

When men reached the southern extremity of America, the *Megatherium,* the giant sloth, and the *Glyptodon,* the giant armadillo, were still living....

There is a considerable imaginative appeal in the obscure story of the early American civilizations. It was largely a separate development.[119] Somewhen at last the southward drift of the Amerindians must have met and mingled with the eastward, canoe-borne drift of the heliolithic culture. But it was the heliolithic culture still at a very lowly stage and probably before the use of metals. It has to be noted as evidence of this canoe-borne origin of American culture, that elephant-headed figures are found in Central American drawings. American metallurgy may have arisen independently of the old-world use of metal, or it may have been brought by these elephant carvers. These American peoples got to the use of bronze and copper, but not to the use of iron; they had gold and silver; and their stonework, their pottery, weaving, and dyeing were carried to a very high level. In all these things the American product resembles the old-world product generally, but always it has characteristics that are distinctive. The American civilizations had picture-writing of a primitive{vi-208} sort, but it never developed even to the pitch of the earliest Egyptian hieroglyphics. In Yucatan only was there a kind of script, the Maya writing, but it was used simply for keeping a calendar. In Peru the beginnings of writing were superseded by a curious and complicated method of keeping records by means of knots tied upon strings of various colours and shapes. It is said that even laws and orders could be conveyed by this code. These string bundles were called *quipus*, but though quipus are still to be found in collections, the art of reading them is altogether lost. The Chinese histories, Mr. L. Y. Chen informs us, state that a similar method of record by knots was used in China before the invention of writing there. The Peruvians also got to making maps and the use of counting-frames. "But with all this there was no means of handing on knowledge and experience from one generation to another, nor was anything done to fix and summarize these intellectual possessions, which are the basis of literature and science."[120]

When the Spaniards came to America, the Mexicans knew nothing of the Peruvians nor the Peruvians of the Mexicans. Intercourse there was none. Whatever links had ever existed were lost and forgotten. The Mexicans had never heard of the potato, which was a principal article of Peruvian diet. In 5000 B.C. the Sumerians and Egyptians probably knew as little of one another. America was 6000 years behind the Old World.{v1-209}

XVII

SEA PEOPLES AND TRADING PEOPLES

§ 1. *The Earliest Ships and Sailors.* § 2. *The Ægean Cities before History.* § 3. *The First Voyages of*

Exploration. §   4. *Early*   *Traders.* §   5. *Early*
Travellers.

T HE first boats were made very early indeed in the Neolithic stage of culture by riverside and lakeside peoples. They were no more than trees and floating wood, used to assist the imperfect natural swimming powers of men. Then came the hollowing out of the trees, and then, with the development of tools and a primitive carpentry, the building of boats. Men in Egypt and Mesopotamia also developed a primitive type of basket-work boat, caulked with bitumen. Such was the "ark of bulrushes" in which Moses was hidden by his mother. A kindred sort of vessel grew up by the use of skins and hides expanded upon a wicker framework. To this day cow-hide wicker boats (coracles) are used upon the west coast of Ireland, where there is plenty of cattle and a poverty of big trees. They are also still used on the Euphrates, and on the Towy in South Wales. Inflated skins may have preceded the coracle, and are still used on the Euphrates and upper Ganges. In the valleys of the great rivers, boats must early have become an important means of communication; and it seems natural to suppose that it was from the mouths of the great rivers that man, already in a reasonably seaworthy vessel, first ventured out upon what must have seemed to him then the trackless and homeless sea.

No doubt he ventured at first as a fisherman, having learnt the elements of seacraft in creeks and lagoons. Men may have{v1-210} navigated boats upon the Levantine lake before the refilling of the Mediterranean by the Atlantic waters. The canoe was an integral part of the heliolithic culture, it drifted with that culture upon the warm waters of the earth from the Mediterranean to (at last) America. There were not only canoes, but Sumerian boats and ships upon the Euphrates and Tigris, when these rivers in 7000 B.C. fell by separate mouths into the Persian Gulf. The Sumerian city of Eridu, which stood at the head of the Persian Gulf (from which it is now separated by a hundred and thirty miles of alluvium[121]), had ships upon the sea then. We also find evidence of a fully developed sea life six thousand years ago at the eastern end of the Mediterranean, and possibly at that time there were already canoes on the seas among the islands of the nearer East Indies. There are pre-dynastic Neolithic Egyptian representations of Nile ships of a fair size, capable of carrying elephants.[122]

Very soon the seafaring men must have realized the peculiar freedom and opportunities the ship gave them. They could get away to islands; no chief nor king could pursue a boat or ship with any certainty; every captain was a king. The seamen would find it easy to make nests upon islands and in strong positions on the mainland. There they could harbour, there they could carry on a certain agriculture and fishery; but their speciality and their main business was, of course, the expedition across the sea. That was not usually a trading expedition; it was much more frequently a piratical raid. From what we know of mankind, we are bound to conclude that the first sailors plundered when they could, and traded when they had to.

Because it developed in the comparatively warm and tranquil waters of the eastern Mediterranean, the Red Sea, the Persian Gulf, and the western horn of the Indian Ocean, the shipping of the ancient world retained throughout certain characteristics that make it differ very widely from the ocean-going sailing shipping, with its vast spread of canvas, of the last four hundred years. "The Mediterranean," says Mr. Torr,[123] "is a sea where a{vi-211} vessel with sails may lie becalmed for days together, while a vessel with oars would easily be traversing the smooth waters, with coasts and islands everywhere at hand to give her shelter in case of storm. In that sea, therefore, oars became the characteristic instruments of navigation, and the arrangement of oars the chief problem in shipbuilding. And so long as the Mediterranean nations dominated Western Europe, vessels of the southern type were built upon the northern coasts, though there generally was wind enough here for sails and too much wave for oars.... The art of rowing can first be discerned upon the Nile. Boats with oars are represented in the earliest pictorial monuments of Egypt, dating from about 2500 B.C.; and although some crews are paddling with their faces towards the bow, others are rowing with their faces towards the stern. The paddling is certainly the older practice, for the hieroglyph chen depicts two arms grasping an oar in the attitude of paddling, and the hieroglyphs were invented in the earliest ages. And that practice may really have ceased before 2500 B.C., despite the testimony of monuments of that date; for in monuments dating from about 1250 B.C. crews are represented unmistakably rowing with their faces towards the stern and yet grasping their oars in the attitude of paddling, so that even then Egyptian artists mechanically followed the turn of the hieroglyph to which their hands were accustomed. In these reliefs there are twenty rowers on the boats on the Nile, and thirty on the ships on the Red Sea; but in the earliest reliefs the number{vi-212} varies considerably, and seems dependent on the amount of space at the sculptor's disposal."

Egyptian ship on the Red Sea, about 1250 B.C. (From Torr's "Ancient Ships.")
Mr. Langton Cole calls attention to the rope truss in this illustration, stiffening the beam of the ship. No other such use of the truss is known until the days of modern engineering.

The Aryan peoples came late to the sea. The earliest ships on the sea were either Sumerian or Hamitic; the Semitic peoples followed close upon these pioneers. Along the eastern end of the Mediterranean, the Phœnicians, a Semitic people, set up a string of independent harbour towns of which Acre, Tyre, and Sidon were the chief; and later they pushed their voyages westward and founded Carthage and Utica in North Africa. Possibly

Phœnician keels were already in the Mediterranean by 2000 B.C. Both Tyre and Sidon wee originally on islands, an so easily defensible against a land raid. But before we go on to the marine exploits of this great sea-going race, we must note a very remarkable and curious nest of early sea people whose remains have been discovered in Crete.[124]

§ 2

These early Cretans were of unknown race, but probably of a race akin to the Iberians of Spain and Western Europe and the dark whites of Asia Minor and North Africa, and their language is unknown. This race lived not only in Crete, but in Cyprus, Greece, Asia Minor, Sicily, and South Italy. It was a civilized people for long ages before the fair Aryan Greeks spread southward through Macedonia. At Cnossos, in Crete, there have been found the most astonishing ruins and remains, and Cnossos, therefore, is apt to overshadow the rest of these settlements in people's imaginations, but it is well to bear in mind that, though Cnossos was no doubt a chief city of this Ægean civilization, these "Ægeans" had in the fullness of their time many cities and a wide range. Possibly, all that we know of them now are but the vestiges of a far more extensive heliolithic Neolithic civilization which is now submerged under the waters of the Mediterranean.

At Cnossos there are Neolithic remains as old or older than any of the pre-dynastic remains of Egypt.

The Bronze Age began in Crete as soon as it did in Egypt, and there have been vases found by Flinders Petrie in Egypt and referred by him to the Ist Dynasty, which he declared to be importations from Crete. Stone vessels have been found in Crete of forms characteristic of the IVth (pyramid-building) Dynasty, and there can be no doubt that there was a vigorous trade between Crete and Egypt in the time of the XIIth Dynasty. This continued until about 1000 B.C. It is clear that this island civilization arising upon the soil of Crete is at least as old as the Egyptian, and that it was already launched upon the sea as early as 4000 B.C.

The great days of Crete were not so early as this. It was only about 2500 B.C. that the island appears to have been unified under one ruler. Then began an age of peace and prosperity unexampled in the history of the ancient world. Secure from invasion, living in a delightful climate, trading with every civilized community in the world, the Cretans were free to develop all the arts and amenities of life. This Cnossos was not so much a town as the vast palace of the king and his people. It was not even fortified.{vi-214} The kings, it would seem, were called Minos always, as the kings of Egypt were all called Pharaoh; the king of Cnossos figures in the early legends of the Greeks as King Minos, who lived in the Labyrinth and kept there a horrible monster, half man, half bull, the Minotaur, to feed which he levied a tribute of youths and maidens from the Athenians. Those stories are a part of Greek literature, and have always been known, but it is only in the last few decades that the excavations at Cnossos have revealed how close these legends were to the reality. The Cretan labyrinth was a building as stately, complex, and luxurious as any in the ancient world. Among other details we find waterpipes, bathrooms, and the like conveniences, such as have hitherto been regarded as the latest refinements of modern life. The pottery, the textile manufactures, the sculpture and painting of these people, their gem and ivory work, their metal and inlaid work, is as admirable as any that mankind has produced. They were much given to festivals and shows, and, in particular, they were addicted to bull-fights and gymnastic entertainments. Their female costume became astonishingly "modern" in style; their women wore corsets and flounced dresses. They had a system of writing which has not yet been deciphered.

It is the custom nowadays to make a sort of wonder of these achievements of the Cretans, as though they were a people of incredible artistic ability living in the dawn of civilization. But[vi-215] their great time was long past that dawn; as late as 2000 B.C. It took them many centuries to reach their best in art and skill, and their art and luxury are by no means so great a wonder if we reflect that for 3000 years they were immune from invasion, that for a thousand years they were at peace. Century after century their artizans could perfect their skill, and their men and women refine upon refinement. Wherever men of almost any race have been comparatively safe in this fashion for such a length of time, they have developed much artistic beauty. Given the opportunity, all races are artistic. Green legend has it that it was in Crete that Dædalus attempted to make the first flying machine. Dædalus (= cunning artificer) was a sort of personified summary of mechanical skill. It is curious to speculate what germ of fact lies behind him and those waxen wings that, according to the legend, melted and plunged his son Icarus in the sea.

–

Faience figure from Cnossos ... A votary of the Snake Goddess....
J.F.H. from photos by British School at Athens

There came at last a change in the condition of the lives of these Cretans, for other peoples, the Greeks and the Phœnicians, were also coming out with powerful fleets upon the seas. We do not know what led to the disaster nor who inflicted it; but somewhen about 1400 B.C. Cnossos was sacked and burnt, and though the Cretan life struggled on there rather lamely for another four centuries, there came at last a final blow about 1000 B.C. (that is to say, in the days of the Assyrian ascendancy in the East). The palace at Cnossos was destroyed, and never rebuilt nor reinhabited. Possibly this was done by the ships of those newcomers{v1-216} into the Mediterranean, the barbaric Greeks, a group of Aryan tribes, who may have wiped out Cnossos as they wiped out the city of Troy. The legend of Theseus tells of such a raid. He entered the Labyrinth (which may have been the Cnossos

Palace) by the aid of Ariadne, the daughter of Minos, and slew the Minotaur.

The *Iliad* makes it clear that destruction came upon Troy because the Trojans stole Greek women. Modern writers, with modern ideas in their heads, have tried to make out that the Greeks assailed Troy in order to secure a trade route or some such fine-spun commercial advantage. If so, the authors of the *Iliad* hid the motives of their characters very skilfully. It would be about as reasonable to say that the Homeric Greeks went to war with the Trojans in order to be well ahead with a station on the Berlin to Bagdad railway. The Homeric Greeks were a healthy barbaric Aryan people, with very poor ideas about trade and "trade routes"; they went to war with the Trojans because they were thoroughly annoyed about this stealing of women. It is fairly clear from the Minos legend and from the evidence of the Cnossos remains, that the Cretans kidnapped or stole youths and maidens to be slaves, bull-fighters, athletes, and perhaps sacrifices. They traded fairly with the Egyptians, but it may be they did not realize the gathering strength of the Greek barbarians; they "traded" violently with them, and so brought sword and flame upon themselves.[125]

Another great sea people were the Phœnicians. They were great seamen because they were great traders. Their colony of Carthage (founded before 800 B.C. by Tyre) became at last greater than any of the older Phœnician cities, but already before 1500 B.C. both Sidon and Tyre had settlements upon the African coast. Carthage was comparatively inaccessible to the Assyrian[vI-217] and Babylonian hosts, and, profiting greatly by the long siege of Tyre by Nebuchadnezzar II, became the greatest maritime power the world had hitherto seen. She claimed the Western Mediterranean as her own, and seized every ship she could catch west of Sardinia. Roman writers accuse her of great cruelties. She fought the Greeks for Sicily, and later (in the second century B.C.) she fought the Romans. Alexander the Great formed plans for her conquest; but he died, as we shall tell later, before he could carry them out.

§ 3

At her zenith Carthage probably had the hitherto unheard-of population of a million. This population was largely industrial, and her woven goods were universally famous. As well as a coasting trade, she had a considerable land trade with Central Africa,[126] and she sold negro slaves, ivory, metals, precious stones and the like, to all the Mediterranean people; she worked Spanish copper mines, and her ships went out into the Atlantic and coasted along Portugal and France northward as far as the Cassiterides (the Scilly Isles, or Cornwall, in England) to get tin. About 520 B.C. a certain Hanno made a voyage that is still one of the most notable in the world. This Hanno, if we may trust the *Periplus of Hanno*, the Greek translation of his account which still survives, followed the African coast southward from the Straits of Gibraltar as far as the confines of Liberia. He had sixty big ships, and his main task was to found or reinforce certain Carthaginian stations upon the Morocco coast. Then he pushed southward. He founded a settlement in the Rio de Oro (on Kerne or Herne Island), and sailed on past the Senegal river.{v1-218} The voyagers passed on for seven days beyond the Gambia, and landed at last upon some island. This they left in a panic, because, although the day was silent with the silence of the tropical forest, at night they heard the sound of flutes, drums, and gongs, and the sky was red with the blaze of the bush fires. The coast country for the rest of the voyage was one blaze of fire, from the burning of the bush. Streams of fire ran down the hills into the sea, and at length a blaze arose so loftily that it touched the skies. Three days further brought them to an island containing a lake (? Sherbro Island). In this lake was another island (? Macaulay Island), and on this were wild, hairy men and women, "whom the interpreters called gorilla." The Carthaginians, having caught some of the females of these "gorillas"—they were probably chimpanzees—turned back and eventually deposited the skins of their captives—who had proved impossibly violent guests to entertain on board ship—in the Temple of Juno.

A still more wonderful Phœnician sea voyage, long doubted, but now supported by some archæological evidence, is related by Herodotus, who declares that the Pharaoh Necho of the XXVIth Dynasty commissioned some Phœnicians to attempt the circumnavigation of Africa, and that starting from the Gulf of Suez southward, they did finally come back through the Mediterranean to the Nile delta. They took nearly three years to complete their voyage. Each year they landed, and sowed and harvested a crop of wheat before going on.

§ 4

The great trading cities of the Phœnicians are the most striking of the early manifestations of the peculiar and characteristic gift of the Semitic peoples to mankind, trade and exchange.[127] While the Semitic Phœnician peoples were spreading themselves upon the seas, another kindred Semitic people, the Arameans, whose occupation of Damascus we have already noted, were developing the caravan routes of the Arabian and Persian deserts, and becoming the chief trading people of Western Asia. The{v1-219} Semitic peoples, earlier civilized than the Aryan, have always shown, and still show to-day, a far greater sense of quality and quantity in marketable goods than the latter; it is to their need of account-keeping that the development of alphabetical writing is to be ascribed, and it is to them that most of the great advances in computation are due. Our modern numerals are Arabic; our arithmetic and algebra are essentially Semitic sciences.

The Semitic peoples, we may point out here, are to this day *counting peoples* strong in their sense of equivalents and reparation. The moral teaching of the Hebrews was saturated by such ideas. "With what measure ye mete, the same shall be meted unto you." Other races and peoples have imagined diverse and fitful and marvellous gods, but it was the trading Semites who first began to think of God as a Righteous Dealer, whose promises were kept, who failed not the humblest creditor, and called to account every spurious act.

The trade that was going on in the ancient world before the sixth or seventh century B.C. was almost entirely a barter trade. There was little or no credit or coined money. The ordinary standard of value with the early Aryans was cattle, as it still is with the Zulus and Kaffirs to-day. In the *Iliad*, the respective values of two shields are stated in head of cattle, and the Roman word for moneys, *pecunia*, is derived from *pecus*, cattle. Cattle as money had this advantage; it did not need to be carried from one owner to another, and if it needed attention and food, at any rate it bred. But it was inconvenient for ship or caravan transit. Many other substances have at various times been found convenient as a standard; tobacco was once legal tender in the colonial days in North America, and in West Africa fines are paid and bargains made in bottles of trade gin. The early Asiatic trade included metals; and weighed lumps of metal, since they were in general demand and were convenient for hoarding and storage, costing nothing for fodder and needing small house-room, soon asserted their superiority over cattle and sheep. Iron, which seems to have been first reduced from its ores by the Hittites, was, to begin with, a rare and much-desired substance.[128]{v1-220} It is stated by Aristotle to have supplied the first currency. In the collection of letters found at Tel-el-Amarna, addressed to and from Amenophis III (already mentioned) and his successor Amenophis IV, one from a Hittite king promises iron as an extremely valuable gift. Gold, then as now, was the most precious and therefore most portable, security. In early Egypt silver was almost as rare as gold until after the XVIIIth Dynasty. Later the general standard of value in the Eastern world became silver, measured by weight.

To begin with, metals were handed about in ingots and weighed at each transaction. Then they were stamped to indicate their fineness and guarantee their purity. The first recorded coins were minted about 600 B.C. in Lydia, a gold-producing country in the west of Asia Minor. The first-known gold coins were minted in Lydia by Crœsus, whose name has become a proverb for wealth; he was conquered, as we shall tell later, by that same Cyrus the Persian who took Babylon in 539 B.C. But very probably coined money had been used in Babylonia before that time. The "sealed shekel," a stamped piece of silver, came very near to being a coin. The promise to pay so much silver or gold on "leather" (= parchment) with the seal of some established firm is probably as old or older than coinage. The Carthaginians used such "leather money." We know very little of the way in which small traffic was conducted. Common people, who in those ancient times were in dependent positions, seem to have had no money at all; they did their business by barter. Early Egyptian paintings show this going on.[129]

5

When one realizes the absence of small money or of any conveniently portable means of exchange in the pre-Alexandrian world, one perceives how impossible was private travel in those days.[130] The first "inns"—no doubt a sort of caravanserai—[vi-221]are commonly said to have come into existence in Lydia in the third or fourth century B.C. That, however, is too late a date. They are certainly older than that. There is good evidence of them at least as early as the sixth century. Æschylus twice mentions inns. His word is "all-receiver," or "all-receiving house."[131] Private travellers must have been fairly common in the Greek world, including its colonies, by this time. But such private travel was a comparatively new thing then. The early historians Hecatæus and Herodotus travelled widely. "I suspect," says Professor Gilbert Murray, "that this sort of travel 'for Historie' or 'for discovery' was rather a Greek invention. Solon is supposed to have practiced it; and even Lycurgus."... The earlier travellers were traders travelling in a caravan or in a shipload, and carrying their goods and their minas and shekels of metal or gems or bales of fine stuff with them, or government officials travelling with letters of introduction and a proper retinue. Possibly there were a few mendicants, and, in some restricted regions, religious pilgrims.

That earlier world before 600 B.C. was one in which a lonely "stranger" was a rare and suspected and endangered being. He might suffer horrible cruelties, for there was little law to protect such as he. Few individuals strayed therefore. One lived and died attached and tied to some patriarchal tribe if one was a nomad, or to some great household if one was civilized, or to one of the big temple establishments which we will presently discuss. Or one was a herded slave. One knew nothing, except for a few monstrous legends, of the rest of the world in which one lived. We know more to-day, indeed, of the world of 600 B.C. than any single living being knew at that time. We map it out, see it as a whole in relation to past and future. We begin to learn precisely what was going on at the same time in Egypt and Spain and Media and India and China. We can share in imagination, not only the wonder of Hanno's sailors, but of the men who lit{v1-222} the warning beacons on the shore. We know that those "mountains flaming to the sky" were only the customary burning of the dry grass at that season of the year. Year by year, more and more rapidly, our common knowledge increases. In the years to come men will understand still more of those lives in the past until perhaps they will understand them altogether.{v1-223}

XVIII

WRITING

§ 1. *Picture Writing.* § 2. *Syllable Writing.* § 3. *Alphabet Writing.* § 4. *The Place of Writing in Human Life.*

§ 1

IN the five preceding chapters (XIII to XVII) we have sketched in broad outline the development of the chief human communities from the primitive beginnings of the heliolithic culture to the great historical kingdoms and empires in the sixth century B.C. We must now study a little more closely the general process of social change, the growth of human ideas, and the elaboration of human relationships that were going on during these ages between 10,000 B.C. and 500 B.C. What we have done so far is to draw the map and name the chief kings and empires, to define the relations in time and space of Babylonia, Assyria, Egypt, Phœnicia, Cnossos, and the like; we come now to the real business of history, which is to get down below these outer forms to the thoughts and lives of individual men.

By far the most important thing that was going on during those fifty or sixty centuries of social development was the invention of writing and its gradual progress to importance in human affairs. It was a new instrument for the human mind, an enormous enlargement of its range of action, a new means of continuity. We have seen how in later Palæolithic and early Neolithic times the elaboration of articulate speech gave men a mental handhold for consecutive thought and a vast enlargement of their powers of co-operation. For a time this new acquirement seems to have overshadowed their earlier achievement of drawing, and possibly it checked the use of gesture. But drawing presently{vl-224}reappeared again, for record, for signs, for the joy of drawing. Before real writing came picture-writing, such as is still practised by the Amerindians, the Bushmen, and savage and barbaric people in all parts of the world. It is essentially a drawing of things and acts, helped out by heraldic indications of proper names, and by strokes and dots to represent days and distances and such-like quantitative ideas.

Quite kindred to such picture-writing is the pictograph that one finds still in use to-day in international railway time-tables upon the continent of Europe, where a little black sign of a cup indicates a stand-up buffet for light refreshments; a crossed knife and fork, a restaurant; a little steamboat, a transfer to a steamboat; and a postilion's horn, a diligence. Similar signs are used in the well-known Michelin guides for automobilists in Europe, to show a post-office (envelope) or a telephone (telephone receiver). The quality of hotels is shown by an inn with one, two, three, or four gables, and so forth. Similarly, the roads of Europe are marked with wayside signs representing a gate, to indicate a level crossing ahead, a sinuous bend for a dangerous curve, and the like. From such pictographic signs to the first elements of Chinese writing is not a very long stretch.

In Chinese writing there are still traceable a number of pictographs. Most are now difficult to recognize. A mouth was originally written as a mouth-shaped hole and is now, for convenience of brushwork, squared; a child, originally a recognizable little mannikin, is now a hasty wriggle and a cross; the sun, originally a large circle with a dot in the centre, has been converted, for the sake of convenience of combination, into a crossed oblong, which is easier to make with a brush. By combining these pictographs, a second order of ideas is expressed. For example, the pictograph for mouth combined with pictograph for vapour expressed "words."[132]

Specimens of American Indian picture-writing
(after Schoolcraft ...)

No. 1, painted on a rock on the shore of Lake Superior, records an expedition across the lake, in which five canoes took part. The upright strokes in each indicate the number of the crew, and the bird represents a chief, "The Kingfisher." The three circles (suns) under the arch (of heaven) indicate that the voyage lasted three days, and the tortoise, a symbol of land, denotes a safe arrival. No. 2 is a petition sent to the United States Congress by a group of Indian tribes, asking for fishing rights in certain small lakes. The tribes are represented by their totems, martens, bear, manfish, and catfish, led by the crane. Lines running from the heart and eye of each animal to the heart and eye of the crane denote that they are all of one mind; and a line runs from the eye of the crane to the lakes, shown in the crude little "map" in the lower left-hand corner.

From such combinations one passes to what are called *ideograms*: the sign for "words" and the sign for "tongue" combine to make "speech"; the sign for "roof" and the sign for "pig" make "home"—for in the early domestic economy of China the pig was as important as it used to be in Ireland. But,{v1-225} as we have already noted earlier, the Chinese language consists of a comparatively few elementary monosyllabic sounds, which are all used in a great variety of meanings, and the Chinese soon discovered that a number of these *pictographs* and *ideographs* could be used also to express other ideas, not so conveniently pictured, but having the same sound. Characters so used are called *phonograms*. For example, the sound fang meant not only "boat," but "a place," "spinning," "fragrant," "inquire," and several other meanings according to the context. But while a boat is easy to draw most of the other meanings are undrawable. How can one draw "fragrant" or "inquire"? The Chinese, therefore, took the same sign for all these meanings of *fang*, but added to each of them another distinctive sign, the determinative, to show what sort of *fang* was intended. A "place" was indicated by the same sign as for "boat" (*fang*) and the determinative sign for "earth"; "spinning" by the sign for *fang* and the sign for{v1-226} "silk"; "inquire" by the sign for *fang* and the sign for "words," and so on.

One may perhaps make this development of pictographs, ideographs, and phonograms a little clearer by taking an analogous case in English. Suppose we were making up a sort of picture-writing in English, then it would be very natural to use a square with a slanting line to suggest a lid, for the word and thing *box*. That would be a pictograph. But now suppose we had a round sign for money, and suppose we put this sign inside the box sign, that would do for "cash-box" or "treasury." That would be an ideogram. But the word "box" is used for other things than boxes. There is the box shrub which gives us boxwood. It would be hard to draw a recognizable box-tree distinct from other trees, but it is quite easy to put our sign "box," and add our sign for shrub as a determinative to determine that it is that sort of box and not a common box that we want to express. And then there is "box," the verb, meaning to fight with fists. Here, again, we need a determinative; we might add the two crossed swords, a sign which is used very often upon maps to denote a battle. A box at a theatre needs yet another determinative, and so we go on, through a long series of phonograms.

Now it is manifest that here in the Chinese writing is a very peculiar and complex system of sign-writing. A very great number of characters have to be learnt and the mind habituated to their use. The power it possesses to carry ideas and discussion is still ungauged by western standards, but we may doubt whether with this instrument it will ever be possible to establish such a wide, common mentality as the simpler and swifter alphabets of the western civilizations permit. In China it created a special reading-class, the mandarins, who were also the ruling and official class. Their necessary concentration upon words and classical forms, rather than upon ideas and realities, seems, in spite of her comparative peacefulness and the very high individual intellectual quality of her people, to have greatly hampered the social and economic development of China. Probably it is the complexity of her speech and writing, more than any other imaginable cause, that has made China to-day politically, socially, and{vi-227} individually a vast pool of backward people rather than the foremost power in the whole world.[133]

§ 2

But while the Chinese mind thus made for itself an instrument which is probably too elaborate in structure, too laborious in use, and too inflexible in its form to meet the modern need for simple, swift, exact, and lucid communications, the growing civilizations of the west were working out the problem of a written record upon rather different and, on the whole, more advantageous lines. They did not seek to improve their script to make it swift and easy, but circumstances conspired to make it so. The Sumerian picture-writing, which had to be done upon clay and with little styles, which made curved marks with difficulty and inaccurately, rapidly degenerated by a conventionalized dabbing down of wedged-shaped marks (cuneiform = wedge-shaped) into almost unrecognizable hints of the shapes intended. It helped the Sumerians greatly to learn to write, that they had to draw so badly. They got very soon to the Chinese pictographs, ideographs, and phonograms, and beyond them.

Most people know a sort of puzzle called a rebus. It is a way of representing words by pictures, not of the things the words represent, but by the pictures of other things having a similar sound. For example, two gates and a head is a rebus for Gateshead; a little streamlet (beck), a crowned monarch, and a ham, Beckingham. The Sumerian language was a language well adapted to this sort of representation. It was apparently a language of often quite vast polysyllables, made up of very distinct inalterable syllables; and many of the syllables taken separately were the names of concrete things. So that this cuneiform writing developed very readily into a syllabic way of writing, in which each sign conveys a syllable just as each act in a {v1-228} charade conveys a syllable. When presently the Semites conquered Sumeria, they adapted the syllabic system to their own speech, and so this writing became entirely a sign-for-a-sound writing. It was so used by the Assyrians and by the Chaldeans. But it was not a letter-writing, it was a syllable-writing. This cuneiform script prevailed for long ages over Assyria, Babylonia, and the Near East generally; there are vestiges of it in some of the letters of our alphabet to-day.

§ 3

But, meanwhile, in Egypt and upon the Mediterranean coast another system of writing grew up. Its beginnings are probably to be found in the priestly picture-writing (hieroglyphics) of the Egyptians, which also in the usual way became partly a sound-sign system. As we see it on the Egyptian monuments, the hieroglyphic writing consists of decorative but stiff and elaborate forms, but for such purpose as letter-writing and the keeping of recipes and the like, the Egyptian priests used a much simplified and flowing form of these characters, the *hieratic script*. Side by side with this hieratic script rose another, probably also derivative from the hieroglyphs, a script now lost to us, which was taken over by various non-Egyptian peoples in the Mediterranean, the Phœnicians, Libyans, Lydians, Cretans, and Celt-Iberians, and used for business purposes. Possibly a few letters were borrowed from the later cuneiform. In the hands of these foreigners this writing was, so to speak, cut off from its roots; it lost all but a few traces of its early pictorial character. It ceased to be pictographic or ideographic; it became simply a pure sound-sign system, an *alphabet*.

There were a number of such alphabets in the Mediterranean differing widely from each other.[134] It may be noted that the Phœnician alphabet (and perhaps others) omitted vowels. Possibly they pronounced their consonants very hard and had rather{v1-229} indeterminate vowels, as is said to be still the case with tribes of South Arabia. Quite probably, too, the Phœnicians used their alphabet at first not so much for writing as for single initial letters in their business accounts and tallies. One of these Mediterranean alphabets reached the Greeks, long after the time of the Iliad, who presently set to work to make it express the clear and beautiful sounds of their own highly developed Aryan speech. It consisted at first of consonants, and the Greeks added the vowels. They began to write for record, to help and fix their bardic tradition....

§ 4

So it was by a series of very natural steps that writing grew out of the life of man. At first and for long ages it was the interest and the secret of only a few people in a special class, a mere accessory to the record of pictures. But there were certain very manifest advantages, quite apart from the increased expressiveness of mood and qualification, to be gained by making writing a little less plain than straightforward pictures, and in conventionalizing and codifying it. One of these was that so messages might be sent understandable by the sender and receiver, but not plain to the uninitiated. Another was that so one might put down various matters and help one's memory and the memory of one's friends, without giving away too much to the common herd. Among some of the earliest Egyptian writings, for example, are medical recipes and magic formulæ. Accounts, letters, recipes, name lists, itineraries; these were the earliest of written documents. Then, as the art of writing and reading spread, came that odd desire, that pathetic desire so common among human beings, to astonish some strange and remote person by writing down something striking, some secret one knew, some strange thought, or even one's name, so that long after one had gone one's way, it might strike upon the sight and mind of another reader. Even in Sumeria men scratched on walls, and all that remains to us of the ancient world, its rocks, its buildings, is plastered thickly with the names and the boasting of those foremost among human advertisers, its kings. Perhaps half the early inscriptions in that ancient world are of this nature, if, that is, we group with the{vi-230} name-writing and boasting the epitaphs, which were probably in many cases prearranged by the deceased.

For long the desire for crude self-assertion of the name-scrawling sort and the love of secret understandings kept writing within a narrow scope; but that other, more truly social desire in men, the desire to *tell*, was also at work. The profounder possibilities of writing, the possibilities of a vast extension and definition and settlement of knowledge and tradition, only grew apparent after long ages. But it will be interesting at this point and in this connection to recapitulate certain elemental facts about life, upon which we laid stress in our earlier chapters, because they illuminate not only the huge value of writing in the whole field of man's history, but also the rôle it is likely to play in his future.

1. Life had at first, it must be remembered, only a discontinuous repetition of consciousness, as the old died and the young were born.

Such a creature as a reptile has in its brain a capacity for experience, but when the individual dies, its experience dies with it. Most of its motives are purely instinctive, and all the mental life that it has is the result of heredity (birth inheritance).

2. But ordinary mammals have added to pure instinct *tradition*, a tradition of experience imparted by the imitated example of the mother, and in the case of such mentally developed animals as dogs, cats, or apes, by a sort of mute precept also. For example, the mother cat chastises her young for misbehaviour. So do mother apes and baboons.

3. Primitive man added to his powers of transmitting experience, representative art and speech. Pictorial and sculptured record and *verbal tradition* began.

Verbal tradition was developed to its highest possibility by the bards. They did much to make language what it is to the world to-day.

4. With the invention of writing, which developed out of pictorial record, human tradition was able to become fuller and much more exact. Verbal tradition, which had hitherto changed from age to age, began to be fixed. Men separated by hundreds of miles could now communicate their thoughts. An increasing number of human beings began to share a common written knowledge[vi-231] and a common sense of a past and a future. Human thinking became a larger operation in which hundreds of minds in different places and in different ages could react upon one another; it became a process constantly more continuous and sustained....

5. For hundreds of generations the full power of writing was not revealed to the world, because for a long time the idea of multiplying writings by taking prints of a first copy did not become effective. The

only way of multiplying writings was by copying one copy at a time, and this made books costly and rare. Moreover, the tendency to keep things secret, to make a cult and mystery of them, and so to gain an advantage over the generality of men, has always been very strong in men's minds. It is only nowadays that the great masses of mankind are learning to read, and reaching out towards the treasures of knowledge and thought already stored in books.

Nevertheless, from the first writings onward a new sort of tradition, an enduring and immortal tradition, began in the minds of men. Life, through mankind, grew thereafter more and more distinctly conscious of itself and its world. It is a thin streak of intellectual growth we trace in history, at first in a world of tumultuous ignorance and forgetfulness; it is like a mere line of light coming through the chink of an opening door into a darkened room; but slowly it widens, it grows. At last came a time in the history of Europe when the door, at the push of the printer, began to open more rapidly. Knowledge flared up, and as it flared it ceased to be the privilege of a favoured minority. For us now that door swings wider, and the light behind grows brighter. Misty it is still, glowing through clouds of dust and reek.

The door is not half open; the light is but a light new lit. Our world to-day is only in the beginning of knowledge. {v1-232}

XIX

GODS AND STARS, PRIESTS AND KINGS

§ 1. Nomadic and Settled Religion. § 2. The Priest Comes into History. § 3. Priests and the Stars. § 4. Priests and the Dawn of Learning. § 5. King against Priest. § 6. How Bel-Marduk Struggled against the Kings. § 7. The God-Kings of Egypt. § 8. Shi Hwang-ti Destroys the Books.

§ 1

W E have already told what there is to tell of the social life of the Aryan tribes when they were settling down to the beginnings of civilized life; we have seen how they were associated in great households, grouped together under tribal leaders, who made a sort of informal aristocracy rather like that of the sixth form and prefects in an English boys' school; we have considered the rôle of the bards in the creation of an oral tradition, and we have glanced at their not very complex religious ideas. We may note one or two points of difference from the equivalent life of the nomadic Semites.

Like the early Aryan life, it was a life in a sort of family-tribe household. But it had differences due originally perhaps to the warmer, drier climate. Though both groups of races had cattle and sheep, the Aryans were rather herdsmen, the Semites, shepherds. The Semites had no long winter evenings and no bardic singing. They never sat in hall. They have consequently no epics. They had stories, camp-fire stories, but not verbally beautified story-recitations. The Semite also was more polygamous than the Aryan, his women less self-assertive,[135] and the{v1-233} tendency of his government more patriarchal. The head of the household or the tribe was less of a leader and more of a master, more like the Palæolithic Old Man. And the Semitic nomads were closer to the earlier civilizations, a thing that fitted in with their greater aptitude for trade and counting. But the religion of the nomadic Semite was as little organized as the religion of the Aryan. In either case the leading man performed most of the functions of the priest. The Aryan gods were little more than a kind of magical super-prince; they were supposed to sit in hall together, and to talk and make scenes with one another under Jupiter or Thor. The early Semitic gods, on the other hand, were thought of as tribal patriarchs. As peoples develop towards nomadism, they seem to lose even such primitive religion and magic as their Neolithic ancestors professed. Nomadism cuts men off from fixed temples and intense local associations; they take a broader and simpler view of the world. They tend towards religious simplification.

We write here of the nomadic peoples, the Aryan herdsmen and Semitic shepherds, and we write in the most general terms. They had their undercurrent of fables and superstitions, their phases of fear and abjection and sacrificial fury. These people were people like ourselves, with brains as busy and moody and inconsistent, and with even less training and discipline. It is absurd to suppose—as so many writers about early religion do seem to suppose—that their religious notions can be reduced to the consistent logical development of some one simple idea. We have already glanced, in Chapter XII, at the elements of religion that must have arisen necessarily in the minds of those early peoples. But for most of the twenty-four hours these nomads were busy upon other things, and there is no sign that their houses, their daily routines, their ordinary acts, were dominated or their social order shaped, by any ideas that we should now call religious. As yet life and its ideas were too elementary for that.

But directly we turn our attention to these new accumulations of human beings that are beginning in Egypt and Mesopotamia, we find that one of the most conspicuous objects in every city is a temple or a group of temples. In some cases there arises[vi-234] beside it in these regions a royal palace, but as often the temple towers over the palace. This presence of the temple is equally true of the Phœnician cities and of the Greek and Roman as they arise. The palace of Cnossos, with its signs of comfort and pleasure-seeking, and the kindred cities of the Ægean peoples, include religious shrines, but in Crete there are also temples standing apart from the palatial city-households. All over the ancient civilized world we find them; wherever primitive civilization set its foot in Africa, Europe, or western

Asia, a temple arose, and where the civilization is most ancient, in Egypt and in Sumer, there the temple is most in evidence. When Hanno reached what he thought was the most westerly point of Africa, he set up a temple to Hercules. We have, in fact, come now to a new stage in the history of mankind, the temple stage.

§ 2

In all these temples there was a shrine; dominating the shrine there was commonly a great figure, usually of some monstrous half-animal form, before which stood an altar for sacrifices. This figure was either regarded as the god or as the image or symbol of the god, for whose worship the temple existed. And connected with the temple there were a number, and often a considerable number, of priests or priestesses, and temple servants, generally wearing a distinctive costume and forming an important part of the city population. They belonged to no household, as did the simple priest of the primitive Aryan; they made up a new kind of household of their own. They were a caste and a class apart, attracting intelligent recruits from the general population.

The primary duty of this priesthood was concerned with the worship of and the sacrifices to the god of the temple. And these things were done, not at any time, but at particular times and seasons. There had come into the life of man with his herding and agriculture a sense of a difference between the parts of the year and of a difference between day and day. Men were beginning to work—and to need days of rest. The temple, by its festivals, kept count. The temple in the ancient city was like the clock and calendar upon a writing-desk.{v1-235}

But it was a centre of other functions. It was in the early temples that the records and tallies of events were kept and that writing began. And there was knowledge there. The people went to the temple not only *en masse* for festivals, but individually for help. The early priests were also doctors and magicians. In the earliest temples we already find those little offerings for some private and particular end, which are still made in the chapels of Catholic churches to-day, *ex votos*, little models of hearts relieved and limbs restored, acknowledgment of prayers answered and accepted vows.

It is clear that here we have that comparatively unimportant element in the life of the early nomad, the medicine-man, the shrine-keeper, and the memorist, developed, with the development of the community and as a part of the development of the community from barbarism to civilized settlement, into something of very much greater importance. And it is equally evident that those primitive fears of (and hopes of help from) strange beings, the desire to propitiate unknown forces, the primitive desire for cleansing and the primitive craving for power and knowledge have all contributed to crystallize out this new social fact of the temple.

The temple was accumulated by complex necessities, it grew from many roots and needs, and the god that dominated the temple was the creation of many imaginations and made up of all sorts of impulses, ideas, and half ideas. Here there was a god in which one sort of ideas predominated, and there another. It is necessary to lay some stress upon this confusion and variety of origin in gods, because there is a very abundant literature now in existence upon religious origins, in which a number of writers insist, some on this leading idea and some on that—we have noted several in our Chapter XII on "Early Thought"—as though it were the only idea. Professor Max Müller in his time, for example, harped perpetually on the idea of sun stories and sun worship. He would have had us think that early man never had lusts or fears, cravings for power, nightmares or fantasies, but that he meditated perpetually on the beneficent source of light and life in the sky. Now dawn and sunset are very moving facts in the daily life, but they are only two among many.{v1-236}

{v1-237}

Early men, three or four hundred generations ago, had brains very like our own. The fancies of our childhood and youth are perhaps the best clue we have to the ground-stuff of early religion, and anyone who can recall those early mental experiences will understand very easily the vagueness, the monstrosity, and the incoherent variety of the first gods. There were sun gods, no doubt, early in the history of temples, but there were also hippopotamus gods and hawk gods; there were cow deities, there were monstrous male and female gods, there were gods of terror and gods of an adorable quaintness, there were gods who were nothing but lumps of meteoric stone that had fallen amazingly out of the sky, and gods who were mere natural stones that had chanced to have a queer and impressive shape. Some gods, like Marduk of Babylon and the Baal (= the Lord) of the Phœnicians, Canaanites, and the like, were quite probably at bottom just legendary wonder beings, such as little boys will invent for themselves to-day. The early Semites, it is said, as soon as they thought of a god, invented a wife for him; most of the Egyptian and Babylonian gods were married. But the gods of the nomadic Semites had not this marrying disposition. Children were less eagerly sought by the inhabitants of the food-grudging steppes.

Even more natural than to provide a wife for a god is to give him a house to live in to which offerings can be brought. Of this house the knowing man, the magician, would naturally become the custodian. A certain seclusion, a certain aloofness, would add greatly to the prestige of the god. The steps by which the early temple and the early priesthood developed so soon as an agricultural population settled and increased are all quite natural and understandable, up to the stage of the long temple with the image, shrine and altar at one end and the long nave in which the worshippers stood. And this temple, because it had records and secrets, because it was a centre of power, advice, and instruction, because it sought and attracted imaginative and clever people for its service, naturally became a kind of brain in the growing community. The attitude of the common people who tilled the fields and herded the beasts towards the temple would remain simple and credulous. There, rarely seen and so imaginatively enhanced, lived the god whose approval{v1-238} gave prosperity, whose anger meant misfortune; he could be propitiated by little presents and the help of his servants could be obtained. He was wonderful, and of such power and knowledge that it did not do to be disrespectful to him even in one's thoughts. Within the priesthood, however, a certain amount of thinking went on at a rather higher level than that.

§ 3[136]

And now we have to note a very interesting fact about the chief temples of Egypt and, so far as we know—because the ruins are not so distinct—of Babylonia, and that is that they were "oriented"— that is to say, that the same sort of temple was built so that the shrine and entrance always faced in the same direction.[137] In Babylonian temples this was most often due east, facing the sunrise on March 21st and September 21st, the equinoxes; and it is to be noted that it was at the spring equinox that the Euphrates and Tigris came down in flood. The Pyramids of Gizeh are also oriented east and west, and the Sphinx faces due east, but very many of the Egyptian temples to the south of the delta of the Nile

do not point due east, but to the point where the sun rises at the longest day—and in Egypt the inundation comes close to that date. Others, however, pointed nearly northward, and others again pointed to the rising of the star Sirius or to the rising-point of other conspicuous stars. The fact of orientation links up with the fact that there early arose a close association between various gods and the sun and various fixed stars. Whatever the mass of people outside were thinking, the priests of the temples were beginning to link the movements of those heavenly bodies with the power in the shrine. They were thinking about the gods they served and thinking new meanings into them. They were brooding upon the mystery of the stars. It was very natural for them to suppose that these shining bodies, so irregularly distributed and circling so solemnly and silently, must be charged with portents to mankind.{v1-239}
{v1-240}

Among other things, this orientation of the temples served to fix and help the great annual festival of the New Year. On one morning in the year, and one morning alone, in a temple oriented to the rising-place of the sun at Midsummer Day, the sun's first rays would smite down through the gloom of the temple and the long alley of the temple pillars, and light up the god above the altar and irradiate him with glory. The narrow, darkened structure of the ancient temples seems to be deliberately planned for such an effect. No doubt the people were gathered in the darkness before the dawn; in the darkness there was chanting and perhaps the offering of sacrifices;

the god alone stood mute and invisible. Prayers and invocations would be made. Then upon the eyes of the worshippers, sensitized by the darkness, as the sun rose behind them, the god would suddenly shine.

So, at least, one explanation of orientation is found by such students of orientation as Sir Norman Lockyer.[138] Not only is orientation apparent in most of the temples of Egypt, Assyria, Babylonia, and the east, it is found in the Greek temples; Stonehenge is oriented to the midsummer sunrise, and so are most of the megalithic circles of Europe; the Temple of Heaven in Peking is oriented to midwinter. In the days of the Chinese Empire, up to a few years ago, one of the most important of all the duties of the Emperor of China was to sacrifice and pray in this temple upon midwinter's day for a propitious year.

The Egyptian priests had mapped out the stars into the constellations, and divided up the zodiac into twelve signs, by 3000 B.C. ...

§ 4

This clear evidence of astronomical inquiry and of a development of astronomical ideas is the most obvious, but only the most obvious, evidence of the very considerable intellectual activities that went on within the temple precincts in ancient times. There is a curious disposition among many modern writers to deprecate priesthoods and to speak of priests as though they had always been impostors and tricksters, preying upon the simplicity of mankind. But, indeed, they were for long the only writing[VI-241] class, the only reading public, the only learned and the only thinkers; they were all the professional classes of the time. You could have no intellectual life at all, you could not get access to literature or any knowledge except through the priesthood. The temples were not only observatories and libraries and clinics, they were museums and treasure-houses. The original *Periplus* of Hanno hung in one temple in Carthage, skins of his "gorillas" were hung and treasured in another. Whatever there was of abiding worth in the life of the community sheltered there. Herodotus, the early Greek historian (485-425 B.C.), collected most of his material from the priests of the countries in which he travelled, and it is evident they met him generously and put their very considerable resources completely at his disposal. Outside the temples the world was still a world of blankly illiterate and unspeculative human beings, living from day to day entirely for themselves. Moreover, there is little evidence that the commonalty felt cheated by the priests, or had anything but trust and affection for the early priesthoods. Even the great conquerors of later times were anxious to keep themselves upon the right side of the priests of the nations and cities whose obedience they desired, because of the immense popular influence of these priests.

No doubt there were great differences between temple and temple and cult and cult in the spirit and quality of the priesthood. Some probably were cruel, some vicious and greedy, many dull and doctrinaire, stupid with tradition, but it has to be kept in mind that there were distinct limits to the degeneracy or inefficiency of a priesthood. It had to keep its grip upon the general mind. It could not go beyond what people would stand—either towards the darkness or towards the light. Its authority rested, in the end, on the persuasion that its activities were propitious.

§ 5[139]

It is clear that the earliest civilized governments were essentially priestly governments. It was not kings and captains{v1-242} who first set men to the plough and a settled life. It was the ideas of the gods and plenty, working with the acquiescence of common men. The early rulers of Sumer we know were all priests, kings only because they were chief priests. And priestly government had its own weaknesses as well as its peculiar deep-rooted strength. The power of a priesthood is a power over their own people alone. It is a subjugation through mysterious fears and hopes. The priesthood can gather its people together for war, but its traditionalism and all its methods unfit it for military control. Against the enemy without, a priest-led people is feeble.

Moreover, a priest is a man vowed, trained, and consecrated, a man belonging to a special corps, and necessarily with an intense *esprit de corps*. He has given up his life to his temple and his god. This is a very excellent thing for the internal vigour of his own priesthood, his own temple. He lives or dies for the honour of his particular god. But in the next town or village is another temple with another god. It is his constant preoccupation to keep his people from that god. Religious cults and priesthoods are sectarian by nature; they will convert, they will overcome, but they will never coalesce. Our first perceptions of events in Sumer, in the dim uncertain light before history began, is of priests and gods in conflict; until the Sumerians were conquered by the Semites they were never united; and the same incurable conflict of priesthoods scars all the temple ruins of Egypt. It was impossible that it could have been otherwise, having regard to the elements out of which religion arose.

An Assyrian King & his Chief Minister

It was out of those two main weaknesses of all priesthoods, namely, the incapacity for efficient military leadership and their inevitable jealousy of all other religious cults, that the power of secular kingship arose. The foreign enemy either prevailed and set up a king over the people, or the priesthoods who would not give way to each other set up a common fighting captain, who retained more or less power in peace time. This secular king developed a group of officials about him and began, in relation to military organization, to take a share in the priestly administration of the people's affairs. So, growing out of priestcraft and beside the priest, the king, the protagonist of the priest,{vi-243} appears upon the stage of human history, and a very large amount of the subsequent experiences of mankind is only to be understood as an elaboration, complication, and distortion of the struggle, unconscious or deliberate, between these two systems of human control, the temple and the palace. And it was in the original centres of civilization that this antagonism was most completely developed. The Aryan peoples never passed through a phase of temple rule on their way to civilization; they came{vi-244} to civilization late; they found that drama already half-played. They took over the ideas of both temple and kingship, when those ideas were already elaborately developed, from the more civilized Hamitic or Semitic people they conquered.

The greater importance of the gods and the priests in the earlier history of the Mesopotamian civilization is very apparent, but gradually the palace won its way until it was at last in a position to struggle definitely for the supreme power. At first, in the story, the palace is ignorant and friendless in the face of the temple; the priests alone read, the priests alone know, the people are afraid of him. But in the dissensions of the various cults comes the opportunity of the palace. From other cities, from among captives, from defeated or suppressed religious cults, the palace gets men who also can read and who can do magic things.[140] The court also becomes a centre of writing and record; the king thinks for himself and becomes politic. Traders and foreigners drift to the court, and if the king has not the full records and the finished scholarship of the priests, he has a wider and fresher first-hand knowledge of many things. The priest comes into the temple when he is very young; he passes many years as a neophyte; the path of learning the clumsy letters of primitive times is slow and toilsome; he becomes erudite and prejudiced rather than a man of the world. Some of the more active-minded young priests may even cast envious eyes at the king's service. There are many complications and variations in this ages-long drama of the struggle going on beneath the outward conflicts of priest and king, between the made man and the born man, between learning and originality, between established knowledge and settled usage on the one hand, and creative will and imagination on the other. It is not always, as we shall find later, the priest who is the conservative and unimaginative antagonist. Sometimes a king struggles against narrow and obstructive priesthoods; sometimes priesthoods uphold the standards of civilization against savage, egotistical, or reactionary kings.

One or two outstanding facts and incidents of the early stages of this fundamental struggle in political affairs are all that we can note here between 4000 B.C. and the days of Alexander.{vi-245}

6

In the early days of Sumeria and Akkadia the city-kings were priests and medicine-men rather than kings, and it was only when foreign conquerors sought to establish their hold in relation to existing institutions that the distinction of priest and king became definite. But the god of the priests remained as the real overlord of the land and of priest and king alike. He was the universal landlord; the wealth and authority of his temples and establishments outshone those of the king. Especially was this the case within the city walls. Hammurabi, the founder of the first Babylonian Empire, is one of the earlier monarchs whom we find taking a firm grip upon the affairs of the community. He does it with the utmost politeness to the gods. In an inscription recording his irrigation work in Sumeria and Akkadia, he begins: "When Anu and Bel entrusted me with the rule of Sumer and Akkad————." We possess a code of laws made by this same Hammurabi—it is the earliest known code of law—and at the head of this code we see the figure of Hammurabi receiving the law from its nominal promulgator, the god Shamash.

An act of great political importance in the conquest of any city was the carrying off of its god to become a subordinate in the temple of its conqueror. This was far more important than the subjugation of king by king. Merodach, the Babylonian Jupiter, was carried off by the Elamites, and Babylon did not feel independent until its return. But sometimes a conqueror was afraid of the god he had conquered. In the collection of letters addressed to Amenophis III and IV at Tel-Amarna in Egypt, to which allusion has already been made, is one from a certain king, Tushratta, King of Mitani, who has conquered Assyria and taken the statue of the goddess Ishtar. Apparently he has sent this statue into Egypt, partly to acknowledge the overlordship of Amenophis, but partly because he fears her anger. (Winckler.) In the Bible is related (Sam. i. v. 1) how the Ark of the Covenant of the God of the Hebrews was carried off by the Philistines, as a token of conquest, into the temple of the fish god, Dagon, at Ashdod, and how Dagon fell down and was broken, and how the people of Ashdod were smitten with disease. In the latter story {v1-246} particularly the gods and priests fill the scene; there is no king in evidence at all.

Right through the history of the Babylonian and Assyrian empires no monarch seems to have felt his tenure of power secure in Babylon until he had "taken the hand of Bel"—that is to say, that he had been adopted by the priesthood of "Bel" as the god's son and representative. As our knowledge of Assyrian and Babylonian history grows clearer, it becomes plainer that the politics of that world, the revolutions, usurpations, changes of dynasty, intrigues with foreign powers, turned largely upon issues between the great wealthy priesthoods and the growing but still inadequate power of the monarchy. The king relied on his army, and this was usually a mercenary army of foreigners, speedily mutinous if there was no pay or plunder, and easily bribed. We have already noted the name of Sennacherib, the son of Sargon II, among the monarchs of the Assyrian Empire. Sennacherib was involved in a violent quarrel with the priesthood of Babylon; he never "took the hand of Bel"; and finally struck at that power by destroying altogether the holy part of the city of Babylon (691 B.C.) and removing the statue of Bel-Marduk to Assyria. He was assassinated by one of his sons, and his successor, Esarhaddon (his son, but not the son who was his assassin), found it expedient to restore Bel-Marduk and rebuild his temple, and make his peace with the god.[141]

Assurbanipal (Greek, Sardanapalus), the son of this Esarhaddon, is a particularly interesting figure from this point of view of the relationship of priesthood and king. His father's reconciliation with the priests of Bel-Marduk went so far that Sardanapalus was given a Babylonian instead of a military Assyrian education. He became a great collector of the clay documents of the past, and his library, which has been unearthed, is now the most precious source of historical material in the world. But for all his learning he kept his grip on the Assyrian army; he made a temporary conquest of Egypt, suppressed a rebellion in Babylon, and carried out a number of successful expeditions. As we have {v1-247} already told in Chapter XVI, he was almost the last of the Assyrian monarchs. The Aryan tribes, who knew more of war than of priestcraft, and particularly the Scythians, the Medes and Persians, had long been pressing upon Assyria from the north and north-east. The Medes and Persians formed an alliance with the nomadic Semitic Chaldeans of the south for the joint undoing of Assyria. Nineveh, the Assyrian capital, fell to these Aryans in 606 B.C.

Sixty-seven years after the taking of Nineveh by the Aryans, which left Babylonia to the Semitic Chaldeans, the last monarch of the Chaldean Empire (the Second Babylonian Empire), Nabonidus, the father of Belshazzar, was overthrown by Cyrus, the Persian. This Nabonidus, again, was a highly educated monarch, who brought far too much intelligence and imagination and not enough of the short range wisdom of this world to affairs of state. He conducted antiquarian researches, and to his researches it is that we owe the date of 3750 B.C., assigned to Sargon I and still accepted by many authorities. He was proud of this determination, and left inscriptions to record it. It is clear he was a religious innovator; he built and rearranged temples and attempted to centralize religion in Babylon by bringing a number of local gods to the temple of Bel-Marduk. No doubt he realized the weakness and disunion of his empire due to these conflicting cults, and had some conception of unification in his mind.

Events were marching too rapidly for any such development. His innovation had manifestly raised the suspicion and hostility of the priesthood of Bel. They sided with the Persians. "The soldiers of Cyrus entered Babylon without fighting." Nabonidus was taken prisoner, and Persian sentinels were set at the gates of the temple of Bel, "where the services continued without intermission."

Cyrus did, in fact, set up the Persian Empire in Babylon with the blessing of Bel-Marduk. He gratified the conservative instincts of the priests by packing off the local gods back to their ancestral temples. He also restored the Jews to Jerusalem.[142] These were merely matters of immediate policy to him. But in{vi-248} bringing in the irreligious Aryans, the ancient priesthood was paying too highly for the continuation of its temple services. It would have been wiser to have dealt with the innovations of Nabonidus, that earnest heretic, to have listened to his ideas, and to have met the needs of a changing world. Cyrus entered Babylon 539 B.C.; by 521 B.C. Babylon was in insurrection again, and in 520 B.C. another Persian monarch, Darius, was pulling down her walls. Within two hundred years the life had altogether gone out of those venerable rituals of Bel-Marduk, and the temple of Bel-Marduk was being used by builders as a quarry.

§ 7[143]

The story of priest and king in Egypt is similar to, but by no means parallel with, that of Babylonia. The kings of Sumeria and Assyria were priests who had become kings; they were secularized priests. The Pharaoh of Egypt does not appear to have followed precisely that line. Already in the very oldest records the Pharaoh has a power and importance exceeding that of any priest. He is, in fact, a god, and more than either priest or king. We do not know how he got to that position. No monarch of Sumeria or Babylonia or Assyria could have induced his people to do for him what the great pyramid-building Pharaohs of the IVth Dynasty made their people do in those vast erections. The earlier Pharaohs were not improbably regarded as incarnations{v1-249} of the dominant god. The falcon god Horus sits behind the head of the great statue of Chephren. So late a monarch as Rameses III (XIXth Dynasty) is represented upon his sarcophagus (now at Cambridge) bearing the distinctive symbols of the three great gods of the Egyptian system.[144] He carries the two sceptres of Osiris, the god of Day and Resurrection; upon his head are the horns of the cow goddess Hathor, and also the sun ball and feathers of Ammon Ra. He is not merely wearing the symbols of these gods as a devout Babylonian might wear the symbols of Bel-Marduk; he is these three gods in one.

Ramses III as Osiris—between the goddesses Nephthys and Isis....

Relief on the cover of the sarcophagus (at Cambridge). After Sharpe.

Inscription (round the edges of cover), as far as decipherable.

"Osiris, King of Upper and Lower Egypt, lord of the two countries ... son of the Sun, beloved of the gods, lord of diadems, Rameses, prince of Heliopolis, triumphant! Thou art in the condition of a god, thou shalt arise as Usr, there is no enemy to thee, I give to thee triumph among them...." Budge, Catalogue, Egyptian Collection, Fitzwilliam Museum, Cambridge.

The student will find much more in Sir J. G. Frazer's *Golden Bough* about the ancient use of human beings as well as statues to represent gods. Here we have merely to point to an apparent difference of idea between the Asiatic and African monarchies in this respect.

We find also a number of sculptures and paintings to enforce{v1-250} the idea that the Pharaohs were the actual sons of gods. The divine fathering and birth of Amenophis III, for instance (of the

XVIIIth Dynasty), is displayed in extraordinary detail in a series of sculptures at Luxor. Moreover, it was held that the Pharaohs, being of so divine a strain, could not marry common clay, and consequently they were accustomed to marry blood relations within the degrees of consanguinity now prohibited, even marrying their sisters.

The struggle between palace and temple came into Egyptian history, therefore, at a different angle from that at which it came into Babylonia. Nevertheless, it came in. Professor Maspero (in his *New Light on Ancient Egypt*) gives a very interesting account of the struggle of Amenophis IV with the priesthoods, and particularly with priests of the great god, Ammon Ra, Lord of Karnak. The mother of Amenophis IV was not of the race of Pharaoh; it would seem that his father, Amenophis III, made a love match with a subject, a beautiful Syrian named Tii, and Professor Maspero finds in the possible opposition to and annoyance of this queen by the priests of Ammon Ra the beginnings of the quarrel. She may, he thinks, have inspired her son with a fanatical hatred of Ammon Ra. But Amenophis IV may have had a wider view. Like the Babylonian Nabonidus, who lived a thousand years later, he may have had in mind the problem of moral unity in his empire. We have already noted that Amenophis III ruled from Ethiopia to the Euphrates, and that the store of letters to himself and his son found at Tel Amarna show a very wide range of interest and influence. At any rate, Amenophis IV set himself to close all the Egyptian and Syrian temples, to put an end to all sectarian worship throughout his dominions, and to establish everywhere the worship of one god, Aton, the solar disk. He left his capital, Thebes, which was even more the city of Ammon Ra than later Babylon was the city of Bel-Marduk, and set up his capital at Tel Amarna; he altered his name from "Amenophis," which consecrated him to Ammon (Amen) to "Akhnaton," the Sun's Glory; and he held his own against all the priesthoods of his empire for eighteen years and died a Pharaoh.

Opinions upon Amenophis IV, or Akhnaton, differ very widely.{v1-251} There are those who regard him as the creature of his mother's hatred of Ammon and the uxorious spouse of a beautiful wife. Certainly he loved his wife very passionately; he showed her great honour—Egypt honoured women, and was ruled at different times by several queens—and he was sculptured in one instance with his wife seated upon his knees, and in another in the act of kissing her in a chariot; but men who live under the sway of their womenkind do not sustain great empires in the face of the bitter hostility of the most influential organized bodies in their realm.[145] Others write of him as a "gloomy fanatic." Matrimonial bliss is rare in the cases of gloomy fanatics. It is much more reasonable to regard him as the Pharaoh who refused to be a god. It is not simply his religious policy and his frank display of natural affection that seem to mark a strong and very original personality. His æsthetic ideas were his own. He refused to have his portrait conventionalized into the customary smooth beauty of the Pharaoh god, and his face looks out at us across an interval of thirty-four centuries, a man amidst ranks of divine insipidities.

A reign of eighteen years was not long enough for the revolution{v1-252} he contemplated, and his son-in-law who succeeded him went back to Thebes and made his peace with Ammon Ra.

To the very end of the story the divinity of kings haunted the Egyptian mind, and infected the thoughts of intellectually healthier races. When Alexander the Great reached Babylon, the prestige of Bel-Marduk was already far gone in decay, but in Egypt, Ammon Ra was still god enough to make a snob of the conquering Grecian. The priests of Ammon Ra, about the time of the XVIIIth or XIXth Dynasty (*circa* 1400 B.C.), had set up in an oasis of the desert a temple and oracle. Here was an image of the god which could speak, move its head, and accept or reject scrolls of inquiry. This oracle was still flourishing in 332 B.C. The young master of the world, it is related, made a special journey to visit it; he came into the sanctuary, and the image advanced out of the darkness at the back to meet him. There was an impressive exchange of salutations. Some such formula as this must have been used (says Professor Maspero): "Come, son of my loins, who loves me so that I give thee the royalty of Ra and the royalty of Horus! I give thee valiance, I give thee to hold all countries and all religions under thy feet; I give thee to strike all the peoples united together with thy arm!"

So it was that the priests of Egypt conquered their conqueror, and an Aryan monarch first became a god....[146]

§ 8

The struggle of priest and king in China cannot be discussed here at any length. It was different again, as in Egypt it was different from Babylonia, but we find the same effort on the part of the ruler to break up tradition because it divides up the people. The Chinese Emperor, the "Son of Heaven," was himself a high-priest, and his chief duty was sacrificial; in the more disorderly phases of Chinese history he ceases to rule and continues only to sacrifice. The literary class was detached from the priestly class{v1-253} at an early date. It became a bureaucratic body serving the local kings and rulers. That is a fundamental difference between the history of China and any Western history. While Alexander was overrunning Western Asia, China, under the last priest-emperors of the Chow Dynasty, was sinking into a state of great disorder. Each province clung to its separate nationality and traditions, and the Huns spread from province to province. The King of Ts'in (who lived about eighty years after Alexander the Great), impressed by the mischief tradition was doing in the land, resolved to destroy the entire Chinese literature, and his son, Shi Hwang-ti, the "first universal Emperor," made a strenuous attempt to seek out and destroy all the existing classics.[147] They vanished while he ruled, and he ruled without tradition, and welded China into a unity that endured for some centuries; but when he had passed, the hidden books crept out again. China remained united, though not under his descendants, but after a civil war under a fresh dynasty, the Han Dynasty (206 B.C.). The first Han monarch did not sustain this campaign of Shi Hwang-ti against the *literati*, and his successor made his peace with them and restored the texts of the classics.{v1-254}

XX

SERFS, SLAVES, SOCIAL CLASSES, AND FREE
INDIVIDUALS

§ 1. The Common Man in Ancient Times. § 2. The Earliest Slaves. § 3. The first "Independent" Persons. § 4. Social Classes Three Thousand Years Ago. § 5. Classes Hardening into Castes. § 6. Caste in India. § 7. The System of the Mandarins. § 8. A Summary of Five Thousand Years.

§ 1

W E have been sketching in the last four chapters the growth of civilized states out of the primitive Neolithic agriculture that began in Mesopotamia perhaps 15,000, perhaps 20,000, years ago. It was at first horticulture rather than agriculture; it was done with the hoe before the plough, and at first it was quite supplementary to the sheep, goat, and cattle tending that made the "living" of the family tribe. We have traced the broad outlines of the development in regions of exceptional fruitfulness of the first settled village communities into more populous towns and cities, and the growth of the village shrine and the village medicine-man into the city temple and the city priesthood. We have noted the beginnings of organized war, first as a bickering between villages, and then as a more disciplined struggle between the priest-king and god of one city and those of another. Our story has passed on rapidly from the first indications of conquest and empire in Sumer, perhaps 6000 or 7000 B.C., to the spectacle of great empires growing up, with roads and armies, with inscriptions and written documents, with educated priesthoods and kings and rulers sustained by a tradition already ancient. We have traced in broad outline the appearance and{v1-255} conflicts and replacements of these empires of the great rivers. We have directed attention, in particular, to the evidence of a development of still wider political ideas as we find it betrayed by the actions and utterances of such men as Nabonidus and Amenophis IV. It has been an outline of the accumulations of human experience for ten or fifteen thousand years, a vast space of time in comparison with all subsequent history, but a brief period when we measure it against the succession of endless generations that intervenes between us and the first rude flint-using human creatures of the Pleistocene dawn. But for these last four chapters we have been writing almost entirely not about mankind generally, but only about the men who thought, the men who could draw and read and write, the men who were altering their world. Beneath their activities what was the life of the mute multitude?

The life of the common man was, of course, affected and changed by these things, just as the lives of the domestic animals and the face of the cultivated country were changed; but for the most part it was a change suffered and not a change in which the common man upon the land had any voice or will. Reading and writing were not yet for the likes of him. He went on cultivating his patch, loving his wife and children, beating his dog and tending his beasts, grumbling at hard times, fearing the magic of the priests and the power of the gods, desiring little more except to be left alone by the powers above him. So he was in 10,000 B.C.; so he was, unchanged in nature and outlook, in the time of Alexander the Great; so over the greater part of the world he remains to-day. He got rather better tools, better seeds, better methods, a slightly sounder house, he sold his produce in a more organized market as civilization progressed. A certain freedom and a certain equality passed out of human life when men ceased to wander. Men paid in liberty for safety, shelter, and regular meals. By imperceptible degrees the common man found the patch he cultivated was not his own; it belonged to the god; and he had to pay a fraction of his produce to the god. Or the god had given it to the king, who exacted his rent and tax. Or the king had given it to an official, who was the lord of the common man. And sometimes the god or the king or the noble had work to be done, and{v1-256} then the common man had to leave his patch and work for his master.

How far the patch he cultivated was his own was never very clear to him. In ancient Assyria the land seems to have been held as a sort of freehold and the occupier paid taxes; in Babylonia the land was the god's, and he permitted the cultivator to work thereon. In Egypt the temples or Pharaoh-the-god or the nobles under Pharaoh were the owners and rent receivers. But the cultivator was not a slave; he was a peasant, and only bound to the land in so far that there was nothing else for him to do but cultivate, and nowhere else for him to go. He lived in a village or town, and went out to his work. The village, to begin with, was often merely a big household of related people under a patriarch headman, the early town a group of householders under its elders. There was no process of enslavement as civilization grew, but the headmen and leaderly men grew in power and authority, and the common men did not keep pace with them, and fell into a tradition of dependence and subordination.

On the whole, the common men were probably well content to live under lord or king or god and obey their bidding. It was safer. It was easier. All animals—and man is no exception—begin life as dependents. Most men never shake themselves loose from the desire for leading and protection.[148]

Egyptian peasants seized for non-payment of taxes ... (Pyramid Age)

The earlier wars did not involve remote or prolonged campaigns, and they were waged by levies of the common people. But war brought in a new source of possessions, plunder, and a new social factor, the captive. In the earlier, simpler days of war, the captive man was kept only to be tortured or sacrificed to the victorious god; the captive women and children were assimilated into the tribe. But later many captives were spared to be slaves because they had exceptional gifts or peculiar arts. It would be the kings and captains who would take these slaves at first, and{v1-257} it would speedily become apparent to them that these men were much more their own than were the peasant cultivators and common men of their own race.[149] The slave could be commanded to do all sorts of things for his master that the quasi-free common man would not do so willingly because of his attachment to his own patch of cultivation. From a very early period the artificer was often a household slave, and the manufacture of trade goods, pottery, textiles, metal ware, and so forth, such as went on vigorously in the household city of the Minos of Cnossos, was probably a slave industry from the beginning. Sayce, in his *Babylonians and Assyrians*,[150] quotes Babylonian agreements for the teaching of trades to slaves, and dealing with the exploitation of slave products. Slaves produced slave children, enslavement in discharge of debts added to the slave population; it is probable that as the cities grew larger, a larger part of the new population consisted of these slave artificers and slave servants in the large households. They were by no means abject slaves; in later Babylon their lives and property were protected by elaborate laws. Nor were they all outlanders. Parents might sell their children into slavery, and brothers their orphan sisters. Free men who had no means of livelihood would even sell themselves into slavery. And slavery was the fate of the insolvent debtor. Craft apprenticeship, again, was a sort of fixed-term slavery. Out of the slave population, by a converse process, arose the freed-man and freed-woman, who worked for[vi-258]wages and had still more definite individual rights. Since in Babylon slaves could themselves own property, many slaves saved up and bought themselves. Probably the town slave was often better off and practically as free as the cultivator of the soil, and as the rural population increased, its sons and daughters came to mix with and swell the growing ranks of artificers, some bound, some free.

As the extent and complexity of government increased, the number of households multiplied. Under the king's household grew up the households of his great ministers and officials, under the temple grew up the personal households of temple functionaries; it is not difficult to realize how houses and patches of land would become more and more distinctly the property of the occupiers, and more and more definitely alienated from the original owner-god. The earlier empires in Egypt and China both passed into a feudal stage, in which families, originally official, became for a time independent noble families. In the later stages of Babylonian civilization we find an increasing propertied class of people appearing in the social structure, neither slaves nor peasants nor priests nor officials, but widows and descendants of such people, or successful traders and the like, and all *masterless* folk. Traders came in from the outside. Babylon was full of Aramean traders, who had great establishments, with slaves, freed-men, employees of all sorts. (Their book-keeping was a serious undertaking. It involved storing a great multitude of earthenware tablets in huge earthenware jars.) Upon this gathering mixture of more or less free and detached people would live other people, traders, merchants, small dealers, catering for their needs. Sayce (*op. cit.*) gives the particulars of an agreement for the setting up and stocking of a tavern and beerhouse, for example. The passer-by, the man who happened to be about, had come into existence.

But another and far less kindly sort of slavery also arose in the old civilization, and that was gang slavery. If it did not figure very largely in the cities, it was very much in evidence elsewhere. The king was, to begin with, the chief *entrepreneur*. He made the canals and organized the irrigation (*e.g.* Hammurabi's enterprises noted in the previous chapter). He exploited mines. He seems (at Cnossos, *e.g.*) to have organized manufactures for export. The Pharaohs of the 1st Dynasty were already working the copper and{v1-259}turquoise mines in the peninsula of Sinai. For many such purposes gangs of captives were cheaper and far more controllable than levies of the king's own people. From an early period, too, captives may have tugged the oars of the galleys, though Torr (*Ancient Ships*) notes that up to the age of Pericles (450 B.C.) the free Athenians were not above this task. And the monarch also found slaves convenient for his military expeditions. They were uprooted men; they did not fret to go home, because they had no homes to go to. The Pharaohs hunted slaves in Nubia, in order to have black troops for their Syrian expeditions. Closely allied to such slave troops were the mercenary barbaric troops the monarchs caught into their service, not by positive compulsion, but by the bribes of food and plunder and under the pressure of need. As the old civilization developed, these mercenary armies replaced the national levies of the old order more and more, and servile gang labour became a more and more important and significant factor in the economic system. From mines and canal and wall building, the servile gang spread into cultivation. Nobles and temples adopted the gang slave system for their works. Plantation gangs began to oust the patch cultivation of the labourer-serf in the case of some staple products....

§ 3

So, in a few paragraphs, we trace the development of the simple social structure of the early Sumerian cities to the complex city crowds, the multitude of individuals varying in race, tradition, education, and function, varying in wealth, freedom, authority, and usefulness, in the great cities of the last thousand years B.C. The most notable thing of all is the gradual increase amidst this heterogeneous multitude of what we may call *free individuals*, detached persons who are neither priests, nor kings, nor officials, nor serfs, nor slaves, who are under no great pressure to work, who have time to read and inquire. They appear side by side with the development of social security and private property. Coined money and monetary reckoning developed. The operations of the Arameans and such-like Semitic trading people led to the organization of credit and monetary security. In the earlier days almost the only property, except a few movables, consisted of rights in{v1-260} land and in houses; later, one could deposit and lend securities, could go away and return to find one's property faithfully held and secure. Towards the middle of the period of the Persian Empire there lived one free individual, Herodotus, who has a great interest for us because he was among the first writers of critical and intelligent history, as distinguished from a mere priestly or court chronicle. It is worth while to glance here very briefly at the circumstances of his life. Later on we shall quote from his history.

Brawl among boatmen ... (From tomb of Ptah-hetep——Pyramid Age)

We have already noted the conquest of Babylonia by the Aryan Persians under Cyrus in 539 B.C. We have noted, further, that the Persian Empire spread into Egypt, where its hold was precarious; and it extended also over Asia Minor. Herodotus was born about 484 B.C. in a Greek city of Asia Minor, Halicarnassus, which was under the overlordship of the Persians, and directly under the rule of a political boss or tyrant. There is no sign that he was obliged either to work for a living or spend very much time in the administration of his property. We do not know the particulars of his affairs, but it is clear that in this minor Greek city, under foreign rule, he was able to obtain and read and study manuscripts of nearly everything that had been written in the Greek language before his time. He travelled, so far as one can gather, with freedom and comfort about the Greek archipelagoes; he stayed wherever he wanted to stay, and he seems to have found comfortable accommodation; he went to Babylon and to Susa, the new capital the Persians had set up in Babylonia to the east of the Tigris; he toured along the coast of the Black Sea, and [vi-261] accumulated a considerable amount of knowledge about the Scythians, the Aryan people who were then distributed over South Russia; he went to the south of Italy, explored the antiquities of Tyre, coasted Palestine, landed at Gaza, and made a long stay in Egypt. He went about Egypt looking at temples and monuments and gathering information. We know, not only from him, but from other evidence, that in those days the older temples and the pyramids (which were already nearly three thousand years old) were visited by strings of tourists, a special sort of priests acting as guides. The inscriptions the sightseers scribbled upon the walls remain to this day, and many of them have been deciphered and published.

{v1-262}

As his knowledge accumulated, he conceived the idea of writing a great history of the attempts of Persia to subdue Greece. But in order to introduce that history he composed an account of the past of Greece, Persia, Assyria, Babylonia, Egypt, Scythia, and of the geography and peoples of those countries. He then set himself, it is said, to make his history known among his friends in Halicarnassus by reciting it to them, but they failed to appreciate it; and he then betook himself to Athens, the most flourishing of all Greek cities at that time. There his work was received with applause. We find him in the centre of a brilliant circle of intelligent and active-minded people, and the city authorities voted him a reward of ten talents (a sum of money equivalent to £2,400) in recognition of his literary achievement....

But we will not complete the biography of this most interesting man, nor will we enter into any criticism of his garrulous, marvel-telling, and most entertaining history. It is a book to which all intelligent readers come sooner or later, abounding as it does in illuminating errors and Boswellian charm. We give these particulars here simply to show that in the fifth century B.C. a new factor was becoming evident in human affairs. Reading and writing had already long escaped from the temple precincts and the ranks of the court scribes. Record was no longer confined to court and temple. A new sort of people, these people of leisure and independent means, were asking questions, exchanging knowledge and views, and developing ideas. So beneath the march of armies and the policies of monarchs, and above the common lives of illiterate and incurious men, we note the beginnings of what is becoming at last nowadays a dominant power in human affairs, the *free intelligence of mankind.*

Of that free intelligence we shall have more to say when in a subsequent chapter we tell of the Greeks.

§ 4

We may summarize the discussion of the last two chapters here by making a list of the chief elements in this complicated accumulation of human beings which made up the later Babylonian and Egyptian civilizations of from two thousand five hundred to three thousand years ago. These elements grew up and became distinct{vi-263} one from another in the great river valleys of the world in the course of five or six thousand years. They developed mental dispositions and traditions and attitudes of thought one to another. The civilization in which we live to-day is simply carrying on and still further developing and working out and rearranging these relationships. This is the world from which we inherit. It is only by the attentive study of their origins that we can detach ourselves from the prejudices and immediate ideas of the particular class to which we may belong, and begin to understand the social and political questions of our own time.

(1) First, then, came the priesthood, *the temple system*, which was the nucleus and the guiding intelligence about which the primitive civilizations grew. It was still in these later days a great power in the world, the chief repository of knowledge and tradition, an influence over the lives of every one, and a binding force to hold the community together. But it was no longer all-powerful, because its nature made it conservative and inadaptable. It no longer monopolized knowledge nor initiated fresh ideas. Learning had already leaked out to other less pledged and controlled people, who thought for themselves. About the temple system were grouped its priests and priestesses, its scribes, its physicians, its magicians, its lay brethren, treasurers, managers, directors, and the like. It owned great properties and often hoarded huge treasures.

(2) Over against the priesthood, and originally arising out of it, was the *court system*, headed by a king or a "king of kings," who was in later Assyria and Babylonia a sort of captain and lay controller of affairs, and in Egypt a god-man, who had released

himself from the control of his priests. About the monarch were accumulated his scribes, counsellors, record keepers, agents, captains, and guards. Many of his officials, particularly his provincial officials, had great subordinate establishments, and were constantly tending to become independent. The nobility of the old river valley civilizations arose out of the court system. It was, therefore, a different thing in its origins from the nobility of the early Aryans, which was a republican nobility of elders and leading men.

(3) At the base of the social pyramid was the large and most{vl-264} necessary class in the community, *the tillers of the soil.* Their status varied from age to age and in different lands; they were free peasants paying taxes, or serfs of the god, or serfs or tenants of king or noble, or of a private owner, paying him a rent; in most cases tax or rent was paid in produce. In the states of the river valleys they were high cultivators, cultivating comparatively small holdings; they lived together for safety in villages, and had a common interest in maintaining their irrigation channels and a sense of community in their village life. The cultivation of the soil is an exacting occupation; the seasons and the harvest sunsets will not wait for men; children can be utilized at an early age, and so the cultivator class is generally a poorly educated, close-toiling class, superstitious by reason of ignorance and the uncertainty of the seasons, ill-informed and easily put upon. It is capable at times of great passive resistance, but it has no purpose in its round but

crops and crops, to keep out of debt and hoard against bad times. So it has remained to our own days over the greater part of Europe and Asia.

(4) Differing widely in origin and quality from the tillers of the soil was *the artisan class*. At first, this was probably in part a town-slave class, in part it consisted of peasants who had specialized upon a craft. But in developing an art and mystery of its own, a technique that had to be learnt before it could be practised, each sort of craft probably developed a certain independence and a certain sense of community of its own. The artisans were able to get together and discuss their affairs more readily than the toilers on the land, and they were able to form guilds to restrict output, maintain rates of pay, and protect their common interest.

(5) As the power of the Babylonian rulers spread out beyond the original areas of good husbandry into grazing regions and less fertile districts, a class of *herdsmen* came into existence. In the case of Babylonia these were nomadic Semites, the Bedouin, like the Bedouin of to-day. They probably grazed their flocks over great areas much as the sheep ranchers of California do.[151] They were paid and esteemed much more highly than the husbandmen.

(6) The first *merchants* in the world were shipowners, like the people of Tyre and Cnossos, or nomads who carried and traded{vi-265} goods as they wandered between one area of primitive civilization and another. In the Babylonian and Assyrian world the traders were predominantly the Semitic

Arameans, the ancestors of the modern Syrians. They became a distinct factor in the life of the community; they formed great households of their own. Usury developed largely in the last thousand years B.C. Traders needed accommodation; cultivators wished to anticipate their crops. Sayce (*op. cit.*) gives an account of the Babylonian banking-house of Egibi, which lasted through several generations and outlived the Chaldean Empire.

(7) A class of *small retailers*, one must suppose, came into existence with the complication of society during the later days of the first empires, but it was not probably of any great importance. It is difficult to understand how there could be much active retailing without small change, and there is little evidence of small change to be found either in Egypt or Mesopotamia.[152] Shekels and half-shekels of silver, weighing something between a quarter and half an ounce, are the lightest weights of stamped metal of which we find mention.

(8) A growing class of *independent property owners*.

(9) As the amenities of life increased, there grew up in the court, temples, and prosperous private houses a class of *domestic servants*, slaves or freed slaves, or young peasants taken into the household.

(10) *Gang workers.*—These were prisoners of war or debt slaves, or impressed or deported men.

(11) *Mercenary soldiers.*—These also were often captives or impressed men. Sometimes they

were enlisted from friendly foreign populations in which the military spirit still prevailed.

(12) *Seamen.*

In modern political and economic discussions we are apt to talk rather glibly of "labour." Much has been made of the *solidarity of labour* and its sense of community. It is well to note that in these first civilizations, what we speak of as "labour" is represented by five distinct classes dissimilar in origin, traditions, and outlook{v1-266}—namely, classes 3, 4, 5, 9, 10, and the oar-tugging part of 12. The "solidarity of labour" is, we shall find when we come to study the mechanical revolution of the nineteenth century A.D., a new idea and a new possibility in human affairs.

§ 5

Let us, before we leave this discussion of the social classes that were developing in these first civilizations, devote a little attention to their fixity. How far did they stand aloof from each other, and how far did they intermingle? So far as the classes we have counted as 9, 10, 11, and 12 go, the servants, the gang labourers and slaves, the gang soldiers, and, to a lesser extent, the sailors, or at any rate the galley rowers among the sailors, they were largely recruited classes, they did not readily and easily form homes, they were not distinctively breeding classes; they were probably replenished generation after generation by captives, by the failures of other classes, and especially from the failures of the class of small retailers, and by persuasion and impressment from among the cultivators. But so far as the sailors go, we have to distinguish between the mere rower and the navigating and shipowning seamen of such ports as Tyre and Sidon. The shipowners pass, no doubt, by insensible gradations into the mercantile class, but the navigators must have made a peculiar community in the great seaports, having homes there and handing on the secrets of seacraft to their sons. The eighth class we have distinguished was certainly a precarious class, continually increased by the accession of the heirs and dependents, the widows and retired members of the wealthy and powerful, and continually diminished by the deaths or speculative losses of these people and the dispersal of their properties. The priests and priestesses too, so far as all this world west of India went, were not a very reproductive class; many priesthoods were celibate, and that class, too, may also be counted as a recruited class. Nor are servants, as a rule, reproductive. They live in the households of other people; they do not have households and rear large families of their own. This leaves us as the really vital classes of the ancient civilized community:

(*a*) The royal and aristocratic class, officials, military officers, and the like;{vi-267}

(*b*) The mercantile class;

(*c*) The town artisans;

(*d*) The cultivators of the soil; and

(*e*) The herdsmen.

Each of these classes reared its own children in its own fashion, and so naturally kept itself more or less continuously distinct from the others. General education was not organized in those ancient states, education was mainly a household matter (as it is still in many parts of India to-day), and so it was natural and necessary for the sons to follow in the footsteps of their father and to marry women accustomed to their own sort of household. Except during times of great political disturbance therefore, there would be a natural and continuous separation of classes; which would not, however, prevent exceptional individuals from intermarrying or passing from one class to another. Poor aristocrats would marry rich members of the mercantile class; ambitious herdsmen, artisans, or sailors would become rich merchants. So far as one can gather, that was the general state of affairs in both Egypt and Babylonia. The idea was formerly entertained that in Egypt there was a fixity of classes, but this appears to be a misconception due to a misreading of Herodotus. The only exclusive class in Egypt which did not intermarry was, as in England to-day, the semi-divine royal family.

At various points in the social system there were probably developments of exclusiveness, an actual barring out of interlopers. Artisans of particular crafts possessing secrets, for example, have among all races and in all ages tended to develop guild organizations restricting the practice of their craft and the marriage of members outside their guild.

Conquering people have also, and especially when there were marked physical differences of race, been disposed to keep themselves aloof from the conquered peoples, and have developed an aristocratic exclusiveness. Such organizations of restriction upon free intercourse have come and gone in great variety in the history of all long-standing civilizations. The natural boundaries of function were always there, but sometimes they have been drawn sharply and laid stress upon, and sometimes they have been made little of. There has been a general tendency among the Aryan peoples to distinguish noble (patrician) from common {vi-268} (plebeian) families; the traces of it are evident throughout the literature and life of Europe to-day, and it has received a picturesque enforcement in the "science" of heraldry. This tradition is still active even in democratic America. Germany, the most methodical of European countries, had in the Middle Ages a very clear conception of the fixity of such distinctions. Below the princes (who themselves constituted an exclusive class which did not marry beneath itself) there were the:

(*a*) Knights, the military and official caste, with heraldic coats-of-arms;

(*b* and *c*) The Bürgerstand, the merchants, shipping people, and artisans; and

(*d*) The Bauernstand, the cultivating serfs or peasants.

Mediæval Germany went as far as any of the Western heirs of the first great civilizations towards a fixation of classes. The idea is far less congenial both to the English-speaking people and to the French and Italians, who, by a sort of instinct, favour a free movement from class to class. Such exclusive ideas began at first among, and were promoted chiefly by, the upper classes, but it is a natural response and a natural Nemesis to such ideas that the mass of the excluded should presently range themselves in antagonism to their superiors. It was in Germany, as we shall see in the concluding chapters of this story, that the conception of a natural and necessary conflict, "the class war," between the miscellaneous multitudes of the disinherited ("the class-conscious proletariat" of the Marxist) and the rulers and merchants first arose. It was an idea more acceptable to the German mind than to the British or French.... But before we come to that conflict, we must traverse a long history of many centuries.

§ 6

If now we turn eastward from this main development of civilization in the world between Central Asia and the Atlantic, to the social development of India in the 2000 years next before the Christian era, we find certain broad and very interesting differences. The first of these is that we find such a fixity of classes in process of establishment as no other part of the world can present. This fixity of classes is known to Europeans as the institution of{v1-269} *caste*;[153] its origins are still in complete obscurity, but it was certainly well rooted in the Ganges valley before the days of Alexander the Great. It is a complicated horizontal division of the social structure into classes or castes, the members of which may neither eat nor intermarry with persons of a lower caste under penalty of becoming outcasts, and who may also "lose caste" for various ceremonial negligences and defilements. By losing caste a man does not sink to a lower caste; he becomes outcast. The various subdivisions of caste are very complex; many are practically trade organizations. Each caste has its local organization which maintains discipline, distributes various charities, looks after its own poor, protects the common interests of its members, and examines the credentials of newcomers from other districts. (There is little to check the pretensions of a travelling Hindu to be of a higher caste than is legitimately his.) Originally, the four main castes seem to have been:

The Brahmins—the priests and teachers;

The Kshatriyas—the warriors;

The Vaisyas—herdsmen, merchants, money-lenders, and land-owners;

The Sudras;

And, outside the castes, the Pariahs.

But these primary divisions have long been superseded by the disappearance of the second and third primary castes, and the subdivision of the Brahmins and Sudras into a multitude of minor castes, all exclusive, each holding its members to one definite way of living and one group of associates.

Next to this extraordinary fission and complication of the social body we have to note that the Brahmins, the priests and teachers of the Indian world, unlike so many Western priesthoods, are a reproductive and exclusive class, taking no recruits from any other social stratum.

Whatever may have been the original incentive to this extensive fixation of class in India, there can be little doubt of the rôle played by the Brahmins as the custodians of tradition and the only teachers of the people in sustaining it. By some it is supposed that the first three of the four original castes, known also as the "twice{v1-270} born," were the descendants of the Vedic Aryan conquerors of India, who established these hard-and-fast separations to prevent racial mixing with the conquered Sudras and Pariahs. The Sudras are represented as a previous wave of northern conquerors, and the Pariahs are the original Dravidian inhabitants of India. But those speculations are not universally accepted, and it is, perhaps, rather the case that the uniform conditions of life in the Ganges valley throughout long centuries served to stereotype a difference of classes that have never had the same steadfastness of definition under the more various and variable conditions of the greater world to the west.

However caste arose, there can be no doubt of its extraordinary hold upon the Indian mind. In the sixth century B.C. arose Gautama, the great teacher of Buddhism, proclaiming, "As the four streams that flow into the Ganges lose their names as soon as they mingle their waters in the holy river, so all who believe in Buddha cease to be Brahmins, Kshatriyas, Vaisyas, and Sudras." His teaching prevailed in India for some centuries; it spread over China, Tibet, Japan, Burmah, Ceylon, Turkestan, Manchuria; it is to-day the religion of one-third of the human race, but it was finally defeated and driven out of Indian life by the vitality and persistence of the Brahmins and of their caste ideas....

§ 7

In China we find a social system travelling along yet another and only a very roughly parallel line to that followed by the Indian and Western civilizations. The Chinese civilization even more than the Hindu is organized for peace, and the warrior plays a small part in its social scheme. As in the Indian civilization, the leading class is an intellectual one; less priestly than the Brahmin and more official. But unlike the Brahmins, the mandarins, who are the literate men of China, are not a caste; one is not a mandarin by birth, but by education; they are drawn by education and examination from all classes of the community, and the son of a mandarin has no prescriptive right to succeed his father.[154] As a consequence{v1-271} of these differences, while the Brahmins of India are, as a class, ignorant even of their own sacred books, mentally slack, and full of a pretentious assurance, the Chinese mandarin has the energy that comes from hard mental work. But since his education so far has been almost entirely a scholarly study of the classical Chinese literature, his influence has been entirely conservative. Before the days of Alexander the Great, China had already formed itself and set its feet in the way in which it was still walking in the year 1900 A.D. Invaders and dynasties had come and gone, but the routine of life of the yellow civilization remained unchanged.

The traditional Chinese social system recognized four main classes below the priest-emperor.

(*a*) The literary class, which was equivalent partly to the officials of the Western world and partly to its teachers and clerics. In the time of Confucius its education included archery and horsemanship. Rites and music, history and mathematics completed the "Six Accomplishments."

(*b*) The cultivators of the land.

(*c*) The artisans.

(*d*) The mercantile class.

But since from the earliest times it has been the Chinese way to divide the landed possessions of a man among all his sons, there has never been in Chinese history any class of great land-owners, renting their land to tenants, such as most other countries have displayed. The Chinese land has always been cut up into small holdings, which are chiefly freeholds, and cultivated intensively. There are landlords in China who own one or a few farms and rent them to tenants, but there are no great, permanent estates. When a patch of land, by repeated division, is too small to sustain a man, it is sold to some prospering neighbour, and the former owner drifts to one of the great towns of China to join the mass of wage-earning workers there. In China, for many centuries, there have been these masses of town population with scarcely any property at all, men neither serfs nor slaves, but held to their daily work by their utter impecuniousness. From such masses it is that the soldiers needed by the Chinese government are recruited, and also such gang labour as has been needed for the making of canals, the building of walls, and the like has[v1-272] been drawn.[155] The war captive and the slave class play a smaller part in Chinese history than in any more westerly record of these ages before the Christian era.

One fact, we may note, is common to all these three stories of developing social structure, and that is the immense power exercised by the educated class in the early stages before the crown or the commonalty began to read and, consequently, to think for itself. In India, by reason of their exclusiveness, the Brahmins, the educated class, retain their influence to this day; over the masses of China, along entirely different lines and because of the complexities of the written language, the mandarinate has prevailed. The diversity of race and tradition in the more various and eventful world of the West has delayed, and perhaps arrested for ever, any parallel organization of the specially intellectual elements of society into a class ascendancy. In the

Western world, as we have already noted, education early "slopped over," and soaked away out of the control of any special class; it escaped from the limitation of castes and priesthoods and traditions into the general life of the community. Writing and reading had been simplified down to a point when it was no longer possible to make a cult and mystery of them. It may be due to the peculiar elaboration and difficulty of the Chinese characters, rather than to any racial difference, that the same thing did not happen to the same extent in China.

§ 8

In these last six chapters we have traced in outline the whole process by which, in the course of 5000 or 6000 years—that is to say, in something between 150 and 200 generations—mankind passed from the stage of early Neolithic husbandry, in which the primitive skin-clad family tribe reaped and stored in their rude mud huts the wild-growing fodder and grain-bearing grasses with{v1-273} sickles of stone, to the days of the fourth century B.C., when all round the shores of the Mediterranean and up the Nile, and across Asia to India, and again over the great alluvial areas of China, spread the fields of human cultivation and busy cities, great temples, and the coming and going of human commerce. Galleys and lateen-sailed ships entered and left crowded harbours, and made their careful way from headland to headland and from headland to island, keeping always close to the land. Phœnician shipping under

Egyptian owners was making its way into the East Indies and perhaps even further into the Pacific. Across the deserts of Africa and Arabia and through Turkestan toiled the caravans with their remote trade; silk was already coming from China, ivory from Central Africa, and tin from Britain to the centres of this new life in the world. Men had learnt to weave fine linen[156] and delicate fabrics of coloured wool; they could bleach and dye; they had iron as well as copper, bronze, silver, and gold; they had made the most beautiful pottery and porcelain; there was hardly a variety of precious stone in the world that they had not found and cut and polished; they could read and write; divert the course of rivers, pile pyramids, and make walls a thousand miles long. The fifty or sixty centuries in which all this had to be achieved may seem a long time in comparison with the threescore and ten years of a single human life, but it is utterly inconsiderable in comparison with the stretches of geological time. Measuring backward from these Alexandrian cities to the days of the first stone implements, the *rostro-carinate* implements of the Pliocene Age, gives us an extent of time fully a hundred times as long.

We have tried in this account, and with the help of maps and figures and time charts, to give a just idea of the order and shape of these fifty or sixty centuries. Our business is with that outline. We have named but a few names of individuals; though henceforth the personal names must increase in number. But the content of this outline that we have drawn here in a few diagrams and charts cannot but touch the imagination. If only we could look closelier, we should see through all these sixty centuries a procession of lives more and more akin in their fashion to our own. We have shown how the naked Palæolithic savage gave place to the Neolithic{vl-274} cultivator, a type of man still to be found in the backward places of the world. We have given an illustration of Sumerian soldiers copied from a carved stone that was set up long before the days when the Semitic Sargon I conquered the land. Day by day some busy brownish man carved those figures, and, no doubt, whistled as he carved. In those days the plain of the Egyptian delta was crowded with gangs of swarthy workmen unloading the stone that had come down the Nile to add a fresh course to the current pyramid. One might paint a thousand scenes from those ages: of some hawker merchant in Egypt spreading his stock of Babylonish garments before the eyes of some pretty, rich lady; of a miscellaneous crowd swarming between the pylons to some temple festival at Thebes; of an excited, dark-eyed audience of Cretans like the Spaniards of to-day, watching a bull-fight, with the bull-fighters in trousers and tightly girded, exactly like any contemporary bull-fighter; of children learning their cuneiform signs—at Nippur the clay exercise tiles of a school have been found; of a woman with a sick husband at home slipping into some great temple in Carthage to make a vow for his recovery. Or perhaps it is a wild Greek, skin-clad and armed with a bronze axe, standing motionless on some Illyrian mountain crest, struck with amazement at his first vision of a many-oared Cretan galley crawling like a great insect across the amethystine mirror of the Adriatic Sea. He went home to tell his folk a strange story of a monster, Briareus with his hundred arms. Of millions of such stitches in each of these 200 generations is the fabric of this history woven. But unless they mark the presence of a primary seam or join, we cannot pause now to examine any of these stitches.{v1-275}

BOOK IV

JUDEA, GREECE, AND INDIA{v1-277}

XXI

THE HEBREW SCRIPTURES AND THE PROPHETS[157]

§ 1. *The Place of the Israelites in History.* § 2. *Saul, David, and Solomon.* § 3. *The Jews a People of Mixed Origin.* § 4. *The Importance of the Hebrew Prophets.*

§ 1

WE are now in a position to place in their proper relationship to this general outline of human history the Israelites, and the most remarkable collection of ancient documents in the world, that collection which is known to all Christian peoples as the Old Testament. We find in these documents the most interesting and valuable lights upon the development of civilization, and the clearest indications of a new spirit that was coming into human affairs during the struggles of Egypt and Assyria for predominance in the world of men.

All the books that constitute the Old Testament were certainly in existence, and in very much their present form, at latest by the year 100 B.C. They were probably already recognized as sacred writings in the time of Alexander the Great (330 B.C.), and known and read with the utmost respect a hundred years before his time.[158] At that time some of them were of comparatively recent composition; others were already of very considerable antiquity. They were the sacred literature of a people, the Jews, who, except for a small remnant of common people, had recently been deported to Babylonia from their own country in 587 B.C. by Nebuchadnezzar II, the Chaldean. They had returned to their city, Jerusalem, and had rebuilt their temple there under the auspices{v1-278} of Cyrus, that Persian conqueror who, we have already noted, in 539 B.C. overthrew Nabonidus, the last of the Chaldean rulers in Babylon. The Babylonian Captivity had lasted about fifty years, and many authorities are of opinion that there was a considerable admixture during that period both of race and ideas with the Babylonians.

The position of the land of Judea and of Jerusalem, its capital, is a peculiar one. The country is a band-shaped strip between the Mediterranean to the west and the desert beyond the Jordan to the east; through it lies the natural high road between the Hittites, Syria, Assyria, and Babylonia to the north and Egypt to the south. It was a country predestined, therefore, to a stormy history. Across it Egypt, and whatever power was ascendant in the north, fought for empire; against its people they fought for a trade route. It had itself neither the area, the agricultural possibilities, nor the mineral wealth to be important. The story of its people that these scriptures have preserved runs like a commentary to the greater history of the two systems of civilization to the north and south and of the sea peoples to the west.

These scriptures consist of a number of different elements. The first five books, the *Pentateuch*, were early regarded with peculiar respect. They begin in the form of a universal history with a double account of the Creation of the world and mankind, of the early life of the race, and of a great Flood by which, except for certain favoured individuals, mankind was destroyed. Excavations have revealed Babylonian versions of both the Creation story and the Flood story of prior date to the restoration of the Jews, and it is therefore argued by Biblical critics that these opening chapters were acquired by the Jews during their captivity. They constitute the first ten chapters of Genesis. There follows a history of the fathers and founders of the Hebrew nation, Abraham, Isaac, and Jacob. They are presented as patriarchal Bedouin chiefs, living the life of nomadic shepherds in the country between Babylonia and Egypt. The existing Biblical account is said by the critics to be made up out of several pre-existing versions; but whatever its origins, the story, as we have it to-day, is full of colour and vitality. What is called Palestine to-day was at that time the land of Canaan, inhabited by a Semitic people[v1-279] called the Canaanites, closely related to the Phœnicians who founded Tyre and Sidon, and to the Amorites who took Babylon and, under Hammurabi, founded the first Babylonian Empire. The Canaanites were a settled folk in the days—which were perhaps contemporary with the days of Hammurabi—when Abraham's flocks and herds passed through the land. The God of Abraham, says the Bible narrative, promised this smiling land of prosperous cities to him and to his children. To the book of Genesis the reader must go to read how Abraham, being childless, doubted this promise, and of the births of Ishmael and Isaac. And in Genesis too, he will find the lives of Isaac and Jacob, whose name was changed to Israel, and of the twelve sons of Israel; and how in the days of a great famine they went down into Egypt. With that, Genesis, the first book of the Pentateuch, ends. The next book, Exodus, is concerned with the story of Moses.

The story of the settlement and slavery of the children of Israel in Egypt is a difficult one. There is an Egyptian record of a settlement of certain Semitic peoples in the land of Goshen by the Pharaoh Rameses II, and it is stated that they were drawn into Egypt by want of food. But of the life and career of

Moses there is no Egyptian record at all; there is no account of any plagues of Egypt or of any Pharaoh who was drowned in the Red Sea. There is much about the story of Moses that has a mythical flavour, and one of the most remarkable incidents in it, his concealment by his mother in an ark of bulrushes, has also been found in an ancient Sumerian inscription made at least a thousand years before his time by that Sargon I who founded the ancient Akkadian Sumerian Empire. It runs:

"Sargon, the powerful king, the king of Akkadia am I, my mother was poor, my father I knew not; the brother of my father lived in the mountains.... My mother, who was poor, secretly gave birth to me; she placed me in a *basket of reeds*, she shut up the mouth of it with bitumen, she abandoned me to the river, which did not overwhelm me. The river bore me away and brought me to Akki the irrigator. Akki the irrigator received me in the goodness of his heart. Akki the irrigator reared me to boyhood. Akki the irrigator made me a gardener. My service as a gardener was pleasing unto Istar and I became king.{v1-280}"
{v1-281}

This is perplexing. Still more perplexing is the discovery of a clay tablet written by the Egyptian governors of a city in Canaan to the Pharaoh Amenophis IV, who came in the XVIIIth Dynasty before Rameses II, apparently mentioning the Hebrews by name and declaring that they are overrunning Canaan. Manifestly, if the Hebrews were conquering Canaan in the time of the XVIIIth

Dynasty, they could not have been made captive and oppressed, before they conquered Canaan, by Rameses II of the XIXth Dynasty. But it is quite understandable that the Exodus story, written long after the events it narrates, may have concentrated and simplified, and perhaps personified and symbolized, what was really a long and complicated history of tribal invasions. One Hebrew tribe may have drifted down into Egypt and become enslaved, while the others were already attacking the outlying Canaanite cities. It is even possible that the land of the captivity was not Egypt (Hebrew, Misraim), but Misrim in the north of Arabia, on the other side of the Red Sea. These questions are discussed fully and acutely in the *Encyclopædia Biblica* (articles *Moses* and *Exodus*), to which the curious reader must be referred.[159]

Two other books of the Pentateuch, Deuteronomy and Leviticus, are concerned with the Law and the priestly rules. The book of Numbers takes up the wanderings of the Israelites in the desert and their invasion of Canaan.

Whatever the true particulars of the Hebrew invasion of Canaan may be, there can be no doubt that the country they invaded had changed very greatly since the days of the legendary promise, made centuries before, to Abraham. Then it seems to have been largely a Semitic land, with many prosperous trading cities. But great waves of strange peoples had washed along this coast. We have already told how the dark Iberian or Mediterranean peoples of Italy and Greece, the peoples of that

Ægean civilization which culminated at Cnossos, were being assailed by the southward movement of Aryan-speaking races, such as the Italians and Greeks, and how Cnossos was sacked about 1400 B.C., and destroyed altogether about 1000 B.C. It is now evident that the people of these Ægean seaports were crossing the sea in search of securer land nests. They invaded the Egyptian delta and the African{vI-282} coast to the west, they formed alliances with the Hittites and other Aryan or Aryanized races. This happened after the time of Rameses II, in the time of Rameses III. Egyptian monuments record great sea fights, and also a march of these people along the coast of Palestine towards Egypt. Their transport was in the ox-carts characteristic of the Aryan tribes, and it is clear that these Cretans were acting in alliance with some early Aryan invaders. No connected narrative of these conflicts that went on between 1300 B.C. and 1000 B.C. has yet been made out, but it is evident from the Bible narrative, that when the Hebrews under Joshua pursued their slow subjugation of the promised land, they came against a new people, the Philistines, unknown to Abraham,[160] who were settling along the coast in a series of cities of which Gaza, Gath, Ashdod, Ascalon, and Joppa became the chief, who were really, like the Hebrews, newcomers, and probably chiefly these Cretans from the sea and from the north. The invasion, therefore, that began as an attack upon the Canaanites, speedily became a long and not very successful struggle for the coveted and promised land with these much more formidable newcomers, the Philistines.

It cannot be said that the promised land was ever completely in the grasp of the Hebrews. Following after the Pentateuch in the Bible come the books of Joshua, Judges, Ruth (a digression), Samuel I and II, and Kings I and II, with Chronicles repeating with variation much of the matter of Samuel II and Kings; there is a growing flavour of reality in most of this latter history, and in these books we find the Philistines steadfastly in possession of the fertile lowlands of the south, and the Canaanites and Phœnicians holding out against the Israelites in the north. The first triumphs of Joshua are not repeated. The book of Judges is a melancholy catalogue of failures. The people lose heart. They desert the worship of their own god Jehovah,[161] and worship{v1-283} Baal and Ashtaroth (= Bel and Ishtar). They mixed their race with the Philistines, with the Hittites, and so forth, and became, as they have always subsequently been, a racially mixed people. Under a series of wise men and heroes they wage a generally unsuccessful and never very united warfare against their enemies. In succession they are conquered by the Moabites, the Canaanites, the Midianites, and the Philistines. The story of these conflicts, of Gideon and of Samson and the other heroes who now and then cast a gleam of hope upon the distresses of Israel, is told in the book of Judges. In the first book of Samuel is told the story of their great disaster at Ebenezer in the days when Eli was judge.

This was a real pitched battle in which the Israelites lost 30,000 {v1-284}(!) men. They had previously suffered a reverse and lost 4000 men, and then they brought out their most sacred symbol, the Ark of the Covenant of God.

"And when the ark of the covenant of the Lord came into the camp, all Israel shouted with a great shout, so that the earth rang again. And when the Philistines heard the noise of the shout, they said, 'What meaneth the noise of this great shout in the camp of the Hebrews?' And they understood, that the ark of the Lord was come into the camp. And the Philistines were afraid, for they said, 'God is come into the camp,' And they said, 'Woe unto us! for there hath not been such a thing heretofore. Woe unto us! who shall deliver us out of the hand of these mighty Gods? these are the Gods that smote the Egyptians with all the plagues in the wilderness. Be strong, and quit yourselves like men, O ye Philistines, that ye be not servants unto the Hebrews, as they have been to you: quit yourselves like men, and fight.'

"And the Philistines fought, and Israel was smitten, and they fled every man into his tent: and there was a very great slaughter for there fell of Israel thirty thousand[162]footmen. And the ark of God was taken; and the two sons of Eli, Hophni and Phinehas, were slain.

"And there ran a man of Benjamin out of the army, and came to Shiloh the same day with his clothes rent, and with earth upon his head. And when he came, lo, Eli sat upon a seat by the wayside watching: for his heart trembled for the ark of God. And when the man came into the city and told it, all the city cried out. And when Eli heard the noise of the crying, he said, 'What meaneth the noise of this tumult?' And the man came in hastily, and told Eli. Now Eli was ninety and eight years old; and his eyes were dim, that he could not see. And the man said unto Eli, 'I am he that came out of the army, and I fled to-day out of the army.' And he said, 'What is there done, my son?' And the messenger answered and said, 'Israel is fled before the Philistines, and there hath been also a great slaughter among the people, and thy two sons also, Hophni and Phinehas, are dead, and the ark of God is taken.' And it came to pass when he made mention of the ark of God, that Eli fell from off his seat backward by the side of the{v1-285} gate, and his neck brake, and he died: for he was an old man, and heavy. And he had judged Israel forty years.

"And his daughter in law, Phinehas' wife, was with child, near to be delivered: and when she heard the tidings that the ark of God was taken, and that her father in law and her husband were dead, she bowed herself and travailed; for her pains came upon her. And about the time of her death the women that stood by her said unto her, 'Fear not; for thou hast born a son! But she answered not, neither did she regard it. And she named the child I-chabod,[163] saying, 'The glory is departed from Israel:' because the ark of God was taken, and because of her father in law and her husband." (1 Sam., chap. iv.)

The successor of Eli and the last of the Judges was Samuel, and at the end of his rule came an event in the history of Israel which paralleled and was suggested by the experience of the greater nations around. A king arose. We are told in vivid language the plain issue between the more ancient rule of priestcraft and the newer fashion in human affairs. It is impossible to avoid a second quotation.

"Then all the elders of Israel gathered themselves together, and came to Samuel unto Ramah, and said unto him: 'Behold, thou art old, and thy sons walk not in thy ways: now make us a king to judge us like all the nations.'

"But the thing displeased Samuel, when they said, 'Give us a king to judge us.' And Samuel prayed unto the Lord. And the Lord said unto Samuel, 'Hearken unto the voice of the people in all that they say unto thee: for they have not rejected thee, but they have rejected me, that I should not reign over them. According to all the works which they have done since the day that I brought them up out of Egypt even unto this day, wherewith they have forsaken me, and served other gods, so do they also unto thee. Now therefore hearken unto their voice: howbeit yet protest solemnly unto them, and shew them the manner of the king that shall reign over them.'

"And Samuel told all the words of the Lord unto the people that asked of him a king. And he said, 'This will be the manner of the king that shall reign over you: He will take your sons, and {vi-286} appoint them for himself, for his chariots, and to be his horsemen; and some shall run before his chariots. And he will appoint him captains over thousands, and captains over fifties; and will set them to ear his ground, and to reap his harvest, and to make his instruments of war, and instruments of his chariots. And he will take your daughters to be confectioners, and to be cooks, and to be bakers. And he will take your fields, and your vineyards, and your oliveyards, even the best of them, and give them to his servants. And he will take the tenth of your seed, and of your vineyards, and give to his officers, and to his servants. And he will take your menservants, and your maidservants, and your goodliest young men, and your asses, and put them to his work. He will take the tenth of your sheep: and ye shall be his servants. And ye shall cry out in that day because of your king which ye shall have chosen you; and the Lord will not hear you in that day.'

"Nevertheless the people refused to obey the voice of Samuel; and they said, 'Nay; but we will have a king over us; that we also may be like all the nations; and that our king may judge us, and go out before us, and fight our battles.'" (I Sam., chap. viii.)

§ 2

But the nature and position of their land was against the Hebrews, and their first king Saul was no more successful than their judges. The long intrigues of the adventurer David against Saul are told in the rest of the first book of Samuel, and the end of Saul was utter defeat upon Mount Gilboa. His army was overwhelmed by the Philistine archers.

"And it came to pass on the morrow, when the Philistines came to strip the slain, that they found Saul and his three sons fallen in Mount Gilboa. And they cut off his head, and stripped off his armour, and sent into the land of the Philistines round about, to publish it in the house of their idols, and among the people. And they put his armour in the house of Ashtaroth; and they fastened his body to the wall of Beth-shan." (I Sam., chap, xxxi.)

David (990 B.C. roughly) was more politic and successful than his predecessor, and he seems to have placed himself under the{v1-287} protection of Hiram, King of Tyre. This Phœnician alliance sustained him, and was the essential element in the greatness of his son Solomon. His story, with its constant assassinations and executions, reads rather like the history of some savage chief than of a civilized monarch. It is told with great vividness in the second book of Samuel.

The first book of Kings begins with the reign of King Solomon (960 B.C. roughly). The most interesting thing in that story, from the point of view of the general historian, is the relationship of Solomon to the national religion and the priesthood, and his dealings with the tabernacle, the priest Zadok, and the prophet Nathan.

The opening of Solomon's reign is as bloody as his father's. The last recorded speech of David arranges for the murder of Shimei; his last recorded word is "blood." "But his hoar head bring thou down to the grave with blood," he says, pointing out that though old Shimei is protected by a vow David had made to the Lord so long as David lives, there is nothing to bind Solomon in that matter. Solomon proceeds to murder his brother, who has sought the throne but quailed and made submission. He then deals freely with his brother's party. The weak hold of religion upon the racially and mentally confused Hebrews at that time is shown by the ease with which he replaces the hostile chief priest by his own adherent Zadok, and still more strikingly by the murder of Joab by Benaiah, Solomon's chief ruffian, in the Tabernacle, while the victim is claiming sanctuary and holding to the very horns of Jehovah's altar. Then Solomon sets to work, in what was for that time a thoroughly modern spirit, to recast the religion of his people. He continues the alliance with Hiram, King of Sidon, who uses Solomon's kingdom as a high road by which to reach and build shipping upon the Red Sea, and a hitherto unheard-of wealth accumulates in Jerusalem as a result of this partnership. Gang labour appears in Israel; Solomon sends relays of men to cut cedarwood in Lebanon under Hiram, and organizes a service of porters through the land. (There is much in all this to remind the reader of the relations of some Central African chief to a European trading concern.) Solomon then builds a palace for himself, and a temple not nearly as big for Jehovah. Hitherto, the Ark of the Covenant, the divine symbol of these ancient Hebrews, had{v1-288} abode in a large tent, which had been shifted from one high place to another, and sacrifices had been offered to the God of Israel upon a number of different high places. Now the ark is brought into the golden splendours of the inner chamber of a temple of cedar-sheathed stone, and put between two great winged figures of gilded olivewood, and sacrifices are henceforth to be made only upon the altar before it.

This centralizing innovation will remind the reader of both Akhnaton and Nabonidus. Such things as this are done successfully only when the prestige and tradition and learning of the priestly order has sunken to a very low level.[164]

"And he appointed, according to the order of David his father, the courses of the priests to their service, and the Levites to their charges, to praise and minister before the priests, as the duty of every day required; the porters also by their courses at every gate; for so had David the man of God commanded. And they departed not from the commandment of the king unto the priests and Levites concerning any matter, or concerning the treasures."

Neither Solomon's establishment of the worship of Jehovah in Jerusalem upon this new footing, nor his vision of and conversation with his God at the opening of his reign, stood in the way of his developing a sort of theological flirtatiousness in his declining years. He married widely, if only for reasons of state and splendour, and he entertained his numerous wives by sacrificing to their national deities, to the Sidonian goddess Ashtaroth (Ishtar), to

Chemosh (a Moabitish god), to Moloch, and so forth. The Bible account of Solomon does, in fact, show us a king and a confused people, both superstitious and mentally unstable, in no way more religious than any other people of the surrounding world.

A point of considerable interest in the story of Solomon, because it marks a phase in Egyptian affairs, is his marriage to a daughter of Pharaoh: This must have been one of the Pharaohs of the XXIst Dynasty: In the great days of Amenophis III, as the Tel Amarna letters witness, Pharaoh could condescend to receive a Babylonian princess into his harem, but he refused absolutely{v1-289} to grant so divine a creature as an Egyptian princess in marriage to the Babylonian monarch. It points to the steady decline of Egyptian prestige that now, three centuries later, such a petty monarch as Solomon could wed on equal terms with an Egyptian princess. There was, however, a revival with the next Egyptian dynasty (XXII); and the Pharaoh Shishak, the founder, taking advantage of the cleavage between Israel and Judah, which had been developing through the reigns of both David and Solomon, took Jerusalem and looted the all-too-brief splendours both of the new temple and of the king's house.

Shishak seems also to have subjugated Philistia. From this time onward it is to be noted that the Philistines fade in importance. They had already lost their Cretan language and adopted that of the Semites they had conquered, and although their cities remain more or less independent, they merge gradually into the general Semitic life of Palestine.

There is evidence that the original rude but convincing narrative of Solomon's rule, of his various murders, of his association with Hiram, of his palace and temple building, and the extravagances that weakened and finally tore his kingdom in twain, has been subjected to extensive interpolations and expansions by a later writer, anxious to exaggerate his prosperity and glorify his wisdom. It is not the place here to deal with the criticism of Bible origins, but it is a matter of ordinary common sense rather than of scholarship to note the manifest reality and veracity of the main substance of the account of David and Solomon, an account explaining sometimes and justifying sometimes, but nevertheless relating facts, even the harshest facts, as only a contemporary or almost contemporary writer, convinced that they cannot be concealed, would relate them, and then to remark the sudden lapse into adulation when the inserted passages occur. It is a striking tribute to the power of the written assertion over realities in men's minds that this Bible narrative has imposed, not only upon the Christian, but upon the Moslim world, the belief that King Solomon was not only one of the most magnificent, but one of the wisest of men. Yet the first book of Kings tells in detail his utmost splendours, and beside the beauty and wonder of the buildings and organizations of such great monarchs as Thotmes III or Rameses II or half{vl-290} a dozen other Pharaohs, or of Sargon II or Sardanapalus or

Nebuchadnezzar the Great, they are trivial. His temple, measured internally, was twenty cubits broad, about 35 feet[165]—that is, the breadth of a small villa residence—and sixty cubits, say, 100 feet, long. And as for his wisdom and statescraft, one need go no further than the Bible to see that Solomon was a mere helper in the wide-reaching schemes of the trader-king Hiram, and his kingdom a pawn between Phœnicia and Egypt. His importance was due largely to the temporary enfeeblement of Egypt, which encouraged the ambition of the Phœnician and made it necessary to propitiate the holder of the key to an alternate trade route to the East. To his own people Solomon was a wasteful and oppressive monarch, and already before his death his kingdom was splitting, visibly to all men.

With the reign of King Solomon the brief glory of the Hebrews ends; the northern and richer section of his kingdom, long oppressed by taxation to sustain his splendours, breaks off from Jerusalem to become the separate kingdom of Israel, and this split ruptures that linking connection between Sidon and the Red Sea by which Solomon's gleam of wealth was possible. There is no more wealth in Hebrew history. Jerusalem remains the capital of one tribe, the tribe of Judah, the capital of a land of barren hills, cut off by Philistia from the sea and surrounded by enemies.

The tales of wars, of religious conflicts, of usurpations, assassinations, and of fratricidal murders to secure the throne goes on for three centuries. It is a tale frankly barbaric. Israel wars with Judah and the neighbouring states; forms alliances first with one and then with the other. The power of Aramean Syria burns like a baleful star over the affairs of the Hebrews, and then there rises behind it the great and growing power of the last Assyrian Empire. For three centuries the life of the Hebrews was like the life of a man who insists upon living in the middle of a busy thoroughfare, and is consequently being run over constantly by omnibuses and motor-lorries.

"Pul" (apparently the same person as Tiglath Pileser III) is, according to the Bible narrative, the first Assyrian monarch{vi-291} to appear upon the Hebrew horizon, and Menahem buys him off with a thousand talents of silver (738 B.C.). But the power of Assyria is heading straight for the now aged and decadent land of Egypt, and the line of attack lies through Judea; Tiglath Pileser III returns and Shalmaneser follows in his steps, the King of Israel intrigues for help with Egypt, that "broken reed," and in 721 B.C., as we have already noted, his kingdom is swept off into captivity and utterly lost to history. The same fate hung over Judah, but for a little while it was averted. The fate of Sennacherib's army in the reign of King Hezekiah (701 B.C.), and how he was murdered by his sons (II Kings xix. 37), we have already mentioned. The subsequent subjugation of Egypt by Assyria finds no mention in Holy Writ, but it is clear that before the reign of Sennacherib, King Hezekiah had carried on a diplomatic correspondence with Babylon (700 B.C.), which was in revolt against Sargon II of Assyria.

There followed the conquest of Egypt by Esarhaddon, and then for a time Assyria was occupied with her own troubles; the Scythians and Medes and Persians were pressing her on the north, and Babylon was in insurrection. As we have already noted, Egypt, relieved for a time from Assyrian pressure, entered upon a phase of revival, first under Psammetichus and then under Necho II.

Again the little country in between made mistakes in its alliances. But on neither side was there safety. Josiah opposed Necho, and was slain at the battle of Megiddo (608 B.C.). The king of Judah became an Egyptian tributary. Then when Necho, after pushing as far as the Euphrates, fell before Nebuchadnezzar II, Judah fell with him (604 B.C.). Nebuchadnezzar, after a trial of three puppet kings, carried off the greater part of the people into captivity in Babylon (586 B.C.), and the rest, after a rising and a massacre of Babylonian officials, took refuge from the vengeance of Chaldea in Egypt.

"And all the vessels of the house of God, great and small, and the treasures of the house of the Lord, and the treasures of the king, and of his princes; all these he brought to Babylon. And they burnt the house of God and brake down the wall of Jerusalem, and burnt all the palaces thereof with fire, and destroyed all the goodly vessels thereof. And them that had escaped from the {v1-292} sword carried he away to Babylon; where they were servants to him and his sons until the reign of the kingdom of Persia." (II Chron. xxxvi. 18, 19, 20.)

So the four centuries of Hebrew kingship comes to an end. From first to last it was a mere incident in the larger and greater history of Egypt, Syria, Assyria, and Phœnicia. But out of it there were now to arise moral and intellectual consequences of primary importance to all mankind.

§ 3

The Jews who returned, after an interval of more than two generations, to Jerusalem from Babylonia in the time of Cyrus were a very different people from the warring Baal worshippers and Jehovah worshippers, the sacrificers in the high places and sacrificers at Jerusalem of the kingdoms of Israel and Judah. The plain fact of the Bible narrative is that the Jews went to Babylon barbarians and came back civilized. They went a confused and divided multitude, with no national self-consciousness; they came back with an intense and exclusive national spirit. They went with no common literature generally known to them, for it was only about forty years before the captivity that king Josiah is said to have discovered "a book of the law" in the temple (II Kings xxii.), and, besides that, there is not a hint in the record of any reading of books; and they returned with most of their material for the Old Testament. It is manifest that, relieved of their bickering and murderous kings, restrained from politics and in the intellectually stimulating atmosphere of that Babylonian world, the Jewish mind made a great step forward during the captivity.

It was an age of historical inquiry and learning in Babylonia. The Babylonian influences that had made Sardanapalus collect a great library of ancient writings in Nineveh were still at work. We have already told how Nabonidus was so preoccupied with antiquarian research as to neglect the defence of his kingdom against Cyrus. Everything, therefore, contributed to set the exiled Jews inquiring into their own history, and they found an inspiring leader in the prophet Ezekiel. From such hidden and forgotten records as they had with them, genealogies, contemporary histories{v1-293} of David, Solomon, and their other kings, legends and traditions, they made out and amplified their own story, and told it to Babylon and themselves. The story of the Creation and the Flood, much of the story of Moses, much of Samson, were probably incorporated from Babylonian sources.[166] When the Jews returned to Jerusalem, only the Pentateuch had been put together into one book, but the grouping of the rest of the historical books was bound to follow.

The rest of their literature remained for some centuries as separate books, to which a very variable amount of respect was paid. Some of the later books are frankly post-captivity compositions. Over all this literature were thrown certain leading ideas. There was an idea, which even these books themselves gainsay in detail, that all the people were pure-blooded children of Abraham; there was next an idea of a promise made by Jehovah to Abraham that he would exalt the Jewish race above all other races; and, thirdly, there was the belief first of all that

Jehovah was the greatest and most powerful of tribal gods, and then that he was a god above all other gods, and at last that he was the only true god. The Jews became convinced at last, as a people, that they were the chosen people of the one God of all the earth.

And arising very naturally out of these three ideas, was a fourth, the idea of a coming leader, a saviour, a Messiah who would realize the long-postponed promises of Jehovah.

This welding together of the Jews into one tradition-cemented people in the course of the "seventy years" is the first instance in history of the new power of the written word in human affairs. It was a mental consolidation that did much more than unite the people who returned to Jerusalem. This idea of belonging to a chosen race predestined to pre-eminence was a very attractive one. It possessed also those Jews who remained in Babylonia. Its literature reached the Jews now established in Egypt. It affected the mixed people who had been placed in Samaria, the old capital of the kings of Israel when the ten tribes were deported to Media. It inspired a great number of Babylonians and the like to claim Abraham as their father, and thrust their company upon the{v1-294} returning Jews. Ammonites and Moabites became adherents. The book of Nehemiah is full of the distress occasioned by this invasion of the privileges of the chosen. The Jews were already a people dispersed in many lands and cities, when their minds and hopes were unified and they became an exclusive people. But at first their exclusiveness is merely to preserve soundness of doctrine and worship, warned by such lamentable lapses as those of King Solomon. To genuine proselytes of whatever race, Judaism long held out welcoming arms.

To Phœnicians after the falls of Tyre and Carthage, conversion to Judaism must have been particularly easy and attractive. Their language was closely akin to Hebrew. It is possible that the great majority of African and Spanish Jews are really of Phœnician origin. There were also great Arabian accessions. In South Russia, as we shall note later, there were even Mongolian Jews.

§ 4

The historical books from Genesis to Nehemiah, upon which the idea of the promise to the chosen people had been imposed later, were no doubt the backbone of Jewish mental unity, but they by no means complete the Hebrew literature from which finally the Bible was made up. Of such books as Job, said to be an imitation of Greek tragedy, the Song of Solomon, the Psalms, Proverbs, and others, there is no time to write in this *Outline*, but it is necessary to deal with the books known as "the Prophets" with some fullness. For those books are almost the earliest and certainly the best evidence of the appearance of a new kind of leading in human affairs.[167]

These prophets are not a new class in the community; they are of the most various origins—

Ezekiel was of the priestly caste and of priestly sympathies, and Amos was a shepherd; but they have this in common, that they bring into life a religious force outside the sacrifices and formalities of priesthood and temple. The earlier prophets seem most like the earlier priests, they are oracular, they give advice and foretell events; it is quite possible that at{v1-295} first, in the days when there were many high places in the land and religious ideas were comparatively unsettled, there was no great distinction between priest and prophet. The prophets danced, it would seem, somewhat after the Dervish fashion, and uttered oracles. Generally they wore a distinctive mantle of rough goat-skin. They kept up the nomadic tradition as against the "new ways" of the settlement. But after the building of the temple and the organization of the priesthood, the prophetic type remains over and outside the formal religious scheme. They were probably always more or less of an annoyance to the priests. They became informal advisers upon public affairs, denouncers of sin and strange practices, "self-constituted," as we should say, having no sanction but an inner light. "Now the word of the Lord came unto"—so and so; that is the formula.

In the latter and most troubled days of the kingdom of Judah, as Egypt, North Arabia, Assyria, and then Babylonia closed like a vice upon the land, these prophets became very significant and powerful. Their appeal was to anxious and fearful minds, and at first their exhortation was chiefly towards repentance, the pulling down of this or that high place, the restoration of worship in Jerusalem, or the like. But through some of the prophecies there runs already a note like the note of what we call nowadays a "social reformer." The rich are "grinding the faces of the poor"; the luxurious are consuming the children's bread; influential and wealthy people make friends with and imitate the splendours and vices of foreigners, and sacrifice the common people to these new fashions; and this is hateful to Jehovah, who will certainly punish the land.

But with the broadening of ideas that came with the Captivity, the tenour of prophecy broadens and changes. The jealous pettiness that disfigures the earlier tribal ideas of God give place to a new idea of a god of universal righteousness. It is clear that the increasing influence of prophets was not confined to the Jewish people; it was something that was going on in those days all over the Semitic world. The breaking down of nations and kingdoms to form the great and changing empires of that age, the smashing up of cults and priesthoods, the mutual discrediting of temple by temple in their rivalries and disputes—all these influences were{v1-296} releasing men's minds to a freer and wider religious outlook. The temples had accumulated great stores of golden vessels and lost their hold upon the imaginations of men. It is difficult to estimate whether, amidst these constant wars, life had become more uncertain and unhappy than it had ever been before, but there can be no doubt that men had become more conscious of its miseries and insecurities. Except for the weak and the women, there remained little comfort or assurance in the sacrifices, ritual and formal devotions of the temples. Such was the world to which the later prophets of Israel began to talk of the One God, and of a Promise that some day the world should come to peace and unity and happiness. This great God that men were now discovering lived in a temple "not made with hands, eternal in the heavens." There can be little doubt of a great body of such thought and utterance in Babylonia, Egypt, and throughout the Semitic east. The prophetic books of the Bible can be but specimens of the prophesyings of that time....

We have already drawn attention to the gradual escape of writing and knowledge from their original limitation to the priesthood and the temple precincts, from the shell in which they were first developed and cherished. We have taken Herodotus as an interesting specimen of what we have called the free intelligence of mankind. Now here we are dealing with a similar overflow of moral ideas into the general community. The Hebrew prophets, and the steady expansion of their ideas towards one God in all the world, is a parallel development of the free conscience of mankind. From this time onward there runs through human thought, now weakly and obscurely, now gathering power, the idea of one rule in the world, and of a promise and possibility of an active and splendid peace and happiness in human affairs. From being a temple religion of the old type, the Jewish religion becomes, to a large extent, a prophetic and creative religion of a new type. Prophet succeeds prophet. Later on, as we shall tell, there was born a prophet of unprecedented power, Jesus, whose followers founded the great universal religion of Christianity. Still later Muhammad, another prophet, appears in Arabia and founds Islam. In spite of very distinctive features of their own, these two teachers do in a manner arise out of, and in succession to these Jewish{v1-297} prophets. It is not the place of the historian to discuss the truth and falsity of religion, but it is his business to record the appearance of great constructive ideas. Two thousand four hundred years ago, and six or seven or eight thousand years after the walls of the first Sumerian cities arose, the ideas of the moral unity of mankind and of a world peace had come into the world.[168]

XXII

THE GREEKS AND THE PERSIANS[169]

AND now our history must go back again to those Aryan-speaking peoples of whose early beginnings we have given an account in Chapters XIV and XV. We must, for the sake of precision, repeat here two warnings we have already given the reader: first, that we use the word Aryan in its widest sense, to express all the early peoples who spoke languages of the "Indo-Germanic" or "Indo-European" group; and, secondly, that when we use the word Aryan we do not imply any racial purity.

The original speakers of the fundamental Aryan language, 2000 or 3000 years B.C., were probably a specialized and distinctive Nordic race of fair white men, accustomed to forests and cattle, who wandered east of the Rhine and through the forests of the Danube valley, the Balkan peninsula, Asia Minor, and eastward to the north and west of the great Central Asian Sea; but very early they had encountered and mixed themselves extensively, and as they spread they continued to mix themselves with other races, with races of uncertain affinities in Asia Minor and with Iberian and Mediterranean peoples of the dark-haired white race.{v1-299} For instance, the Aryans, spreading and pressing westward in successive waves of Keltic-speaking peoples through Gaul and Britain and Ireland, mixed more and more with Iberian races, and were affected more and more by that Iberian blood and their speech by the characteristics of the language their Keltic tongue superseded. Other waves of Keltic peoples washed with diminishing force into Spain and Portugal, where to this day the pre-Keltic strain is altogether dominant although the languages spoken are Aryan. Northward, in Europe, the Aryan peoples were spreading into hitherto uninhabited country, and so remaining racially more purely Nordic blonds. They had already reached Scandinavia many centuries B.C.

From their original range of wandering, other Aryan tribes spread to the north as well as to the south of the Black Sea, and ultimately, as these seas shrank and made way for them, to the north and east of the Caspian, and so began to come into conflict with and mix also with Mongolian peoples of the Ural-Altaic linguistic group, the horse-keeping people of the grassy steppes of Central Asia. From these Mongolian races the Aryans seem to have acquired the use of the horse for riding and warfare. There were three or four prehistoric varieties or sub-species of horse in Europe and Asia, but it was the steppe or semi-desert lands that first gave horses of a build adapted to other than food uses.[170] All these peoples, it must be understood, shifted their ground rapidly, a succession of bad seasons might drive them many hundreds of miles, and it is only in a very rough and provisional manner that their "beats" can now be indicated. Every summer they went north, every winter they swung south again. This annual swing covered sometimes hundreds of miles. On our maps, for the sake of simplicity, we represent the shifting of nomadic peoples by a straight line; but really they moved in annual swings, as the broom of a servant who is sweeping out a passage swishes from side to side as she advances. Spreading round the north of the Black Sea, and probably to the north of the Caspian, from the range of the original Teutonic tribes of Central and North-central Europe to the Iranian peoples who became the Medes and Persians and (Aryan) Hindus, were the grazing lands[v1-300] of a confusion of tribes, about whom it is truer to be vague than precise, such as the Cimmerians, the Sarmatians, and those Scythians who, together with the Medes and Persians, came into effective contact with the Assyrian Empire by 1000 B.C. or earlier.

East and south of the Black Sea, between the Danube and the Medes and Persians, and to the north of the Semitic and Mediterranean peoples of the sea coasts and peninsulas, ranged another series of equally ill-defined Aryan tribes, moving easily from place to place and intermixing freely—to the great confusion of historians. They seem, for instance, to have broken up and assimilated the Hittite civilization, which was probably pre-Aryan in its origin. They were, perhaps, not so far advanced along the nomadic line as the Scythians of the great plains.

The general characteristics of the original Aryan peoples we have already discussed in Chapter XV. They were a forest people, not a steppe people, and, consequently, wa

Made in the USA
Las Vegas, NV
10 March 2021